A Lost Cause

to Miley

Bethany Hulbrick

A Lost Cause

Bethany Hentrich

Print information available on the last page.

Rev. date: 02/13/2020

To order additional copies of this book, contact:
Xlibris
1-888-795-4274
www.Xlibris.com
Orders@Xlibris.com
807341

CONTENTS

Hello Everyone! My name is Bethany Hentrich. And the title of this book pretty much describes the main point of why I wrote this story. I wrote this story in high school and have spent the last four years, off and on, working on it. It was meant to be a short story, but it ended up being quote "not so short". So because of that it has finally gotten to this point.. Publication. Something I had been dreaming of for this book, for years now. I've been a writer for all of my life, always finding joy in the creation of stories and characters, and the lives they lead. Writing is almost an escape from the pain and sorrows of the real world, and therefore has become a thing I do in my spare time, other than spending time with my Lord, God. For it is He who gives me this ability to create and has led me this far. All praise and glory to Him for bringing this to life for me, with the help of Xlibris and their helpful team of representatives, editors and designers. And to all, thank you for taking the time to enjoy this heartfelt story, and with that.. I hope you enjoy!

Chapter One

A New Challenge

"Bring him out, Matt!" Jenna Tyler called. A warm, gentle wind blew through her golden blonde hair, her green eyes watching for the silhouette of the person in question.

Matthew Bartlett finally emerged from the stables leading Skipper, a young quarter horse who was being boarded here at Sunshine Ridge Ranch to be cured of his fear of flapping objects.

"I have returned." Matt announced cheekily, gesturing his hands out in a proud manner.

"What would we have done without meeting you all that *year* or so ago?" Jenna replied with a smirk, only slightly sarcastic in saying so. And Matt just shrugged, their smiles glowing with an added chuckle of fondness.

Ryan Tyler strode up to them from the house as Matt went to unlatch the round pen gate for Jenna to lead the horse into.

"So what are we going to try today?" he asked his daughter thoughtfully.

Jenna had Skipper standing in the middle of the pen, standing directly in front of him at his head.

"I guess the same thing we've *been* doing." Jenna sighed, stroking the gelding's shaggy forelock.

Matt dropped his shoulders reluctantly and strolled toward the fence. He reached for an old blanket that was draped over the fence rung and carefully slid it down from it. While Jenna held Skipper, he held the blanket out to the horse so he could sniff it briefly. Then, when Skipper looked away, Matt walked back to the fence. Facing Skipper and taking small, slow steps toward him, he gently shook the blanket.

At first, Skipper tensed, but when Jenna spoke soothingly to him, he soon relaxed.

"Good boy," Jenna praised softly as Matt stood right in front of him and shook it.

Skipper perked his ears forward but stayed calm.

"Making any progress with him?" Franklin Tyler asked, leaning against the fence of the round pen, peering through it next to Ryan.

"Yep," Jenna answered proudly, playing with the horse's mane. "He may be able to go home soon." She smiled at her grandfather.

"Good," he said, returning one, his hazel eyes oozing with pride for his granddaughter's accomplishment.

"Jenna's worked really hard to get him used to it. His owners are gonna be very happy," Ryan added, shooting a fond smirk in her direction.

"Was there ever any doubt?" Matt joked sarcastically as Jenna nudged her elbow at him playfully.

"Well, keep it up." Frank smiled. "Cause we're proud of ya."

"Thanks, Grandpa," Jenna thanked him thoughtfully. "But Matt and Dad have been a huge help too."

Matt just laughed.

"Just part of the job." He shrugged, grinning at Skipper.

"Oh, but we're blessed to have you here, son," Frank commented.

"Ain't nothin' truer than that," added Rosemary Tyler, hugging her husband. "So what are ya'll up to now?"

"Well, I think I'll take Bentley out for a ride. Wanna come?" Jenna answered.

"I'll go," Matt offered.

"Me too," said a voice from behind them.

Jenna turned to see her best friend, Katherine Morgan, trudging toward them as a maroon truck drove away.

"Hey, Kate. What's up?" Jenna greeted as the African American girl reached them.

"Us in a few minutes," Kate replied jokingly.

Everyone laughed at this response, knowing that Kate always loved kidding around when she comes to visit.

"Okay, Katherine," Jenna chuckled, recovering from the laughter. "Other than that?"

"Now, now, Jenna, you know I hate being called Katherine," Kate complained, her humorous swagger indicating her friendly distaste for her full name addressing her.

"Yeah, yeah, sure," Jenna responded, waving her off playfully. "What's going on, *Kate*?"

The lighter-skinned girl smirked as she reemphasized her previous statement.

"Not much. Just giving you a hard time, sweetie. That's all." Kate shrugged, unable to hide a smile.

"As always." Jenna rolled her eyes knowingly. "Anyway, you can ride Princeton, then if you want."

"Girl, you know me too well." Kate sighed, waving a hand at her friend in a sarcastically scoffing manner.

Everyone looked up at the sound of barking as a fancy black Tahoe SUV pulled into the driveway. Fergus and Penny, their two golden retrievers, began to bark like crazy from their fenced-in yard. The car pulled to a stop, and a middle-aged woman, about five foot seven, with light, wavy brunette hair and sunglasses stepped out of the driver seat.

"Is Ryan Tyler here?" The woman asked kindly as the family came to meet her.

"That's me." Jenna's father replied, shaking the woman's hand firmly. "This is my wife, Ann, my parents, Frank and Rose, our stable hand, Matt, and our daughter, Jenna. Oh, and Jenna's best friend, Kate."

"Pleased to meet you all." The woman smiled, taking her glasses off. "I'm Vanessa Whitely. I'm a riding instructor, trainer and breeder. And owner of Briar Meadow Ranch and Riding Academy. I breed a wide range of horses for my clients."

"The pleasure is all ours, Ms. Whitely." Frank smiled.

"Please." The woman chuckled. "Call me Vanessa."

"Well alrighty then, *Vanessa*," Frank corrected himself respectfully. "What brings you to our humble home here at Sunshine Ridge Ranch?"

"Yes, what can we do for you?" Ryan asked, smiling warmly.

"Well," Vanessa sighed. "I have a horse I just bought from a rescue center for my nephew who practically *begged* me to buy her. But we can't get her to let us ride her or even get anywhere near her with a saddle. And I've heard stories about this place and thought I'd bring her here as a last resort. Other stables have tried, but even *they* can't seem to help her."

"We'll do our best," Ryan replied confidently.

"Is there anything you can tell us about this horse?" Jenna asked.

Vanessa smiled thoughtfully at her, intrigued by the girl's immediate interest.

"Yes, this horse was found in a rickety old shed out in the open. Some say this horse was abused and left to die, but they'd also said she was very well bred wherever she came from. That is one of the only reasons I bought her. I only buy the most high-quality-bred horses."

"Thank you so much. That information will be most helpful." Ann smiled sweetly.

"Anytime, and Hope Shines really is a fine-looking animal," Vanessa remarked, then she turned to Jenna. "And I believe I've seen you before. You look very familiar to me." She thought for a brief moment. "Oh yes, I remember now. It was in a magazine I read once. I didn't think much about it at the time, but I read this article about a girl who saved a difficult horse from going to the slaughterhouse. People have been talking about it nonstop ever since. And now I know where I can find her. I hope you can do something for Hope. She means a lot to my nephew already. He absolutely refuses to give her up."

"Yep, you got the right girl." Frank laughed, putting a hand on Jenna's shoulder.

"Oh yeah, she's a gift from God—that's for sure." Ryan kissed his daughter's forehead and gave Skipper a gentle pat. Skipper nuzzled Jenna's arm and blew in her hair gently.

"You're my hero!" he seemed to say, and she scratched him between the ears.

"Well I'd better go. When should I bring Hope down?" Vanessa asked.

"Oh, whenever you get the chance, honey." Rose smiled. "Just be sure to call ahead to be sure we know you're coming."

"All right then. I'll see you.. sometime," Vanessa answered, getting into her SUV and starting the engine.

"I guess I better put this guy away if we're gonna go anywhere," Jenna said as Vanessa's Tahoe disappeared down the lane.

"Uh, yeah. So whatcha still doin' here, girl? Get a move on." Kate giggled as Jenna kicked dust at her friend playfully, the darker-skinned girl screaming and retreating in a fit of laughter.

When Jenna led Skipper into his stall, she gave him one last pat as she unclipped the lead then hung it up around the door post and closed the door.

****

Bentley tossed his head and whinnied at Jenna as she approached his stall. The blue roan stallion rested his chin on her shoulder and snorted welcomingly. Jenna tenderly chuckled as she scratched her horse behind the ears in his favorite spot.

"How ya doin', Ben?" she asked him. She unlatched his stall and let herself in.

His dark eyes shimmered through his flowing, silky black forelock, which delicately waterfalled over his face, drowning it in shiny locks. She unsnapped the straps and slid his stable blanket off his handsomely muscular back.

The flecks of bluish grays, white, and other shades of gray and black all flowed together in a panorama of snowy color across his well-formed body, fading into midnight black socks on his thick, sturdy legs. His tails flowed as richly as his mane did, spouting and falling over his beautifully arched neck and rump. To Jenna, he was the most beautiful thing in the world, and many would agree. His beauty never ceased to amaze her, and she loved every moment she got to spend with him. She draped the blanket over the door and let herself out just long enough to grab her tack and grooming kit.

When she returned, the horse perked his ears forward and snorted excitedly. Jenna quickly brushed him down and checked each hoof for anything stuck in them, clearing anything she found. Bentley scraped his hoof on the ground once she set the last hoof down again.

"You know, don't you, smart boy?" She laughed, positioning the saddle correctly on top of the saddle pads already on his back.

She tightened the girth and ran her hand up his neck to his head. The bridle hung on her shoulder, the bit clicking at her side as she walked. When she reached the horse's head, he gently pressed his forehead to her chest in a loving horse hug. Jenna couldn't resist his gesture and wrapped her arms around his head. And when he raised it a little, she placed her forehead to his and gave him a quick kiss, her hand on his cheeks.

Bentley took the bit with no problems, and she slipped the straps up over his head with ease, fastening them snugly. As she secured the last strap, she adjusted the noseband, her fingers finding the golden nameplate on it with the word *Bentley* inscribed in the metal. The plate glinted in the sunlight sneaking through the open stable door and windows.

Jenna smiled at it proudly. Taking up her helmet and putting it on, she turned and opened the stall door to lead Bentley out into the cool morning air.

****

Jenna led him out into the yard, where Matt and Kate were waiting.

"'Bout time you showed up," Kate stated sarcastically, smirking.

"Very funny," Jenna replied as she mounted.

Matt was riding Pinto Beanz. The Appaloosa-painted filly shook the bit in her mouth and scraped her hoof on the ground. She whinnied impatiently and pranced sideways. Kate giggled, seeing the filly's reaction.

"She's right—let's go already!" She clicked her tongue to Princeton who pranced regally away as Bentley and Pinto Beanz trotted up alongside him.

Together, the three friends immersed themselves in conversation about summer vacation, horses, and many other topics. And came to a halt, when they arrived at a fork in the trail.

"Which way should we go, guys?" Matt asked.

"How 'bout the right trail," Jenna suggested. She patted Bentley's strong neck as she continued, "I'll bet these guys are tired of walking and really want to stretch their legs."

"That leads to the meadow," Matt replied, thinking for a moment.

"Good idea," Kate agreed. "Hey, and while we're at it, why not make a race out of it? Prince and I'll win!"

"No way!" protested Matt. "Everyone knows Pinto Beanz is the fastest horse on the whole ranch." He patted Pinto firmly, the horse tossing her head in agreement.

"Well, we'll see about that." Jenna grinned tauntingly.

So they headed down the right trail. And when they arrived at the clearing, they dug their heels gently into the horses' sides, each of them lengthening their strides as they surged across the open ground. The rush of the wind pumped adrenaline through all of them. Their hearts pounded to the beat of the horses' thundering hooves, and their hair flailed violently in the air. Laughs and cheers rang out as they flew on across the field of lush green, all of them feeling like jockeys on a professional grass track.

Nature, in all its glory, acted as their audience, cheering them on, the forest being their finish line coming up far ahead of them. Jenna and Bentley were lagging behind the other two teens. But all Jenna had to do was lengthen the reins, giving Bentley his head so he could dig his hooves deeper into the ground, plunging past Kate and Matt in a matter of seconds.

Jenna glanced back briefly as they reached the meadow, and she pulled him down to a halt.

"All right, you magnificent boy!" she praised triumphantly, hugging his damp neck. "We did it!"

"Ah, shoot!" Kate remarked, snapping her fingers in defeat as soon as she pulled Prince down as well.

"Looks like we *both* lost!" Matt laughed. "Nice ride, Jenna. You and Ben don't waste time."

"And that's why I love him," Jenna replied teasingly.

"You're a great team—that's for sure," Kate commented.

Bentley snorted happily and bobbed his head as if to agree.

The three friends laughed then continued on their way, but when they came out of the woods again, they stopped and gasped.

"Oh no!" cried Kate, putting her head on Prince's crest.

Matt scratched the back of his neck and sighed, and Jenna rolled her eyes in frustration. Right in front of them, on their side of the road, was Prairie Rock Stables. All of them stared for what seemed like days, not sure that they should say anything.

"Do we *really* have to pass by . . . *there?*" Kate asked.

"Yep." Jenna sighed, feeling her friend's dread rub off on her.

"Maybe if we hurry, we can get past without having to see Katrina," Matt suggested after another awkward pause.

"Worth a shot." Jenna sighed reluctantly, gathering and readjusting the reins.

But as they approached, a fancy red car drove up, and Katrina Williams stepped smugly from the driver seat. "Well, well, if it isn't Jenna Tyler and her mish-mash pony club," she purred coolly.

"Give it a rest, Katrina," Jenna snapped. "You know we're better than that."

"Temper, temper." Katrina scoffed tauntingly. "But seriously if you think that *that* abomination of a horse is better than any of mine, you've got another thing coming."

Jenna's hands gripped the reins slightly tighter, but she managed to conceal it behind Bentley's neck.

"Yeah right!" exclaimed Kate, getting a little sassy about it. "Ben and Jenna were made for each other! And Bentley's a fine horse!"

"And there's nothing you can say that will change that," Matt snarled.

"Says who?" Katrina questioned, glaring daggers at both of them. "And who even asked you? Oh wait! No one. So I would stay out of it if I were you."

"Leave them alone, Katrina!" Jenna replied. "They aren't hurting you. Besides we didn't even come to see you anyway."

"Then, if that's the case, why are you here?" Katrina sniffed.

"We were just passing through and forgot that your ranch was by this trail. That's all," Jenna answered, a burning fire of anger beginning to rise up in her.

"Well, I'll have you know my mother just bought me a new horse. His name is Napoleon Bonahoof. He's a professional jumper, way better than Sam—I mean *Bentley*." Katrina's mix-up was clearly intentional, and it stung exactly where it hurt.

Jenna couldn't stand it. Katrina was really getting on her nerves. She clicked her tongue to Bentley and galloped away as fast as they could go with Matt and Kate right behind them.

Chapter Two

Past Endeavors

The three friends galloped back into the ranch, their hearts pounding from the adrenaline and their minds troubled with thoughts of Katrina.

Ryan and Frank were waiting for them when they arrived.

"Have fun?" Frank asked brightly.

"Yeah," Jenna responded dryly, sliding down off Bentley's back.

She slid his reins back over his head and led him away to the stables abruptly, brushing past them as she went by. Ryan stared after her, then looked at Matt and Kate. The two teens glanced at each other, guilt crossing their faces. And Frank just stared after Jenna in a puzzled sort of way.

"Was it something I said?" Frank asked after a pause.

"Not exactly." Matt sighed, meeting Kate's glance once more.

****

Jenna briskly brushed the dust off of Bentley's bluish-gray hide, her hands firmly gripping the brush as the bristles scraped against the horse's thick skin, her thoughts a mess, and her hair in chaos. Loose strands of her dusty golden blonde hair escaped from her carelessly pulled back ponytail. She softly murmured the words to her favorite song "He Knows My Name" by Francesca Battistelli. As she gently sang, she couldn't help but recall a time, not long ago, that she had wished to forget and many others like it that she would wish she could say never happened. But this one in particular she felt she would never escape . . .

She galloped round the ring, the steed beneath her practically floating over the sandy ground. The solid-white horse calmly sailed over the fence, his ears twitching gently back and forth between the jumps and the rider on his back. Jenna's silent chuckle echoed like the distant dream that she wished she would get to experience over and over again. She was happy . . . until that dream ended when her vision whipped about and she found she was staring at the ceiling. Painful squeals and screeches echoed in place of her laugh, a white blob shifting fearfully to her left. And another sound was ringing in the air; drowsily shifting her head to the right, she caught a slight glimpse of the distinct shape of Katrina. She was laughing, Jenna's whole world seeming to continue in slow motion. A slight movement like a hand went to Katrina's mouth as she seemed to peer over at another competitor, possibly whispering something to her. Tears blurred Jenna's vision as she began to hear her own cries. She suddenly felt warm hands touching her. She heard the muffled voices of her parents and saw blue and red lights flashing from the corner of her eye. The squealing continued and her chest jerked violently, painful sobs ringing out and were gone in a flash.

Jenna stood frozen; tears pooled in her eyes, but none had fallen yet. Her chin quivered, and she tightened her jaw to stop it. Blinking the tears away a couple times, she shook her head slightly, pushing the thoughts away, and resumed her singing and brushing. She was finding it a bit more difficult now than before, and she knew exactly why.

Unbeknownst to her, Frank strolled in to lean his forearms on Bentley's stall, her back to him. Bentley's ears twitched gently, listening to her singing.

"Katrina spewing her nonsense again?" Frank asked, leaning his weight further on to the door.

Jenna's jaw tensed again, fighting the tears harder.

"Did she make fun of our work again?"

Jenna didn't even turn around. She just rolled her eyes up and blinked, trying to stop herself from crying. Biting her lip, she realized that her hands were shaking almost too much for her to do her work.

Her body stiffened, and she cocked her head slightly to the left then straightened out again.

"Look . . . Jenna . . . whatever Katrina said about us or our work here on the farm, it doesn't make it any less true. You can't just—"

"Katrina insulted Bentley and me!" Jenna blurted out, whirling around to stare him straight in the eye, frustration and anger written all over her face, that final string of resistance finally snapping and giving way to tears in her glassy green eyes, those tears beginning to pour down her face and dripping off her chin.

Frank let himself into the stall. He took her in his arms and held her tight. He stroked her soft blond hair as she sobbed painfully into his chest, shakily hugging him back.

"Now you know that whatever she said about you and Ben aren't true," he whispered, gazing off in front of him, his eyes glazing over a little as well. "She's just trying to tear you down. That's how her mother taught her to be. Don't let her rob you of your dignity. She does not define you. Only God does. And he has made you to be an amazingly talented, hardworking and compassionate young lady who has a heart for the Lord, a heart for people and a heart for the horses. No person can take that away from you, not even Katrina." He held her head in his hands. His hazel eyes met hers. "You just have to believe in yourself and Bentley. Stay true to what God says and trust in Him. He'll help make it better. He will work it out for our good."

Jenna wiped her tears away, then she hugged her grandfather again. "Thank you."

They broke their embrace, and she hugged Bentley's neck tightly, breathing in his sweet scent. Feeling his warm breath in her ear, she resumed her grooming.

Frank gently kissed her forehead and strode casually back toward the house.

When she was finished, she helped take care of the other horses. And by the time all the horses were fed, watered, and groomed, the sun was nearly gone.

"Well, I guess I'd better head home. There's my ride. See you guys tomorrow," Kate said as she headed toward her dad's old truck.

Matt, Jenna, and Ryan waved 'til the truck was out of sight.

"Jenna! Matt! Ryan! Time for dinner!" Ann called from the house.

"Try to keep up!" Matt teased, running off.

"No problem," Jenna joked, sprinting after him.

The two friends raced ahead of Ryan as fast as they could go toward the gently lit house in the dim light of the coming dusk.

****

The whole family sat down for dinner together at the long table in the dining room. Jenna helped Ann and Rose set the table and place the food on the table.

"I think it's your turn to pray tonight, Dad." Jenna laughed.

The family sat down and bowed their heads for the prayer.

"Father," Ryan began, "thank you for all the things you have given us and for helping us through the rough patches in life. We thank you for the opportunity for our beautiful and talented daughter, Jenna, to work with this special horse. Please bless this food that my lovely wife and mother have prepared for us, and I thank you for giving me an amazing family. Help us to remain focused on you. We love you and serve you with all our hearts. Help us to continue sharing the message of your son, Jesus, even to those who don't seem to deserve it. Give us strength to stand up for what we believe and lead others down the path back to you. In your name, we pray. Amen."

Everyone agreed with an echo of *amen*, and they began to eat and talk.

****

Jenna lay awake in her bed with her arms laid up around and above her head, one hand in the other. Her train of thought was on Hope and what she planned to do when she got here. *Maybe I can use some essential oils on her to help her settle in,* she thought.

Jenna wondered what Hope might look like and what her personality was like. The burning fire of anticipation seemed to flare up inside her every time she thought about it. Excitement was another emotion that accompanied this feeling as well as a hint of concern and . . . doubt? She couldn't know for sure because she felt this every time a new horse came to Sunshine, yet this time it *did* seem different. The last thought she remembered thinking as she drifted off to sleep was, *God, give me the wisdom to help Hope.*

****

The screeches and squeals were partially drowned out by the blare of the screaming sirens. Jenna's obscured vision only caught the flashing glow of the lights. Her breathless sobs attacked her chest as the pain in her side erupted, sending it all throughout her body. A sharp, stabbing pain originating from one of her extremities gained her attention as the sweat and blood of her wounds mixed, birthing an incredibly painful sting. Her sobs became a bawling groan as more tears flowed down her cheeks. Crying others around her, she knew, were her parents. Through her tears, she vaguely saw one familiar shape pull another one into them. Unmistakable sobs informed her of all she needed to know. Beyond the shapes to her left was a larger white blob that was lying still on the ground, and it made her heart leap in her chest.

Jenna thrust herself up out of bed, her breaths fast and abrupt and her eyes full of disoriented panic. She peered around into the darkness, slowly becoming aware of what had happened. The darkness was a calming factor to her at that moment, seeing as how the sight of the blue and red lights were still freshly visible in the back of her mind. She realized she was shaking and hunched over, bracing her elbows on her legs and resting her forehead on her hands, a couple tears slipping down her cheeks.

****

The covers appeared disorganized, while chaotically covering Jenna's body. Her blonde hair lay sprawled out across the pillow. Her right arm was exposed over the blankets holding them on to her upper body. Her hand supported her left cheek as she peeled her eyes open. The harsh rays of the sun were thankfully being dulled by the thin white drapes that hid the windows from view, creating a welcoming environment for the sleeping teenager to return to.

She sat up slowly, and the covers dropped into her lap because of it. She sleepily stretched then lifted the covers to slide out of bed. Heading to her dresser, she began to pull out her clothes and tossed them onto her bed to put them on. And as she grabbed the last few things, her eyes looked up to find her favorite silver locket on top of the dresser. Jenna picked up the heart-shaped pendant on the sterling silver chain and opened it. Knowing already what was in it, she still couldn't help but smile memorably at the sight of it. Snapping it closed, she delicately fingered the clasp open and secured it around her neck. Looking forward into the mirror, she smiled and then turned to get dressed.

****

Ann looked up from the table as Jenna came noisily down the stairs from here room.

"Ah, Jenna, you're up. Good, I just got a call from Vanessa," she told her daughter. "She's bringing Hope over right now. Matt already went out to get a stall ready for her."

"Oh, great!" Jenna said happily, smiling at her mother. Jenna quickly grabbed a banana and hurried out to help Matt with the morning chores.

****

"Come on, Hiccup!" Jenna hissed, nudging the pinto forward into a canter.

Hiccup snorted, and she could feel him slightly resist, but she kept her leg on him. He obediently broke into a steady canter for her. After circling the ring for the third time, she pulled him down to a walk and then a halt, realizing the loud barking coming from the house and looked out toward the road.

The pinto scraped his hooves on the ground anxiously but stayed put as Jenna caught sight of a big truck hauling an expensive decently small trailer behind it. Fergus and Penny continued to bark from the front porch on either side of Rose.

"Oh, calm down, you two. We see them," she told them, stroking their golden coats.

Vanessa stepped carefully from the passenger side, standing on the footplate to glance over at them on the other side of the vehicle. Jenna had dismounted and led Hiccup out to meet them with her family.

"Hello, everyone," Vanessa called kindly, smiling over at them, the warm gentle wind blowing at a few loose strands of her auburn hair. She hopped out off of the truck and strolled around in front of it. "Well, here I am again," she said, gesturing with her hands out then slapping them against her hips and sliding them into the back pockets of her fancy jeans. Her casual manner only partially masked her slightly anxious demeanor.

"Everything alright, Vanessa?" Frank wondered, catching on to her feelings immediately.

"Oh . . . yeah." Vanessa sighed. "It's just that . . . I think I've gotten my nephew's hopes up when I'm not sure that it'll . . . turn out the way we want it to . . . Ya know?" The way she spoke was almost breathless, showing her dread quite clearly.

"Well, don't you worry." Frank smiled warmly back at her. "Whatever the case, we'll do our *very* best to fix your horse up for him."

"Thank you," Vanessa breathed, rolling her neck down to the right, the stress seeming to drain from her a little bit, putting her more at ease now. "I just hope that Hope *can* be fixed, you know?"

"Absolutely." Frank smirked, laying a hand on her shoulder. "And we'll figure that out soon enough."

Vanessa smiled back at him thankfully, her demeanor seeming to be much calmer and more focused now. She then turned toward Jenna and Matt. "And who is this guy?" Vanessa asked, gesturing toward Hiccup.

"Oh, this is Hiccup," Jenna replied, adjusting the brow-bands, the horse shaking his head to shoo away the flies after she did so. "He's been staying with us to be treated for a sour behavior. We've been doing some basic behavior training on him and using essential oils and herbs to help calm him down too. And it seems to be working."

"You use oils and herbs on the horses?" Vanessa asked, her tone lightening.

"Sure," Matt replied. "We've learned that horses respond to oils and herbs similar to how humans do. They can help them heal and give them vitamins and stuff."

"My mom makes all sorts of blends and oils for use on them," Jenna explained. "Plus, we also have a remedy book in the medicine cabinet next to the tack room."

"Huh," Vanessa replied thoughtfully. "That's amazing. I never thought oils worked on horses."

"Well, of course," Ryan confirmed, smiling. "All animals can benefit from natural oils just like humans do."

Their conversation was brought to an abrupt halt by a shrill whinny and the clatter of hooves inside the trailer.

"Well, she sounds friendly," Jenna remarked sarcastically, smiling at Vanessa who humorously returned one.

"Yep, she's somethin' else—that's for sure," she tenderly responded.

"Well then, let's have a look, shall we?" Ryan remarked, glancing over at Vanessa.

They exchanged smiles, and Vanessa looked back at the driver of the truck. "We're ready," she told him.

The tall young man with silky brunette curls gave a nod and stepped down off the truck's footplate. He loosely strode toward them, standing at Vanessa's left side.

"This is Myles," Vanessa addressed the man by putting her hand on his shoulder and gestured to him with her other one. "He is my head groomsman at my stable. He's been the only one able to handle Hope safely, seeing as how she's too dangerous for anyone to be around. Hopefully we can get her off the trailer and into a stall to calm down without too much trouble."

"That's the plan," Frank nodded, grinning.

"Well then, let us begin," Myles said, his bold Argentinian accent sounding like a symphony of nonexistent instruments playing a tune with every word he spoke. The melody of his tone spoke with utmost authority over his national origin. The man was quite handsome and very masculine in stature, his eyes gentle and caring as Jenna'd hoped they'd be. She had to guess he was in his upper twenties, but he hadn't lost much of his youthful charm and looks.

As they all headed for the back of the trailer, the clatter of hooves sounded again, and a distinctly agitated snort soon followed. Ryan assisted Myles in unlatching and lowering the ramp down.

As soon as it hit the dusty ground, Jenna was completely blown away with what she saw. Hope Shines was a beautiful silvery gray horse with solid grays, blacks, and whites in a snowy blizzard across her shimmery, soft-looking hide. While the pattern of Bentley's coat had a dappled look, Hope had no pattern whatsoever. She had a chaotic mess of beauty beyond anything even the greatest of artists could design. Her almond-shaped eyes were bright, her ears attentive; the blackness of her mane and tail flowed down across her well sculpted neck and out behind her. The elegant locks of both hung in loose gentle waves similar to that of Bentley's hair.

She was definitely smaller than Bentley from what Jenna could see. And she clearly did not possess the same draft horse build as her beloved horse. She looked to be just a couple inches shorter than Bentley and wasn't quite as muscular as he was, but she was very well built from what she could tell in the dimmed light of the closed-in trailer.

Hope turned to looked at her as soon as the ramp went down, her eyes almost seeming to lock with her own. At the sight of Hope, the first thing that came to Jenna's mind was, *Wow!*

Jenna could tell just by the look in her dark eyes and the way she held herself that she was tense and untrusting, and she completely understood why.

"Vanessa, she's gorgeous!!" Jenna commented, finally unable to take her eyes off the horse.

"Yes, I have to agree." Vanessa smiled, looking from Hope to Jenna then back again.

"What type is she?" Ann asked, also mesmerized by her beauty.

"Morgan, I think," Vanessa replied. "Might even have parts of other good breeds."

"Okay, let's get her out of there and into a stall," Jenna decided.

"Myles?" Vanessa said, diverting her gaze to the man to which he nodded.

Entering the trailer, he edged toward her, Hope tensing more as he approached. Myles walked slowly and carefully, avoiding any sudden movements. Keeping along the left wall, he reached for the lead rope tied up on the ring three-quarters up the wall. But while he was attempting to pull it loose, Hope suddenly lurched forward and Myles had to step back. Jenna could have sworn she'd seen the flames of anger in the horse's eyes as she reacted this way. Myles made another attempt, but the beautiful gray half reared and squealed at him. Her ears laid back, she pawed a hoof at him, backing herself against the back of the trailer. Jenna observed this behavior carefully and knew of something to do.

"Mind if I take a crack at it?" she asked and looked from Myles to Vanessa.

"I don't know." Vanessa sighed uneasily, peering over at her parents. "Are you sure that's a good idea?" she wondered.

"It'll be fine." Jenna smiled. "I know what needs to be done." She glanced back over her shoulder at her family. "Please?" she gently begged.

Ryan and Ann looked to each other.

"Is there somewhere you have to be?" Rose asked, looking at Vanessa.

"Take all the time you need. I've got plenty of time," she replied.

"All right." Ryan sighed reluctantly, turning to his daughter. "But take it *very* slowly."

Vanessa gave Myles a nod, and he backed away from Hope. Jenna shot her a smile and turned back to Hope who stared at her with cautious eyes. Reaching into her pocket, she pulled out a packet of sugar cubes. She took one out and put the rest back into her pocket. Then she edged toward the ring on the wall. The horse tensed and stared but stayed still, twitching her ears nervously. Jenna eased up and pulled the slip-knotted lead lose, Hope jumping slightly at the jolt. Moving to the middle of the trailer, she let the rope hang loose so as not to spook her. And, dropping it, showed her the sugar cube she'd been concealing this whole time. Hope sniffed and perked her ears forward.

"You want it?" she whispered. "Well, ya have to come get it and take it from me. But you'll have to trust me."

Jenna turned away and held the cube so Hope could see it. As she stood there and held the cube out to Hope, the horse stood there staring at her, stiff as a board. Jenna dropped her eyes away from her, while tracking her carefully with her peripheral vision. She was relieved when a sound of slow cautious hoof steps edged toward her. A soft, velvety muzzle lipped up the cube, Hope's warm breath on her hands. Jenna turned back to her, the horse's eyes shimmering through her parted forelock as the filly gave a sighing snort at her. Jenna calmly reached for the rope. She was able to take it and let it hang loosely in her grasp.

You know just because I came to you, doesn't mean I trust you yet, Hope seemed to say. Jenna smiled. *We'll see,* she thought to herself. Jenna then proceeded to lead her out; Hope jumped slightly at the slight tug on her halter, but walked on nonetheless. As soon as the breeze hit her, she hopped forward and pranced anxiously about. Jenna simply remained calm and spoke to her soothingly, and she eventually calmed again, though her ears still twitched. Her dark eyes darted about nervously, her muscular body tensing at anything and everything.

Jenna smoothly pointed her toward Vanessa and Myles, who both remained still and calm. Hope perked her ears forward at them. Taking a cautious step forward, she began to stretch her neck out to Vanessa, who was the closest. Vanessa leaned in to come nearly nose to nose with the horse, delicately blowing air in her nostril. Hope's nose twitched, and her ears flicked back and forth toward her. And for a moment, she looked more curious than afraid.

Jenna instantly caught on to this and felt an amazing sense of optimism for the filly. Hope seemed to notice Myles standing there as well, since she turned to him and edged forward to reach him just enough to snuffle his glossy, dark hair. Myles just remained still and calm, speaking to her in a low gentle voice, as she explored him for only a few seconds, before pulling away to sigh and shake her head and neck, almost as though she had completely calmed down.

Seeing this, Jenna tenderly led her on, letting her explore her surroundings as they went. She would allow the horse to stop occasionally to inspect whatever may have concerned or spooked her, then would slowly make their way farther into the barn.

"No one who has ever handled her has ever gotten her to do that so quickly before," Vanessa remarked thoughtfully, while watching Jenna return to them.

"I've just learned to observe and listen to what they need and give it to them in the best way I can," Jenna replied as she reached them again.

"Well, I'm impressed already," Vanessa articulated. "I think you've already made progress with her. And she hasn't even been here an hour."

"So do you have a deadline?" Rose asked as they strode toward the front of the vehicle.

"No, not really," Vanessa answered. "I honestly don't care how long it takes. I just want the horse my nephew loves so much to finally be manageable for us. Most folks say she's *a lost cause*, but I don't. I do believe she could be a good horse, once we figure out how she operates."

"We'll do our best to try and help her," Jenna told her confidently.

"Good." Vanessa smiled. "Thanks again. This may well be her last chance to become a good horse. She seems to be the kind of horse that would do well in the show ring in all events. Oh, and by the way, would it be okay if my nephew stops by once in a while to see her?"

"Absolutely," Ryan answered, grinning.

"That would be great!" Jenna spoke up positively. "Having him stop by can also be helpful for Hope's training. It could help us establish a bond between them and allow them to get to know each other."

"We have high hopes for her already," Matt remarked.

"Wonderful!" Vanessa smiled. "Well, we should be getting going," she said after a short pause. "We have other business to attend to. Let's go, Myles."

The two opened the doors to the truck.

"You take care now, ya hear?" Frank called after them, hugging his wife close.

The family watched Vanessa drive away and waved as she disappeared down the road.

Chapter Three

Establishing Bonds

"So what do ya think of Hope already?" Ryan asked over dinner that night.

Rose had prayed, and they'd been eating and talking ever since.

"I think she has a lot of potential," Jenna returned, passing the carrots to her mother. "I think if we calm her down and work with her a little bit, her real temperament and personality will start to show through."

"So you think there *is* more to her then," Frank speculated, winking at her.

"I think so, yeah." Jenna nodded. "I think she's just a bit too fearful and anxious right now. I bet if we curb that nervousness and establish trust, we'll hopefully start to see her come out of her shell. Start to see her true personality."

"Well, I think that sounds wonderful, dear," Rose remarked.

"So what do you think we should do with her first?" Matt asked from across the table after swallowing a mouthful of potatoes.

"I'm not sure yet," Jenna admitted, grasping her fork loosely in her right hand, resting on the table's surface. "I'm praying that God'll help me figure out what to do."

"I don't doubt that He won't." Frank smiled proudly.

Jenna returned one, as they resumed eating.

****

Jenna shot herself upright. Her breath jerked her at chest, as she became aware of her surroundings. She gave a soft groan, as she rolled her eyes up and plopped back against the pillow, pulling the covers over her face, in hopes of escaping the sunlight pushing through the light drapes.

Jenna trekked down the stairs a short time later, meeting Matt sitting at the dining room table eating; the rest of her family congregated around the large cedar table with him. As soon as she hit the bottom step, they all glanced up at her.

"Well, good morning, sunshine." Ryan grinned, half-jokingly.

"Get enough rest, sleepyhead?" Matt teased, fighting back the urge to laugh out loud.

"Very funny, Matt," Jenna returned, shaking her head at him humorously. "But I didn't sleep *that* much. Couldn't if I tried."

"Sure you couldn't." Matt smirked.

Jenna batted a hand at him, which he dodged. Then, picking up his bowl, he retreated into the kitchen, the girl following without hesitation.

Eventually bursting out the front door, they raced to the barn, slowing as they neared the closed door. They pried the door to the first barn, closest to the fencing extending along the right of the buildings to the arena, open after unlatching it. The silent, startled snorts and shifting of hooves and hay met them. As the sunlight cut out a long square out of the darkened corridor, with only their own shadows defining their presence in the doorway, Matt and Jenna strode into the barn, glancing at each stall as they went.

The horses were all aware of the newcomers by now, and most of them were becoming very curious and expectant, given the time of day it was. Hope whinnied nervously and pranced about in her stall, her flowing mane flopping in her face.

"Shhh, easy, girl," Jenna soothed from a distance.

Matt strode past the tack room, and turned to face the small hall of feed bins and counterspace, connecting the two identical barns together.

Looking up to Jenna, while still holding the broom that he'd grabbed when they entered.

"We've got a remedy for that, Horse Girl." Matt joked, smirking.

"I know." Jenna shrugged one shoulder. "I'm just trying to get her used to the sound of my voice."

"Good point." The younger boy shrugged, holding the broom with both hands by now.

"Let's work on feeding the horses first," Jenna decided after a pause. "We can clean up while they're eating, then we can run them out into the paddocks for the day."

"Yeah, good plan," Matt agreed, giving her a thumbs-up.

****

"That's the last one," Matt called, closing the gate behind the horses.

"All except for Hope, Dani, Checkers, and Bentley. But I'll let Bentley out myself." Jenna returned, feeding Dani a carrot. "I also kept Micah, Zelda, and Violet in too," she added. "Barn two." She reached up to scratch the tiny half-star on the black mare's forehead, which she welcomed with a pleased sigh.

"Is there a reason you wanted to keep them inside?" Matt wondered curiously. "I mean Hope I understand, but the rest of them?" He trailed off to leave it open for Jenna to respond.

"I wanted to keep Dani in because I noticed some bumps on her back the other day when we brought her in. I think the bugs went to town on her, and the bites got a bit irritated. I wanna be sure they heal before we send her out again. Got any oils that might speed up the process?"

"Sure do," Matt conveyed, tossing a tiny spray bottle in her direction; which she easily caught. "It's an oil blend of several anti-inflammatories that'll clear the infection right up."

"Great, thanks!" Jenna smiled, opening the stall and letting herself in.

"Once you spray the infected areas, use the *actual* fly spray oil blend on her," Matt called, poking his head around the corner again. "Then put on her extra-light summer blanket. That'll hopefully keep the bugs off of her, so you can still let her out with the other mares when you're done."

"Good idea, thanks," Jenna called over her shoulder.

"No prob!" Matt called, turning with a wave over his shoulder to head down to the other end of the corridor, starting the sweeping from there.

Finishing up with Dani, Jenna let the mare out with the other horses. Matt was almost halfway done with the sweeping by the time she returned.

"Oh and by the way," Jenna spoke up, hanging Dani's halter on the doorpost next to her stall, between hers and Checkers's stalls. "I kept Bentley in because he's great with new client horses. He seems to have a way with helping them settle in while they're here."

****

"Makes sense I guess," Matt realized.

"Yep, and Zelda and Micah both have lessons today." Jenna finished, coming closer to him. "So we kinda need them in for that, easier for mom's students."

"Guess what day it is!" Kate's voice called, as she suddenly jumped out into the doorway in sight. Matt and Jenna looked up and immediately leapt forward toward her cheering.

"Hump day!"

Both landed a stance, much like Kate's. The three kids made their way closer to each other, each cheering and showcasing their own little jig as they went. The three danced 'til they were laughing so hard, they could hardly breathe.

"So." Kate sighed, finally recovering from the laughter. "What did I miss?"

"Not much." Jenna shrugged, grabbing a pitchfork. "Just doing some cleanup." She grabbed another handle. "Ready to chip in?" she asked, abruptly tossing a fork at her friend.

The girl flinched but still caught it. "Sure, yeah, I'm ready." Kate sighed, rolling her eyes humorously, staking the end of the fork's handle

to the concrete floor. "Boy, did I pick a good time to show up. And here
I thought I was gonna miss out on all the fun."

It was now Jenna's turn to roll her eyes knowingly at her friend's
sarcasm. "Heh, you didn't think we wouldn't save some for you, did
you?" Jenna teased.

"Okay, you got me," Kate surrendered, dropping her shoulders in
defeat, still smiling. "I love helping out even with the jobs that *aren't*
as fun."

"I know." Jenna winked at her friend. "But we always seem to find
ways to make it fun."

"I'll say," Matt called from the far end of the corridor. "We can be
pretty creative when we wanna be," he finished, as he strode up to the
two girls. "Okay, you guys work on the stalls, and I'll. . . go kick back
and drink some lemonade with Fergus and Penny." He then started to
walk off toward the house.

"Matt!" the two girls shouted after him, half-laughing.

"What?" Matt called back, turning to continue by walking
backward, shrugging his shoulders. "I'm joking. I'm just going to see
if Ann and Ryan have anything else they want us to do." Kate staked
her fork once more.

"He's *your* friend," she said, sassily craning her neck toward Jenna.

"Well, he's yours too," Jenna deadpanned, jabbing her elbow into
her friend's arm.

Kate just withdrew, laughing as she and Jenna headed back to their
work.

****

"So why's Ben and Hope still in?" Kate asked, finally noticing the
two horses sniffing noses through the rungs of the stalls. "And is that
Checkers?"

"Yeah, Hope's not used to human contact yet, so I think if we
just hang around here. She'll begin to get used to our presence,"
Jenna explained, leaning the fork against the stall, and picked up

the wheelbarrow handles. "Then we can start to build trust with her through touch and smell."

Kate fell in line with her as they wheeled the manure out to the large pile. "So what'll we do when chores are done?" Kate asked, shaking the wheelbarrow vigorously.

"Well, I guess we could just hang out. Try to see if we can get closer to her," Jenna guessed, letting her wheelbarrow drop back on to its back legs. The two girls turned back, dragging the wheelbarrows along behind them with one hand as they trudged back to the stable.

"Hey, guys, the hay load'll be here soon!" Matt called from the other side of the barn as they entered. "Ryan wants us to clear a space in both barns."

"Okay, coming!" Jenna yelled back. "Let's start in here then move on to barn two," she finished, when they joined Matt.

"Sounds like a plan," the younger boy said, pulling himself up onto the higher bales. "Kate, stay low. You and Jenna can stack from the ground up. I'll handle the higher ones."

"Sure thing." The black girl nodded.

They were just finishing up the stacking in the second barn, when a truck hauling a big hay rack pulled in, honking its horn.

"Hay's here," Matt said, brushing his hand across his brow.

"You sure it even left?" Jenna asked jokingly, picking off a few strands of golden wisps that were roughly sticking out of his dark hair.

"You've got so much hay on you, the horses might think *you* are lunch," Kate added, snickering.

"Well then, just call me the King of Hay!" Matt joked, adopting a regal persona.

"Well, all right then, Your Majesty," Jenna stated, bowing with Kate.

"More like hay fever," Kate murmured to Jenna, earning herself a giggle from her friend, muffling it into her hand. They both straightened up, just as Ryan and the rest of the family strode up to join them.

"Ready to get this done?" Ryan asked, pulling on his last work glove.

"Yep, we're all set," Jenna reported happily. Ryan climbed up onto the rig and singlehandedly helped heave Frank up as well.

"Your grandpa and I'll drop the bales, and Ann and Rose can stack them," Ryan told his daughter. "You kids can bridge the gap from here to the barns."

"You got it, Dad," Jenna replied, nodding.

Frank pushed a bale to the edge with his leg. "Ready?" he called. "Timber!" He pushed the bale over the edge and went on to the next one.

Amongst the lot of them, they finished the hay stacking in less than an hour and a half and sent the truck on its way. Jenna combed through her dusty blonde hair, shaking the hay strands that had intertwined themselves in her loose ponytail. She suddenly heard a snort and turned around.

Hope was peering over the door at her, her ears forward and attentive and her eyes curious. Jenna turned toward her, and Hope flinched but remained where she was. Jenna stopped and remembered what she had to do. Taking out a sugar cube, she approached slowly, holding it where she could see it.

"It's okay, girl. You can trust me," Jenna murmured softly to the filly.

Hope stepped anxiously from side to side, ears twitching, but then she slightly calmed down, raising her nose to sniff the air. Jenna had managed to get close enough, now that she could now stand nose to nose with her. Hope leaned forward to sniff her, and Jenna blew gently into her nostril. Hope remained a bit tense, but once Jenna offered her the cube, she relaxed a little more.

"Good girl, Hope," Jenna whispered to her. She put her hand up to the filly and allowed her to explore it.

Hope's nose was soft to the touch, and Jenna kept her hand still so as not to scare her away. Hope eventually became disinterested with this and looked away. Jenna withdrew her hand, knowing that she had to build a little more trust with her before trying to pet her.

****

The next couple days were much like the first two; Jenna would take time to hang out around the filly's stall and even come by to visit. Jenna held her hand up to Hope again, and the filly inspected it again. Jenna eased her hand forward ever so slightly, her fingertips being the only thing to touch her soft face. Hope jolted at the sudden feeling but didn't seem to mind otherwise. She then attempted to rub her fingers in a gentle circular motion, working her way around her face.

Jenna's heart leapt in her chest. She never thought she could get this far after only a few days, but the pride and relief she felt bubbled up in her as she calmly continued.

****

"So how's Hope doing?" Kate asked when she arrived one morning.

"She's actually been doing really well," Jenna responded, half astonished herself. "She's been slowly accepting me and getting used to me being around her."

She opened Zelda's stall, and the leopard-print mare came to her instantly. The horse snorted welcomingly, setting her head in Jenna's hands, as she began slip the halter off her shoulder.

"I haven't been able to comfortably pet her yet, but she's definitely getting used to my fingers on her face, so that's a start."

"Sounds like she's improving already," Kate reasoned.

"She is." Jenna sighed, adjusting the halter straps on Zelda's head. "Believe it or not."

"Well, you sound optimistic," Matt noted cheekily.

"Yeah, sorry. I guess I've just been surprised by her progress so far." Jenna sighed, leading Zelda out of her stall and out toward the round pen. "I can't help but wonder why nobody has been able to make progress with her anywhere else. I mean, she seems like a really good horse once you really get to know her."

"Maybe it just takes a special person to get them there," Matt suggested. "Hint, hint." He elbowed her knowingly.

"That's how it was with Amir," Kate reminded her.

"That was different," Jenna replied earnestly, as she led Zelda into the round pen. "Amir would have been sent to the slaughterhouse for no reason if I didn't help him. He was a good horse, but people ultimately gave up on him because he wouldn't jump like he was bred to do."

"Right, but he was also a severe danger to the competitors and staff because he was so highly strung, no one could be around him," Kate recalled.

"That's 'cause they didn't understand him," Jenna answered definitively. She clicked her tongue and sent the mare around the circle, one hand holding the lunge line and leaving the other extended out from her body. "Amir had suffered a traumatic experience the summer before we met him and, since then, had not been given the appropriate amount of time and effort in getting him back in the game. He needed some extra TLC in order to fully heal and start jumping again, and his owners didn't give him that. That's why he responded the way he did. They needed to work with him a bit more often to help him overcome his injury and the emotional trauma of the experience. Sending him to the slaughterhouse was too extreme and needed to be stopped. No sense in destroying a perfectly good horse with a very fixable issue."

"But that's exactly why *you* did," Matt reinforced. "You've gotta gift that no one I know has."

"A gift that sets you apart from the rest," Kate added.

"Heck! They wrote an entire article for a magazine about it!" Matt disclosed, waving his hand in the air and gazing up into the clear blue sky.

"Yeah, but it still seems to be a bit too easy to gain her trust," Jenna articulated thoughtfully, signaling Zelda to stop and come to her. "At least for how *messed up* she's supposed to be."

"Maybe getting to know her isn't the issue," Kate guessed.

"Maybe," Jenna thought, "but then if that's not it, what is?"

All Kate and Matt could do was shrug. Jenna heaved a deep sigh and looked at Zelda, who gently nuzzled her shoulder.

****

Jenna hung her jacket up on its hook, and slipped off her boots. She stepped out of the mud room and glanced to the her left. At that moment, Matt and Kate came in the front door behind her, as she found her parents and grandparents all lounging together in the living room.

"Coming in for a break?" Ann asked her when she looked up from her book, peering over her reading glasses at her daughter.

Jenna nodded, then turned toward the kitchen.

"There should be some fresh homemade muffins on the counter you can have," Rose called after her. "You and your friends can help yourselves to them, just made them today."

"Sweet." Kate smiled coolly.

"Oh and by the way, the annual Huntington's Exhibition is today. We still need to decide if we're going or not," Frank called into the kitchen.

"Decide? I thought you always go?" Kate asked, through a small bite of muffin.

"We do," Jenna confirmed. "Every year. But—"

"It's at Prairie Rock Stables," Matt shouted in a strained whisper, the back of his hand to his mouth.

"Oh," Kate realized sensitively. "So are you still going?"

"I don't know." Jenna sighed. "I want to, but I'm also afraid we'll see Katrina there."

"Of course we'll see her.." Matt groaned, "..without a doubt."

"Well, seeing as how she *lives* there, then yes," Jenna replied dryly.

"Oh, come on now, kids. Katrina may be a bully, but that doesn't mean we lose our humility," Rose stated, setting her coffee mug into the sink to rinse it off. "She is still a person, a person who needs the love of the Father just like we do. You can't expect everyone to be perfectly just. That is only God's job."

"Yeah well, I don't think that girl has one just bone in her body," Kate muttered.

"Maybe so," Rose returned, still focusing on her work. "But we still must carry ourselves with the light and love that God gives us." And with that, Rose left the room, heading back into the living room.

"I enjoy the Huntington's Exhibition," Kate remarked, turning to her friends. "But I don't know that I could go if *she's* gonna be there."

"I'm not a big fan of her either," Jenna agreed slowly, as they emerged from the kitchen into the living room. "But we shouldn't let that ruin all our fun. And we don't have to talk to her if we don't want to. We can avoid her as best we can and still enjoy the Exhibition."

"I guess you're right," Matt thought aloud. "All right, we'll go," the boy finally gave in.

"I'll call my dad to see if it's okay," Kate said. "Can I use your home phone?"

"Of course, dear," Rose told her sweetly.

Smiling, Kate dove into the kitchen once more.

"You don't have to do this, but I'm proud of you for making this choice thoughtfully," Ryan told his daughter, standing up to hug her close.

Jenna wrapped her arms around him to return the embrace. Pressing her cheek to his chest, she wistfully gazed out the window at the stable across the yard, beyond the gravel driveway.

Chapter Four

Ridiculed

"Welcome, one and all, to the Forty-sixth Annual Huntington's Exhibition hosted by Carlotta and Tony Williams, owners of this here facility, Prairie Rock Stables," a male announcer declared over the microphone. "I'm your informational host, Carter Sanchez, here with you live, on site on this beautiful day! Boy, is it a good time to enjoy the workmanship of the man we're celebrating today! As many of you know, Samuel J. Huntington was a man of his work and put everything he had into teaching others about good horsemanship and trust. And that today is the day that we get to celebrate and remember this amazing man. Games, activities, and food are available at many designated areas around the farm where you can explore and enjoy all the Exhibition has to offer. And don't forget the *Exhibition* part, which will be starting in just a few moments."

"Who'll wanna bet Katrina's got her hands all over that too?" Kate whispered dryly to her friends.

"Without a doubt," Jenna whispered back. "But at least then maybe we won't run into her."

"You do realize the exhibition part doesn't last the whole time, right?" Matt reminded them.

"And do *you* realize that the exhibition part is the most crucial part of the whole event?"

All three teens turned around to meet the smug grin of Katrina in her fancy riding uniform. She flipped her creamy blonde hair back over her shoulder and strode toward them.

"Oh great, speak of the devil," Kate mumbled, earning her an elbow in the side by Jenna.

"Oh, come now, dear, you *had* to know I would be here," Katrina reminded her sarcastically, gently running her fingers up the black girl's chin.

Kate withdrew intensely, glaring at her, already displaying evidence of annoyance.

"We did," Jenna cut in, pushing her friend's forearm into her body, as if to restrain her from saying or doing something. "We just should've known you'd seek us out."

"Oh please, why would I seek *you* out? You're not *that* special," Katrina scoffed, gesturing a hand at them humorously.

"Because you always do," Jenna returned dryly. "Only so you can insult us or gloat about how great you *think* you are."

"Well, I *am* great," Katrina had to agree, closing her eyes in pleased pride. "But that's not the point. Hope you're ready for a *real* show 'cause I *know* I can deliver even if you couldn't."

Jenna's fist tightened; so did her jaw.

"We've never even hosted the Exhibition before. And frankly, we're perfectly fine with that," she returned tensely.

"Uh-huh, sure like I'm gonna believe that." Katrina sniffed.

"As if you'd actually believe us anyway," Jenna returned innocently.

"Exhibitors, please report to your posts at the main arena. Thank you," the announcer called over the mic.

Katrina looked up toward it and then back to Jenna. "Well, gotta go," she said proudly. "The crowd awaits." With that, she turned on her heel and strode away, her hair flipping around and blowing in the wind as she walked.

"Are we ready to go yet?" Kate sighed in exasperation.

"Come on," Jenna said, sighing herself. "Let's go enjoy the Exhibition before Katrina ruins it for us completely."

Jenna began to head off another way, while her friends stared after Katrina a moment longer before slowly following suit.

****

Cotton candy and popcorn in hand, the three friends took their seats for the Exhibition show. The crowd filled every seat in the stands. So much so that some had to stand at the ground rail running all the way around the ring, which was meant to prevent people from standing too close to the actual fence. Matt shielded his eyes with his hand and squinted in the intense sunlight, gazing down to the gate on the far right side of the arena.

"I think it's starting," he guessed, detecting movement. "Look!"

The gate began to open, and a fabulous liver-chestnut mare pranced out in traditional 18th century attire to match that of its rider. The male rider dug his heels into the horse's sides, and the horse wheeled across the level sandy ground with ease. A flag caught the breeze and flapped violently from its pole, which the rider held firmly in his hand as he galloped the chestnut around the ring. The sheet-white hue encouraged a bolder hue of the purple and teal blue words that read, *The 46th Annual Huntington's Exhibition.*

A buckskin gelding, in similar attire, entered the ring shortly after, bearing a female rider wielding a flag of her own. This one was dripped with crimson and bore the face of the man who started it all: Samuel Huntington. His brown hair and green eyes shone brightly in every detail.

The crowd roared with cheers and applause, as the two horses galloped around the ring. As they came around the first time, they were joined by an army of horses dressed for war. The mob of pounding hooves and flickering tails surged into the arena, a mighty battle cry erupting from their riders, giving them a voice as they made their way around once. All of the horses exited, and only a palomino, a filly Jenna guessed, entered the ring, being led by a blonde-haired woman, who ran at her side as the horse calmly trotted in.

The woman halted the horse in the center of the ring and, lengthening the lunge line, sent the horse around at a gentle walk. The filly seemed to obey well, calmly stepping about the invisible circle quietly, her ears flicking as she gave a soft snort.

Jenna observed the woman carefully, knowing all about lunging herself, watching for the different signals that the woman gave quite subtly. And with each command, the filly would effortlessly obey, executing the best possible gait Jenna had ever seen.

The woman had worked the horse up to a canter, before bringing it down to a steady walk once more. Waving, she began to lead it to one of the six points marked in the way an egg carton would be set up, stopping at the one on the far corner of the ring closest to the stands.

The gate opened, and another horse was led out, a gray horse, a horse so gray, it was almost white with only a bit of dappling on its rump and dark points on its face and legs. It too was brought center stage, so to speak, and performed tricks like the first. Only instead of lunging, this horse's handler, a dark-skinned man, had the horse hold its front hoof out in a sort of wave, pawing the ground upon his command. He had the horse switch legs like this and then proceeded to have it trot in this way, so that with every stride, one hoof was held out in front of it. And as it moved, it would switch legs. He even finished with the horse standing up on its hind legs, before leading it to the next designated spot toward the middle of the arena on the fence closest to the stands.

With each of the proceeding four horses, they, too, did tricks unique to them; no horses performing the same tricks. A bay mare leaped over fire, and a cremello one bowed and lay down for the rider to sit on it like it were a couch. A leopard-print Appaloosa demonstrated a comedy routine of taking his rider's hat and dropping it on the ground only to pick it up again and set it back onto the rider's head lopsided. And the final horse, a strawberry roan mare, allowed its handler to stand up on its back and swing a lasso.

When all six horses had taken their places, the horses closest to the fence facing the ones opposite them, the gate opened once more. Two riders, dressed like generals, entered on bay horses, each leading a group of mounted soldiers by the look of it, heading straight down the middle of the arena. And when they'd reached the end of it, they split ways, circling around the line of three horses on each side, boxing them in. The six horses were now lunging in the same direction by this point, as the troops marched from the center of the arena to the rail by the fence and back out of the arena.

After the arena was cleared, the six horses' riders hopped onto them bareback and rode them out as well, waving to the crowd as they trotted on out the gate.

The two generals from before reentered the arena, this time with only about a dozen riders accompanying them. The two generals gathered their groups on opposite sides of the arena, circling them up for a sort of huddle time, if you will. After a short time, though, they broke the circle into a line and charged forward at each other, one side acting as the British Army and the other acting as American freedom fighters. They charged right through each other's lines, and the first group exited. The one that ended in the opposite side stopped, facing the fence, then the first horse closest to the stands turned to its left to lead the group along the rail to the exit.

****

They ended with one final charge across the open stretch, the American side being slightly larger than the British one this time. This final charge, however, ended in a victory on the American side as the British general waved a small white flag and fled with his army. And the American riders bellowed and jeered with triumph as their flag was hoisted up the flagpole outside the arena opposite the stands. Suddenly they all turned and burst into song, singing the "Star-Spangled Banner," and the crowd, of course, joined in.

When the song had finished, the horses filed out, and only one person entered the ring—Katrina on a jet-black stallion with nothing but a white star and a single sock for color on his ivory coat. The horse regally strode forward, and she took off around the ring, waving and smiling to the crowd like the beauty queen she was, soaking in all the attention, as she brought her horse around. Small poles had been set up, and grassy party banners were hung from them, creating a small chute all the way around the ring. Katrina wore a traditional trick riding suit that shimmered of gold, with red stripes across her chest, arms, and legs. The tassels that hung from it blew in the wind, dancing violently as she turned her horse toward the designated stretch.

Spurring him into a steady gallop, she began her first trick. She twisted her body so that her left knee was under the stirrup, laying across her horse's side demonstrating a left fender. Midway through the lap around the ring, she swiveled around to a reverse fender. Her arm remained extended out the entire time, and she wore a constant smile across her face, which glowed pridefully in the sunshine.

Jenna internally cringed at how proud she was, the memory of Katrina laughing at her from atop her horse being the only thing she could see. She gripped the edge of the bench tightly, mentally biting her lip as she watched trick after trick after trick. Finally, after another hour, it was over; Katrina grandly exited to the crackling crash of fireworks and thundery cheers from the crowd. Jenna released her held breath, realizing now that she'd been holding it for, like, half the performance.

Kate sighed. "Ready?" she asked as they stood to their feet.

"Yeah. My dad's waiting down there with my mom," Jenna replied, glancing down at them. "We should join up with them and get out of here before *you-know-who* finds us." Jenna led the way down the ramp to the ground.

The three friends weaved through the crowd to her parents. Finally reaching them, they pressed themselves against the fence, out of the way of the ever-moving crowd of people.

"Hey, ready to go home, kids?" Ann asked sweetly when they finally realized they'd returned.

"Yeah." Jenna nodded intently.

Ryan grinned and shifted his body to wrap his arm around her shoulders, as they began the short trek back to their car to leave.

****

"Can you believe her!" Jenna complained, brushing vigorously at Bentley's bluish-gray coat after they'd gotten home and eaten dinner. "She's *way* too proud for her own good. What does she have to be proud of! Being a jerk? Doesn't sound like anything I'd wanna be proud of." She threw her hands in the air in saying this and resumed her brushing.

"Having been on the receiving end of her awful nature, I don't blame you for being angry." Kate sighed sympathetically, twirling a strand of Princeton's dark mane in her fingers. "But don't let her get to you 'cause that's what gets you into trouble every time." She, too, resumed her work, combing through it. "You let her get to you, and then the whole thing with Katrina comes up, and then you start to thinking about *the thing* again."

Jenna scoffed. "When have I ever *stopped* thinking about *the thing*," Jenna replied dryly, quoting her friend's emphasized words as she moved on to her horse's midnight locks now too.

"You're *still* hung up on that?" Kate asked in surprise, whipping around to stare at her in disbelief.

"Could you blame her?" Matt put in, stuffing more hay into the net he was preparing.

Kate sighed. "I guess not," she realized after a short while, her eyes wandering down to the floor unfortunately. Kate turned back to her work as they all fell silent.

****

The sun shone brightly down over the earth as a little white van sped down the highway. Jenna yawned and stared out the window as they pulled into the long dirt driveway of their church. Her mind swirled with a million thoughts, none of which she could individually think about for very long.

"We're here, Jenna." Her father's voice jerked her from her thoughts, making her jump in surprise.

"Okay," she replied, slowly getting out of the car. She continued to think as they all strolled toward the door of the large building.

The church was a light tan building with an ocean-blue roof, and a cross hung on the eastern side of it. There were two parking lots, one on the top floor and one on the bottom floor. The greeters stood by the door with warm smiles on their faces.

"Hello, Ryan. Good morning, Ann," Mrs. Sanders greeted. "Hello, Jenna," she said, smiling warmly. "How are you?" The old woman laid a gentle hand on Jenna's shoulder and tucked a strand of her light gray hair away with the other.

Jenna felt a flutter of relief wash over her, thankful someone was there to welcome her and her family after the week she'd had.

"Fine, thanks," Jenna answered.

"Wonderful." Mrs. Sanders smiled wider; her blue eyes sparkled welcomingly.

"Jenna!"

Jenna spun around at the sound of her name. She heaved a sigh of relief at the sight of the tall slim figure of Kate who was standing by a taller dark-skinned figure, waving.

"Hi, Kate. Hey, Brian," Jenna said, coming over to stand with her two friends.

Brian grinned broadly. "Hey," he replied brightly.

The three stood there in silence, watching people conversing amongst themselves in the beautiful fellowship they'd all grown used to.

"Where's Matt today?"

"His week to stay home and keep an eye on the horses," Jenna replied. "How's the money saving been going?" she wondered, turning to Brian thoughtfully.

"Fine, thanks," the young man replied, watching as more people arrived. "Kate told me about your new client horse," he went on, lowering his gaze down over to her now. "Sounds like another challenging one."

"Yeah. She's a bit of a handful," Jenna confirmed, shrugging. "But I think I can help her once we earn her trust."

Kate scoffed. "Too bad you can't do that with Katrina," she replied dryly, crossing her arms.

"If only it were possible." Jenna thought, half sarcastic.

"You know it is," Brian corrected simply, his concise response earning him the glance of both girls. "I know what happened with you and her was totally uncool . . ." Brian ventured sensitively. "But that doesn't write her off as unworthy of love and respect."

The girls suddenly looked toward the sound of bellowing laughter as church friends excitedly welcomed each other with hugs and hellos.

"So glad Katrina's not here right now," Jenna stated blandly. "I don't know how much more of that girl I can take right now."

"You know, treating Katrina like a bully and talking bad about her like this isn't really right or nice, is it?" Brian remarked, questioning the two of them, keeping his tender smile.

Kate and Jenna looked at each other and then at the ground. Jenna crossed her arms.

"I guess not," she said.

"Yeah, I guess we haven't really been acting like *real* Christians lately," Kate agreed in a guilty tone.

Brian looked tenderly at them. "Matthew 5:43–45 says, 'You have heard that it was said, "Hate your enemy—"'"

"But I tell you, 'Love your enemies and pray for those who persecute you,'" Kate and Jenna continued together, staring into space.

"'That you may be sons of the Father of Heaven. He causes the sun to rise on the evil and the good and sends rain on the righteous and unrighteous,'" they all finished together.

Kate and Jenna's eyes met each other's and then Brian's.

"Exactly." Brian grinned, a playful smirk on his face. The two girls lowered their gaze sheepishly. "God tells us that we must love everyone even despite what they do or say. Technically speaking, we are all unworthy of love in some aspect or another, but God loves us anyway. And if he can love us no matter what, we should be able to at least try to love others as well."

"I hear what you're saying." Jenna sighed, letting her arms drop to her sides. "And you're right."

"Thanks, big bro." Kate smiled, hugging her brother.

"No problem, little sis," Brian replied, returning the embrace. "Ya know, I know how you girls feel. I used to know someone who bullied me like that too, someone who aggravated me so bad, I thought I might *actually* break something."

"Really?" Kate said in disbelief.

"Sure," Brian answered, sinking into a chair in the side room lounge, resting his chin on the backs of his hands. He stared across the room and out the window. "I felt like doing what you're doing. But I knew it was wrong, so when Sunday came, I went up front at the end of the service to be prayed for and found a better way." He turned and looked the two girls in the eyes, clearing his throat. "He's my closest friend now if you can imagine that."

"Not in the slightest," Jenna answered thoughtfully.

"How long ago was that again?" Kate asked.

"When I was a junior in high school," Brian replied. "He accepted Christ our senior year."

"Wow, I had no idea," Jenna remarked. "That's awesome."

"Wait, you mean Zack? Like Zachary Bennett?" Kate suddenly realized. "Like Tyler's older brother?"

"That's the one," Brian confirmed, pointing to her with a nod. "It was difficult, but it was well worth it." Brian's brown eyes glowed knowingly.

"Well," Jenna said after a silence, "I guess if you did it—"

"We can too," Kate finished with a sigh.

Brian smiled brightly. "Glad to hear it," he said, placing firm hands on both their shoulders.

****

Jenna and her friends were standing in the front row of the sanctuary. The music team were leading the whole congregation in the song "Oceans" by Hillsong. Jenna was thinking about what Brian had said. *There's no way that could work with Katrina, could it?* she thought. But somehow, she heard this voice inside her saying, *Don't be so sure about that. Don't give up on her now. There's* hope *for her yet.*

She thought some more on this as she listened to the music floating through the air. *Maybe there is hope for her after all,* she thought after a while.

****

Jenna sighed. Her temple was braced to her flattened fist, which was anchored to the window sill by her elbow. Her knee also aided in keeping her weight leaned in to the wall around the window, keeping her from falling off of the bench there. She looked across at Matt, sitting in a similarly awkward position opposite her.

"This Katrina thing is driving me crazy," Jenna told him flatly.

The day was fading into night outside, bathing the room in darkness and shadows, at least other than the small lamp in the small upstairs living area on the others side of the stairs just beyond them.

"So why are you letting it?" Matt asked innocently.

"Maybe because I can't seem to get that day out of my head," Jenna guessed unfortunately.

"Well, let's try to change that tomorrow, okay?" Matt told her, reaching his hand over to place on her knee.

"You got it," Jenna replied, smiling at her friend knowingly. "You know, you're more of a brother to me than I ever imagined before."

Matt just grinned broadly. "Guess I'm just that good," Matt joked, rising from his seat.

Jenna quickly grabbed the small pillow he'd been hiding and threw it at him playfully as he retreated down the hall, chuckling all the while.

"Night, Jenna," he called softly.

"Night, Matt," Jenna replied thoughtfully, now sitting upright, her mind wandering off with her once again.

Chapter Five

Building Trust

The crunch shattered the joy in the air, the pound of her heart drumming in her eardrums as the wind whipped at her hair. Terrified squeals and grunts shrilly pierced the thick atmosphere. Jenna bit her lip, the pain in her entire body burning holes into her flesh. Salty tears stung her cheeks as she tried to scream for help.

Jenna's eyes popped open and the ceiling was the only thing to meet her. *Still home, still safe,* she told herself. But this nagging feeling still gripped her, still coming out as tears down her cheeks, pooling around her ears, and soaking into the sheets.

****

"The Exhibition was fine," Jenna was saying, turning the water on to rinse the lunch dishes she'd just cleaned. "The Exhibition was great," she went on. "It's just that, how could the Williamses of all people be allowed to host an event that is based on loyalty, mutual respect, and trust? They've never cared about good horsemanship. All they ever cared about was having obedient, push-button horses that *always* win."

"We don't always get to know the answers, Jenna. You know that," Rose told her granddaughter simply, taking out a plate to dry. "Only heaven knows, and God will not always share those details with us. That's just how life works."

"I know I should just forget about it since it's done and over with, but—"

"You still can't shake the feeling of how wrong it feels," Frank interjected from his paper on the kitchen counter next to the fridge nestled in the corner behind them to their right. "I understand." He stood up to bring his coffee mug to the counter with the other dirty dishes and took up a towel to help dry the clean ones.

"I know, lame, huh?" Jenna sighed sheepishly as she scrubbed another plate.

"Hardly," her grandfather responded and scoffed. "I must say I agree, but that doesn't mean it's wrong for them to wanna carry on the theatrical element that the Exhibition has become so famous for."

"But that's about the *only* thing they got right," Jenna protested, dropping her gaze from the window to the foamy water in which her hands were submerged.

"Perhaps." Frank shrugged.

"But maybe if we continue to speak into their lives, that'll change," Ryan finished for his father.

"Exactly," Rose concurred, gesturing to her son with a toweled hand.

Jenna lowered her gaze again, thinking about this as open-mindedly as she could manage.

****

Jenna would enter the barn every morning to see Hope first.

As the days went by, Hope seemed to calm down and even allow Jenna to enter her stall. Jenna would praise her and treat her with an occasional sugar cube. Jenna just stood there one day for around fifteen minutes before Hope became curious enough to wander over to her. She sniffed Jenna's thigh up her body to her hair and blew in her ear.

Another day, she introduced the halter. And another day, she managed to get it on her. One of these days, Jenna just stood there with

Hope on the halter, holding the lead rope loosely so as not to frighten her. And the horse lifted her head up to nuzzle her upper arm gently.

You're not too bad after all, she seemed to say. Her eyes shimmering through her thick forelock.

****

Matt cleared the way for Jenna to lead Hope out of the barn. Holding the lead firmly in her hand, she calmly entered into the sunshine, bringing with her the calm, attentive filly. Jenna halted her by the fence and tied the lead to one of its vertical posts.

"These'll hold her just fine," Jenna decided, admiring her work. "I'll tie the knot loose so if she freaks, we can loosen it to calm her down again."

"Then let's get started, shall we?" Ryan said, setting the grooming kit on the stool by the fence in front of Hope.

They all turned when they heard the front door open.

"Ryan, can you come help me with something?" Ann called from the house, holding her cell phone to her chest, away from her face.

"Sure, honey," Ryan called, turning to leave. "You guys—"

"Go," Jenna told him abruptly, standing at Hope's shoulder smiling. "We got this."

Ryan smiled back at her and headed off for the house.

"Okay, girl," Jenna said, turning back to the filly who was sniffing at the grooming box curiously, "let's get started."

Jenna took out a body brush and held it up to the filly's nose. Hope snuffled and poked at it with her nose, her ears twitching back and forth intently. Jenna brushed the course bristles against the palm of her hand to introduce her to the sound it made. The horse twitched back at first but settled a moment later, becoming curious enough to investigate it once more. When she seemed calm enough, Jenna took her hand and rubbed it across her neck in slow, steady strokes. After a short while, she stepped back, brushing her hands once more for her to hear the sound again.

Hope jumped once again and turned to look at her, ears forward. Jenna stood there with brush for a while until Hope eventually looked away calmly. Jenna then stepped up to stroke her again. She repeated this sequence over and over that day.

Ryan had come out to join them as she was doing this and couldn't be prouder of his daughter's work.

"Pretty soon, I don't think you'll need my supervision anymore," he told her as she was finally able to run the brush down Hope's blizzardy coat.

"I'll always need you, Dad," Jenna replied, keeping her eyes on Hope's ears as she slowly ran the brush down her neck. "Maybe not standing right there, but you know what I mean."

"Absolutely." Ryan grinned tenderly.

Hope gave a low snort, her ears gently laid back to listen to their voices. Her dark eyes shimmered as they blinked innocently.

"At least she's getting used to it now," Jenna commented.

Hope jumped again as she began to work down her back. Jenna sighed and stepped back again as the filly nervously stepped about for a bit.

"Well, sort of," Matt corrected.

"She'll get there," Ryan encouraged, placing a hand on Jenna's shoulder.

"Yeah," Jenna agreed slowly, "we will." She stepped up to her again to gently funnel the horse's forelock together on her forehead.

The next couple of days was solely focused on touching and feeling, getting Hope accustomed to being touched. Every day they would reintroduce the brush, and every day Hope would slowly accept it quicker and easier.

When Jenna felt she was ready, she began to the same process over again with the other grooming tools. With each passing day, Jenna became more and more confident with using each tool on Hope though it was when she introduced the hoof pick that things *really* got interesting.

Jenna ran her hands down her left foreleg to get her used to the sensation. She was encouraged by the fact that every time she got close to the base of her leg on her fetlock, Hope would lift her foot up and set it back down again with a gentle stamp. Eventually Jenna went to pick her foot up, and the filly willingly cooperated, her ears flicking about gently. The most interesting part, however, wasn't how calm she was but rather the fact that *she had no shoes!*

"Uh, hey, Dad?" Jenna called, tilting her head toward where he was without breaking her gaze.

Ryan peered around the door of the barn at her.

"She's got no shoes," she told her father, turning her head around to glance at him.

"Well then," Ryan said, beginning an approach, "I guess we'll have to get the farrier in here for her. I'll call Vanessa and get her consent." Then he headed for the house as Jenna set Hope's hoof down and placed her hand on Hope's back.

She exchanged a puzzled look with Matt who had come out of the barn from sweeping the halls still holding his broom in hand.

****

Jenna stood at Hope's head. She stroked the horse's forelock, easing her hand under it to rub her forehead. Hope's eyes flashed in a calm blink; a sudden shift made her jerk her head up a bit, but Jenna gently soothed her. The horse's ears flicked back and forth between her and the farrier working on her right hind leg, smoothing out the edges of the hoof to fit the shoe on properly.

"Easy, girl," the farrier murmured softly, holding the filly's hoof firmly in his highly skilled hands. "You know, for being a major problem horse, she's quite calm right now, considering everything."

"Yeah, she's really improved from being here," Jenna confirmed. "But I feel like she may have had, at least, *some* work done on her before Vanessa and her nephew found her."

"I'd say you're probably on the right track. You have good instincts, Jenna." The farrier smiled back at her.

"Thanks, Rich," Jenna replied, returning a smile of her own as she stroked Hope's blizzardlike neck.

Richard began to hammer in the nails, and Hope jolted her head up once more.

"Steady, girl," Jenna reassured, turning her attention fully on her now.

****

When the sun came up again one morning, Jenna went to see Hope first. To her surprise, the filly came to her door to nicker a greeting right away. Letting herself in, Hope willingly set her nose into the halter and waited patiently for Jenna to secure it into place.

"Wow, I think that's, like, the first time that she has ever done this so willingly," Jenna commented in amazement.

"Yeah! She's like a whole new horse!" Matt put in just as astonished as she was.

Jenna began to lead Hope out, and all the filly did was quietly follow, brightly looking about the world around her. Ryan came to stand by the fence as Matt held the gate for Jenna and Hope to enter it, securing it in place behind them. Ryan leaned his elbows on the fence rungs to peer through at his daughter thoughtfully.

Jenna smoothed down Hope's forelock and attached the long line, tossing aside the short lead. She warmed her up with some simple walk, trot, and canter commands both ways, which the horse performed flawlessly each time. Jenna had to admire the elegance of her smooth-looking gait and even tried to imagine what she felt like to ride. Jenna then turned her the other way and repeated the sequence, changing it up a bit as well. The stormy-patterned filly took every command and responded; all who were watching watched her in utmost amazement. Not just because of the fact that she was calm for once but also because she was sometimes wanting to get ahead of Jenna.

The girl brought her down to a steady walk and began walking herself, letting the long line drag on the ground. Hope came to her shoulder and followed her wherever she went and even stopped and backed up when she did.

"Woah! That's incredible!" Matt breathed, awestruck.

"So what do you want to try this time?" Ryan asked.

"I think we should try the saddle and bridle today," Jenna decided. "She seems to trust me enough, and she seems to trust everyone *else* who handles her. So I think she's ready."

"Hope this works," Matt said, handing her the tack through the fence.

As soon as Hope saw them, she tossed her head and whinnied nervously. Jenna put her arm up to her because it seemed to calm her down. Only this time she didn't calm down; instead she half-reared and whinnied shrilly, prancing about anxiously. Jenna dropped the tack and jogged over to Hope, holding her hands up high.

"Woah, girl, woah," she called soothingly.

When the filly's front hooves hit the ground again, Jenna reached for the lunge line and led her in a few tight circles before she could go up again. She held tight in case she tried to rear again and scratched the filly's long, flowing forelock until she relaxed. Then she tried once more, and again the filly went crazy. Only this time as Jenna came closer and closer to her, Hope's hooves lashed out at her.

"Jenna! Watch out!" Matt cried, leaping over the fence to grab her arm and pull her back.

Once Hope's hooves were on the ground again, Jenna handed the tack back to Matt. She stepped forward cautiously talking soothingly, reaching for the lead she stroked her 'til she relaxed again.

"You have to be more careful, Jenna," Ryan said sternly. "You could've been seriously hurt."

"I know." She sighed sheepishly. "I'm sorry."

"I think it's time we call it a day," he said.

Matt unlatched the fence and opened it for Jenna who flatly led the horse out and to the barn.

****

Jenna firmly commanded Checkers to canter, and after a short act of resistance, she obeyed the command. Matt and Ryan watched as she brought the bay mare around the edge of the ring, which is known as the rail. The bellowing sound of barking made her pull the horse to a halt to look over and shield her eyes from the intense sunlight.

A small strange car came thundering down the driveway, one they didn't recognize. A teenaged boy stepped out of the deep-blue vehicle's driver seat. He was tall with light umberish-brown hair, warm hazel eyes, and a slight dappling of freckles on his face. His frame was quite broad for a young man, and well built at that. Yet his face was tender and sweet and handsome, to say the least. The boy smiled a warm smile as he strode to the fence.

Jenna nudged Checkers forward, and she, surprisingly, listened without any objection.

"Hi! Is this Sunshine Ridge Ranch?" the boy asked politely.

"It is," Jenna replied respectfully. "What can we do for you?"

"My name is Ben Stillman," the young man said. "My aunt told me this was the place where she's boarding my horse for treatment, Hope Shines?"

"That's us." Ryan beamed. "Nice to meet you, Ben." He extended a hand to shake Ben's firmly.

"Thank you, sir." Ben smiled. "The feeling is mutual."

"No need for that." Ryan shrugged in a carefree manner. "Call me Ryan."

"Sure thing." Ben grinned as his hand dropped to his side.

"I'm Jenna," Jenna said. "And this is Matt." She gestured to herself and Matt as she spoke.

"Pleased to meet you both," Ben answered, giving them a welcoming nod.

"Same to you," Jenna replied, dropping her stirrups to slide off the Checkers's back. "So you said you were the one who fell in love with Hope when you first saw her?"

"That's me," Ben confirmed brightly. "I couldn't help myself! I took one look and knew she was special."

"I gotta say I agree with you on that one." Matt beamed, opening the gate for Jenna again. "She's been much improved since she first got here, believe it or not."

"It makes me so thankful to hear you say that," Ben remarked thoughtfully. "You have no idea how much I have wanted to get to ride my new horse. She looks like she has a wonderfully smooth gait, which would be perfect for competition."

"You've got good instincts 'cause I see it too," Jenna commented positively. "We're still struggling to get her tacked up, but she's starting to do good ground work. And she seems very well mannered from what I've seen."

"Guess great minds think alike," Matt remarked as Jenna pulled the reins back over Checkers's head to hold them in both hands to lead her away.

"We're thinking about turning her loose with the other horses and see how they react to each other, but I'm really trying to focus on the human interaction with her first so she doesn't become too unsociable with us."

"Sounds like a solid first step," Ben agreed compliantly.

"More like eighth or ninth steps," Matt corrected. "We've had to make quite a few to get her to this point, but at least now we can handle her. We couldn't go anywhere near her when she first got here."

"Improvement is always a good sign," Ben remarked, his demeanor more at ease than when he'd first arrived.

"Ain't nothin' truer than that," Matt agreed heartily.

"So do you mind if I see her?" Ben asked slowly after a short hesitation. "My aunt told me that I could come here for that. But I don't mean to impose of course. I know I should've called ahead."

"No, no, you're fine," Jenna returned quickly. "Of course you can see her." She swiftly ran the stirrups up and led the way to the barn.

"I'll take care of *her* for you," Matt offered cheerily, gesturing to Checkers and receiving the reins from Jenna.

"Thanks, Matt," Jenna smiled, stepping back to watch him lead the mare away. "Hope has gotten better, but we'll need to slowly introduce you to her so we don't stress her out."

"I totally understand that," Ben concurred understandingly. "I can always come back to see her again, right?"

"I'd actually prefer that you did," Jenna returned certainly. "The more we work with you two together, the more comfortable she'll feel when she goes home with you. A strong bond with your horse is key. Knowing your horse trusts you and you trust her is very important!"

"You know you're the first person who's actually told me that," Ben commented, a hint of astonishment in his gentle tone. "Most other stables we've taken her to don't have the value of trust at heart and often think nothing of it."

"Seems like many people have that problem." Jenna sighed unfortunately.

"Yeah, and then they wonder why their horses don't cooperate with them in the ring *or* on the ground."

Ben and Jenna exchanged glances, like suddenly they knew the other inside and out, almost like they'd known each other forever despite having just met.

"Well, anyway," Jenna said finally, slapping her fisted hands against her legs loosely at her sides, "ready to meet Hope?"

"You bet!" Ben beamed.

"Okay, so have you ever been around spooky horses before?" Jenna wondered.

"All the time." Ben shrugged with a slight nod. "Some of the horses my aunt breeds are a bit skittish, so I have to be careful when dealing with them."

"Okay, cool, so just treat her the same way for a while," Jenna said lightly. "She should get better as you get to know her."

The boy nodded, his eagerness showing in his eyes. They headed into the barn, and as soon as their feet hit the stone floor, they heard the scuffling of hooves. Snorts rippled through the long corridors, one following the others, coming back as light echoes.

Jenna clicked her tongue as she approached the first stall on their left. And Ben was amazed when the blizzard-printed filly poked her head out with a gentle nicker. Jenna put the halter on her in no time and held it to clip the lead rope on. Hope peered around over the door, her ears flicking about curiously. She flinched when she realized someone else was standing there but, after a moment, reached her nose to sniff him.

"Do you think she remembers me?" Ben asked, seeming intrigued by this reaction.

"She might." Jenna shrugged. "Depends on what you've done with her since you got her."

"Well, I've tried feeding her treats and brushing her," Ben recalled. "Does that count?"

"How did you treat her when you did?" Jenna asked.

"Calmly and patiently," the young man replied.

"Good. Horses learn from experiences: good ones *and* bad ones," Jenna explained simply. "By giving her good experiences with you and whatever you're doing with her, you're teaching her that you aren't a threat and what you're doing with her isn't going to harm her. And we need to keep reinforcing the good things while continuously discouraging the bad things so she doesn't develop any bad habits."

"Yeah, good plan," Ben concurred, nodding once more.

****

"Thanks for letting me get to meet my horse," Ben remarked gratefully as they strode back out into the warm sunshine. "I think that's probably the closest I've ever been able to get to her since the day I saw her."

"Well, I'm glad we could help you with that." Jenna smiled. "And the more time you spend getting to know her, the more you'll connect and bond as a team. I have a feeling you guys'll be great together."

"Thanks." The older boy grinned. "I'm glad I have at least *someone* who believes in Hope like I do."

"Nope, you have two *someones*," Matt interjected half-jokingly with a smug grin.

Jenna elbowed him humorously, and he retreated from the blow to his upper arm laughing.

"Just let us know when you can, and we can try to set up times for you to come and work with Hope for an hour or two," she told Ben. "Are you free tomorrow?"

"Wow, that soon?" Ben returned in surprise.

"Is that a problem?" Jenna asked, a bit concerned.

"Not at all," Ben replied, gesturing his hands toward her innocently. "It's just that I've heard stories about you, and I guess I thought you'd be a bit busier than that."

"Oh, believe you me, we are." Matt returned, shrugging simply.

"Exactly," Jenna concurred, looking from him to Ben. "We just happen to have time for you come if you're available to."

"Of course!" Ben smiled brightly. "I'm not as busy in the summertime as I usually am, so I should be able to come sometime tomorrow afternoon." He opened the door of his car and put one foot inside, bracing his arm against the top of the vehicle's door frame. "I'll have to call you later to nail down a time, have to talk to my aunt on when I can get away for a bit to come here. She has me helping out around her ranch, Briar Meadow Ranch, for the summer, so I'll have to let you know later tonight."

"Sounds great." Jenna nodded. "We'll be in touch."

Ben smirked humbly. "I guess we will," he said. "Well, see ya. Nice to meet you both."

"See ya, Ben," Jenna returned. She and Matt waved goodbye as the dark blue car dove into the cloud of dust it created, stringing it along with it down the gravel driveway and on to the open road.

Chapter Six

Making Connections

The crunching sound could've exploded her eardrums, yet she seemed to be the only one in agony from the horrible sound. Echoes of squeals, cries, and blares swelled in and out around her. Her chest felt heavy and shook with the rest of her body, forcing her to lay still. The pain radiating all over her body nipped and stabbed at her with a fierce passion so spiteful that she wondered what she did to deserve it. A piercing rumble released a terrified scream from her throat as she clenched her eyes closed to forcefully perform the act.

Jenna was upright immediately. Her chest jerking in constricted breaths as though she'd been underwater for too long, she realized her cheeks felt damp, likely from the tears fleeing from them, and she pressed her half-fisted hands to her forehead, keeping her forearms together in front of her face as she lowered her elbows onto her knees. She desperately attempted to fight the jerk of her shoulders, which her sobs harshly forced upon her, but to no avail did she succeed.

****

The crow of some animal roused her from sleep. Jenna's eyes blinked open, and they registered the ceiling above her. Rolling them down to the side table, she looked at the clock: 9:00 a.m. Alarmed by this, she was up in a snap, hurriedly stumbling about to dress herself to head down for breakfast and chores.

****

"There you are," Kate vocalized when she noticed her friend finally coming their way. She stood waiting with Matt who stood leaning against the first barn's door post. "For a minute, we didn't think you were gonna show," The African American girl remarked with her arms crossed in a somewhat-stern manner.

"Sorry, I kinda overslept," Jenna apologized, smoothing her hair together with her hands before retrieving the elastic from her teeth to keep it pulled back.

"Sure ya did." Kate shrugged, unconvinced, keeping her position weighted on her left side.

"You look kinda tired, Jenna," Matt noted, leaning forward ever so slightly with the broom in his hand. "Are you okay?"

"Yeah, I'm good." Jenna nodded loosely, a small smile crossing her face. "Let's just get to work. We've got two barns to clean and horses to feed, groom, and let out."

"All right, all right, we're going, Drill Sergeant," Kate mocked with a smirk, turning her shoulder away from her friend to walk into the barn with Matt and then Jenna at her side.

****

"So who's staying in today?" Kate asked from Zelda's stall, slowly working at detangling the mare's colorful mane.

"Not sure, lemme check the board," Jenna called back. Jenna let herself out of Kinnick's stall and approached the whiteboard hanging on the opposite wall to study all the names in the columns of both sides of the barn. "I think other than Kinnick, Chase, Hope, and Bentley, everyone else can go out," Jenna said.

"Actually, Micah stays in again today," Matt interjected, poking his head out of Pinto Beanz's stall. "I noticed his tendon was swollen again.

We should let Ryan and Ann know so we can start treating it again, maybe even have the vet come take a look at it."

"Really? I thought we'd finally got the swelling to go down?" Jenna recalled.

"Well, I thought I felt heat on it again when he came in last night," Matt noted. "I was gonna check this morning, but I got sidetracked."

"I'll go do it real quick," Jenna decided, taking the handle of the tack room door beside the board.

Entering the small room, she walked across the planked floor to the door on the exact opposite side of the room. Grabbing the handle, she paused and looked to her right. The door one over from the corner locker facing her seemed to reach out to her as if calling her name somehow. A flash of her opening its door came, and she flinched as it passed. Then she sighed, quickly turned the handle that her hand was still holding on to, and turned left down the corridor that met her.

Micah nickered her a welcome as she entered the stall. His golden coat and dark eyes contrasted each other perfectly even in the dimmed light of the barn despite the lights hanging in the rafters above them. The older horse came to her calmly, setting his head in her hands willingly, allowing her to scratch his forehead, and she ruffled his forelock gently. She brought her right hand around to the horse's right side and followed his neck down to his shoulder, turning around to stand in line with it. Kneeling down so he could feel her being there, she tenderly pressed her palms to his knee and felt down his leg in gentle squeezes.

Micah's head lifted slightly at her touch, and he attempted to lift his knee away from her, especially when she touched the tenderest point on the joint of the knee. She sighed disappointedly as she now felt the sorrowful agreement with Matt's conclusion. Rising once more, she came up to Micah's head to give him a scratch behind the ears.

"Well, boy," she told the horse with another sigh, "I guess we're back to square one again."

Micah's ears just twitched at the sound of her voice, seeming unaffected by her words and their meaning. Kate and Matt finally wandered over to peer into the small space, Matt now holding a pitchfork in his tender hands.

"Guess we better go tell Mom and Dad," Jenna stated, looking up at her friends flatly, still scratching the horse's face.

Kate and Matt just exchanged glances, wondering what this might mean for Micah.

****

The door slammed shut, and suddenly Jenna stood just inside the doorway from the mudroom.

"Everything okay, dear?" Rose asked, seeing the troubled look on her face, having come from the kitchen through the dining room to Jenna's left.

"Not really." Jenna sighed earnestly. "Micah's tendon is swollen again. I really thought we'd gotten past his injury, but I guess I was wrong."

"How bad is it?" Ryan asked, remaining seated in his chair with the morning paper still in hand.

"About as bad as it *has* been," Jenna returned sadly.

Ryan paused as though thinking.

"Well, he is an old horse, Jenna," he said finally. "He was in rough shape when he first came to us, ya know."

"I remember." Jenna sighed, dropping her gaze to the floor. "It's just that he's been here for five years, and we *still* can't seem to stay ahead of his injury, and the arthritis that has set in hasn't exactly helped much."

"Relax, honey," Ann encouraged, coming to her daughter's side. "He just needs some more TLC—that's all."

"I just wish we didn't *have* to," Jenna protested flatly. "I almost wonder if it'd be easier just to let him go."

"Oh, honey, you can't possibly believe that," Rose implied innocently with just a slight bit of drama in her tone.

"I do," Jenna confirmed. "He's in pain, and I know it even if he doesn't seem to be showing it that much."

"Look, Jenna," Ryan began, now at her side to lay a hand on her other shoulder. "I know Micah's journey hasn't been an easy one, but he still has a lot of life left to live. We just have to maintain his injury a bit better. Hopefully soon we can find him a home where he'll have someone to give him the one-on-one care he needs. But his injury is still *very* treatable and *easily* manageable, and so is his condition."

"We just need to keep a closer eye on him from now on," Frank added surely.

"Okay." Jenna sighed reluctantly. "I'll get the ice pack." Then she turned and headed down the hall behind them.

Entering the first room on the right, she approached the small freezer in the far-right corner of the room. It took no time at all to open the lid and seek out the familiar blue wrap for an ice pack and the black sleeve to cover it in the basket beside the freezer.

"Ready?" Frank asked when she'd returned.

"I guess so," Jenna answered flatly.

Then they all exited the room to head back to the barn.

****

Matt held Micah's halter and lead rope and gently stroked his face while Jenna secured the ice pack to his knee. Micah nudged Matt's shoulder lovingly as if nothing had happened.

"Oh, Micah, you're too sweet a horse to have been dealt such a rotten hand," Kate whined, stepping up to press her forehead to the horse's tenderly.

The gelding steadily chewed on nothing and flicked his sagging ears loosely, further demonstrating how calm he *truly* was about the whole situation. Giving a gentle shake of his head to shoo away the flies, he resumed this calm behavior. And instead of this making Jenna feel better, her heart simply appeared to scream louder. Micah made no attempt to move his leg, well aware of what was happening despite not seeming to notice it at all.

****

Jenna mumbled the words to their favorite song, keeping her fingers focused on the mission at hand. Only she remained now, taking some time to think even though nothing could possibly satisfy the nervous drive to avoid it all she could. Yet still her hands stayed calm and gentle, soothingly gliding over the horse's muscly hide.

Bentley simply enjoyed the attention, turning an ear back toward the heavenly sound in which he greatly adored. But even as he was enjoying his time. Jenna seemed too distracted to truly enjoy it herself. The repetitive circular motion her fingers made against Bentley's bluish-gray coat, she'd gotten all too used to though it still could not deter her mind from the thoughts whirling around her head, and she continued to mumble on through the familiar and beloved melody.

"Hello, pretty girl."

Jenna jumped at the sound of the voice and turned around to face the older boy as he rubbed his horse's flurryish neck. Ben's face lit up at the sight of her.

"Oh, sorry," he apologized immediately. "Did I scare you?"

"Ehh . . . a little, yeah," Jenna admitted sheepishly. "But it's okay."

"Oh, okay, good," he said, smiling broadly.

Silence fell over the two of them. Bentley snuffled her hand as she stood there aimlessly staring at the floor.

"So," Ben ventured, breaking the awkward silence. "What are we going to do with Hope today?"

Jenna thought about her original plan then changed her mind when Bentley nudged her shoulder. "Ya know, I think it's time to actually create a *true* bond between you and Hope," she said.

Ben's brow furrowed, giving her a puzzled look. "What do you mean?" he asked.

Jenna smiled playfully at him. "Get her haltered and follow me," she instructed simply.

****

Jenna, Ben, and Hope were standing in the middle of the round pen in the gentle warm sun.

"So what exactly did you mean back there?" Ben asked as Jenna strode around from Hope's other side, carefully following her hand around behind the filly to join Ben.

"I want to show you something," she answered simply, coming up around him to unclip the filly's lead. She slid the longline down off her shoulder and handed it to Ben.

"Stay in the middle of the ring and keep Hope moving along the outside. Keep your shoulders square to hers. Watch her closely. When her inside ear focuses on you, she lowers her head. Turn your shoulder ninety degrees from hers, and drop your eyes to the ground and wait for her to come to you," she told him.

"Okay," he said, smiling intently.

"Ok,.. so send her out to the rail, along the fence," Jenna instructed.

"Got it." Ben flicked the longline at Hope's hindquarters.

Hope was startled but trotted to the outside of the ring just the same. Ben instructed the filly to go to a canter, and Hope obediently broke into a canter after a couple attempts at the command.

After three laps, Jenna called to Ben. "Now try turning her around."

"Okay." Ben stepped closer and almost in her away.

Hope stopped and turned on her hindquarters and cantered the other way. After five laps, Hope's inside ear turned toward Ben and stayed. Jenna's heart leaped in her chest as the filly lowered her head and began to make chewing motions. Ben caught on to these signs as well and turned his shoulders ninety degrees to the horse like Jenna told him to.

Jenna held her breath as she watched Hope stop and turn toward Ben. She perked her ears toward him, hesitating, then slowly inched closer to him. When she reached Ben, she touched his shoulder with her nose and blew gently into his ear.

"Now what?" Ben wondered aloud.

"Walk around for a few minutes," Jenna answered. "See if she'll follow you anywhere you go."

Ben slowly strode forward, and sure enough, Hope followed right at his shoulder, her ears twitching gently, her steps quiet, and her head gently bobbing in a working walk next to the boy.

"Wow! She really trusts me!" Ben breathed in astonishment.

"That exercise is called *Join Up*," Jenna informed.

"What's that?" Ben asked, lifting a hand to Hope's muzzle as she nosed at his upper chest gently.

"It's an exercise that establishes trust between a horse and a human," Jenna explained, stepping her feet up a rung on the fence to cross her arms on the top one and rest her chin on them.

"Where'd you learn to do *that*?" Ben wondered, now able to hold Hope's halter and tenderly scratch her face.

"My aunt, Miranda Morris," Jenna returned thoughtfully, recalling the years she'd spent training with her.

"She must be really smart and good with horses," Ben guessed admirably, running a knuckled finger across Hope's blizzardy face.

"She is," Jenna confirmed knowingly, her slight smile remaining. "She works with horses that have physical and emotional problems just like I do."

"That's so cool." Ben smiled up at her as Hope continued to stand there calmly next to him.

"I know," Jenna agreed. "She taught me a lot of the stuff she uses on the horses she treats in Texas."

"She lives in Texas?" Ben seemed surprised by this.

"Yeah." Jenna shrugged one shoulder, gazing out into the distance. "My whole family used to live there, but then my dad felt God tell us we needed to move." She looked down to meet his thoughtful gaze. "So we came out here."

"Oh," Ben returned simply. "Guess you guys have a lot of faith in your God to make such a huge change."

"Yeah, we've never had a reason not to," Jenna mentioned. "But trust me—it was not an easy change to make."

"I bet." Ben nodded understandingly. "But you've clearly done well with it. I mean look at this place. It's gorgeous. And you"—he locked eyes with her for a moment—"you've built up quite the reputation around here, and from the sound of it, you weren't even trying to."

Jenna's smile widened ever so slightly as her eyes dropped to the ground below where she now sat on the top rung of the fence.

"Maybe," was all she could respond with. "Now come on," she said, switching gears. "I'll show you something else I learned from her. It'll help strengthen your new relationship." Then Jenna hopped down off the fence and Hope lifted her head in response to the sudden movement, Ben soothing her immediately.

"Okay, let's go." The boy decided, then he and Jenna led Hope back to her stall.

****

"So what was your life like back in Texas? Did you do what you do here?" Ben wondered as he vigorously brushed at Hope's dusty coat.

"It was good," Jenna responded lightly, leaning against the wall of the stall next to its door. "We had a small family farm, not anything like this of course. But we had space to keep two horses. One was my dad's." Her voice slowed as she talked, her eyes lowering to the floor. "The other was my mom's. They were the horses I learned to ride on."

"That sounds nice," Ben commented brightly, slowly bending down to work the crusted dirt off Hope's legs.

"It was. We had space to ride and a ring to practice in locally," Jenna recalled fondly. "My dad set up jumps in along a trail in the woods for a cross-country practice to work on my ability to adapt. I would sometimes go to the ring with one of the horses and practice at night after school instead of study. But still somehow I managed to pass all my tests with flying colors."

"Not a very studious person?" Ben implied thoughtfully, glancing back at her from his work.

"Not really," Jenna had to admit, shrugging one shoulder again. "But I was good at school just the same. Sometimes when I'd get bored with homework but still knew I had to get it done, I'd take it out to the barn and sit with the horses to do it. It was almost like I felt more focused out there. I still do it even to this day sometimes." Her shoulders hung loosely from her body, her arms lightly composed in a crossed form nearly ready to fall apart but they stayed as they were.

"Sounds like a great way to do your homework," Ben remarked, recalling some of his studying sessions.

"Yeah, when I got Bentley, he almost seemed to *prefer* that I stay out with him to study. So for a while, that's what I did. I'd like to think that it actually helped me, growing closer with him than I ever thought could at the time. Things were kinda rough at that time."

"Sorry to hear that," Ben apologized sensitively.

"Thanks," Jenna smiled lightly, her green eyes sparkling. "Now let me show something." She changed gears again, pushing off the wall to join Ben at Hope's right side, which faced her this whole time. "Okay, this is called *T-touch*. All you have to do is massage your finger in light small circles on her neck then work your way up her neck to her ears then go back," she briefly explained.

"Got it. Thanks, Jenna!" Ben smiled gratefully.

"Any time." Jenna beamed back.

"So what does this do?" the boy spoke up after a short time of working on the horse's luscious coat.

"Well, for starters, it helps calm horses down," Jenna returned. "But it can also strengthen the relationship with a horse and its owner."

"I really need that right now," Ben remarked emptily. "I really *do* love Hope."

"Who wouldn't?" Jenna shrugged, admiring Hope's incredible beauty with all the different shades of white, black, and gray that painted her hide in the most artistic and unique way.

"People in my class." The slightly older boy sighed unfortunately, refraining from his task to drop his gaze straight to the floor.

"Really?" Jenna's eyes widened slightly, her eyebrows raising themselves in a surprised arch.

"Yeah, I've told everyone in my class about her, and they came to see her." Ben sighed again, placing a hand on Hope's shoulder. "They all think I'm crazy. They all just laugh and call her *'Hopeless'* or *'A Lost Cause'*. They think I'm wasting my time on her. But I'd like to think that they're wrong, but . . ."

"Well, I don't think you're wasting your time," Jenna assured him. "Hope is a *great* horse. And you're lucky to have her. She just has a problem that we can't quite explain, one we don't fully understand yet either."

"Thanks." Ben smiled meaningfully. "You know, you and your family are the *only* ones who have *really* given Hope a chance."

"We *always* give horses a chance here." The girl returned confidently as she entered Bentley's stall right next to Hope's. "That's practically our motto."

"Well, I'm glad it is," Ben remarked thoughtfully, turning back to Hope to resume his bonding exercise. "I don't know what would have happened to her if we didn't find you guys."

"Well, I guess you don't have to worry about that now, do you?"

Ben just glanced over at her again, his fingers remaining actively focused on their task. "No way."

They shared a smile for a moment. Jenna leaned her head against Bentley's big neck and played with his thick midnight mane."

"Well, girl," Ben said at last, "I'll leave you alone now."

"Well, I was just gonna take Bentley out for a ride," Jenna spoke up as Ben began to exit the filly's stall. "Wanna come?"

"Sure, if you don't mind." Ben shrugged loosely.

"Not at all," Jenna replied, folding Bentley's blanket over and sliding it down off his back and taking up his saddle.

"Okay," the boy complied. "So who can I ride?"

"Um . . ." She looked down the corridor. "How 'bout Dani?"

"Who's Dani?" Ben slowly followed her gaze.

"The black mare on the end, left-hand side. Her tack is right there on the hooks by her stall." She slipped the bridle over her horse's head as she spoke. "She's super friendly and very obedient. She'll be good for you." Jenna then adjusted the noseband, positioning the straps correctly before securing them in place.

"Oh, okay. Great." Ben smiled, happily strolling away.

****

Sunlight drenched them as Jenna led Bentley out into it and tied him to the tether rod just outside the barn to the left of the entrance, bridging the gap between the two.

"I'll be right back, boy," she told him and began a slow jog toward the house.

"Where are you going?"

Jenna stopped short to turn around, finding Ben standing in the entryway of the barn with Dani waiting patiently at his side.

"Just up to the house," Jenna replied simply. "I'm going to ask my mom if we can take our dogs, Fergus and Penny, with us."

"Oh, good idea," Ben smiled, pointing an understanding finger gun at her.

Jenna smiled back and took off once more.

****

"Mom!" Jenna burst into the main hall.

"I'm here, Jenna!" Ann's voice echoed from the office down the hall.

Jenna turned toward the sound and immediately followed it. She soon found her mother sitting at the desk in the corner immediately to her left. Her eyes studied the computer screen through her reading glasses, and her body leaned over some paperwork, which she would look up at her computer often.

"Where's Matt?" Jenna wondered leaning against the doorpost.

"Off with your father." her mother sighed laying her head into her right hand, while still staring at the screen. "Went into town to pick up a few things at the store I think.. they'll be home in a few hours or so."

"Oh.. ok, so, um, Ben and I are going out for a ride." Jenna began again. "We shouldn't be gone too long."

"Okay. Thanks for the heads-up." Ann smiled at her daughter briefly before returning to her work.

"I just wanted to know if we can take Fergus and Penny with us."

Ann looked up at her daughter again and took off her glasses. "Of course you can, honey," she said, seeming rather surprised by this question. "Why would you ask me about that? After all, they are *your* dogs."

"I didn't know you actually considered them *my* dogs," Jenna reasoned with a half shrug. "I always thought that they were the *family's* dogs."

"Well, I didn't actually *want* to get a dog in the first place, much less two," her mother shot back earnestly.

"Oh, right," Jenna recalled.

"Yeah, but you and your father talked *so* much about it that I guess I kinda changed my mind," Ann went on.

"But then how'd we end up with two?" Jenna questioned, bringing to light the strangeness of the result of that day.

"Well, our family couldn't really decide," Ann explained, thinking back now too. "Your grandfather, Matt, and I liked Fergus better, but you, your father, and grandmother liked Penny better."

"So when you couldn't decide . . ." Jenna trailed thoughtfully.

"We got them both," Ann finished for her.

"But it still doesn't make sense why you call them *my* dogs," Jenna ventured once more.

"Well, since they were just young puppies, you decided to spend most of your time taking care of them," her mother told her. "And you did a lot of the training with them."

"Your father and mother were always watchin' ya outside on the porch workin' with 'em," Rose put in, setting a cup of coffee down on the desk next to Ann. "So eventually, they decided to start callin' 'em *your* dogs."

"Oh well, I guess that makes sense." Jenna thought for a moment. "Well, I guess I can get going then. Ben's probably still waiting with Dani."

"Okay, see you later, dear." Ann smiled as her daughter turned to go.

"Have fun!" Rose called cheerily.

And before heading back outside, Jenna fished the dogs' harnesses from the plastic crate under the bench along the one wall, closest to the front door and took off into the clear day once again.

****

As Jenna strode back over to Ben, she noticed that he had tied Dani next to Bentley and appeared to be practicing some T-touch on her. He looked up when he heard her coming across the gravel drive once more.

"What took you so long?" he called, and Jenna could see concern in his eyes.

"Oh nothing," she replied with an awkward shrug. "We just got a little sidetracked." She then turned to look over her shoulder and gave a whistle, short and shrill. She grinned when the two golden retrievers trotted out from around the house and out the open gate toward them.

Jenna knelt down when they got close and took a hold of Penny's collar. She straightened the dog out where she wanted her and lifted up her left foreleg. Slipping her leg through the first loop, she adjusted her stance for the next one.

"What's with the harnesses?" Ben asked curiously.

"We put harnesses on them because they have a built-in flea and tick repellent," Jenna willingly explained. "And for if we have to get a hold them for some reason."

"Like what do you mean by that?" Ben wondered, raising a curious eyebrow at her as she snapped Penny's harness into place and adjusted Fergus to slip his leg into the first hole of his harness.

"Like if we find a trapped and frightened horse on the trails, one of us can hold them so they don't frighten it more," Jenna answered, working on the second leg.

"Oh, gotcha," Ben noted, winking at her.

Jenna finally secured the last strap into place, then stood up and dusted herself off, brushing her hands together. "Okay, are we ready?"

Bentley seemed to understand the question because he threw his head in the air and snorted. He perked his ears toward the fields and dug his hoof in the dirt.

"I think he says yes." Ben chuckled.

"Me too." Jenna laughed, loosening the knot she'd tied with his reins. Gathering them up and pulling them over Bentley's big head and muscular neck, she stuck her foot into the stirrup and hopped up into the saddle.

Bentley tossed his head some more and pranced about excitedly.

"All right, boy. We're going," she told him, leaning down to pat his neck. "Come on, Gus! Let's go, Pen!" she called to the dogs who happily trotted after them.

Chapter Seven

Strength in Numbers

Bentley and Dani walked on slowly down the calm, peaceful trail, their step completely in sync with one another and their heads bobbing at the same time despite the height difference between them. Fergus and Penny trotted alongside Bentley, panting quite audibly as they weaved through the tall grass next to the blue roan stallion and a short distance ahead of them. Jenna turned them on a trail where a creek ran on the right side and tall and shady trees on the left, creating tall, skinny windows to the open spaces just beyond them. The massive plain could vaguely be seen—its size created a hole like a giant's footprint in the middle of the forest, giving the land a break from the massive swat of tree territory. Only about eight to ten feet separated them from this clearing, but Jenna knew that wouldn't be for long. The rest of the forest loomed openly around them. The small creek ran peacefully at their side. Its peaceful sound brought a comforting atmosphere that they wished could stay forever in their midst despite the chaos of what their lives involved.

Jenna and Ben remained silent for a good long while, both searching for something to say. The only sound that could be heard was the creek gurgling gently, the horses' hooves tromping along the dry dirt path, and Fergus and Penny steadily panting. Finally, Ben broke the silence.

"So, Jenna," he spoke up cautiously, "what is it that you see in Bentley?"

Jenna turned to look at the slightly older boy beside her, noting the genuine curiosity in his eyes. "What do you mean?" she returned mindfully.

"Just curious." The boy shrugged, keeping his eyes on the path ahead.

"I don't know." Jenna shrugged herself, looking ahead now as well. "I guess it's just that we have some kind of special connection. Ya know?"

"I can understand that." Ben nodded meaningfully, lowering his gaze slightly.

"Really?" Jenna turned to him once again, her eyes flashing.

"Yeah," Ben confirmed brightly. "For some reason, I felt that same way when I first saw Hope at the rescue center I visited with my aunt. That's why I wanted her so badly. Plus, I also noticed some physical potential in her. She could be a great competition horse."

The sincerity of Ben's words warmed Jenna's heart, knowing that she wasn't alone because for so long she felt that she was. "It seems to be the reason why some people have such strong relationships with their horses," Jenna commented. "But some people don't know what to call it or have other reasons for why they're so drawn to them."

They smiled and shared a chuckle.

"So what are you planning on doing with Hope?" Jenna wondered, finding it to be her turn to be genuinely curious as they took a right at a fork in the trail. "When we're done treating her, I mean."

"Well, I wanted to have her trained to be a jumper," Ben answered thoughtfully as if unsure until this moment. "But I also hope to ride her in Western-style riding too. I guess you could say I want her for an all-around horse."

"Well, your aunt says she might be part Morgan," Jenna recalled knowingly.

"I know," Ben agreed. "And Morgans are known to be—"

"Natural jumpers," they finished in unison. The two looked up at one another abruptly and burst into a lighthearted laugh.

"Yeah." Ben chuckled. "You sure know your horse breeds, Jenna."

"Studied them for years," Jenna replied, shrugging a shoulder.

Ben shook his head and laughed again.

"What?" Jenna chuckled, unable to maintain a serious composure with her new friend laughing at her. Ben laughed some more 'til they were both laughing so hard to the point of coughing a bit.

When they finally settled down, Jenna nudged Bentley into a trot. Dani snorted, and Ben allowed her to catch up to him, and the dogs bounded after them.

"You know you're the closest person I've managed to have as a true friend," Ben commented. "Even though we haven't really known each other that long."

"Really?" Jenna blinked excessively. "But you're a kind, humble, and talented rider. How have you not been able to make friends?"

"Well, I have," Ben countered. "I just haven't really found any *real* friends, not like you."

Jenna's heart swelled in a prideful satisfaction, knowing that she'd done well, and that sense of humble pride seemed to suddenly make everything in her life seem so much smaller.

"Well, I'm glad I could give you that piece of mind." Jenna smiled.

"It's more than a piece of mind," Ben returned earnestly. "It's true."

Jenna just beamed and half-laughed, dropping her gaze bashfully. And when she looked up again, she pulled Bentley up, and they stopped, coming to yet another fork in the trail.

"Which way should we go?" Jenna asked. She searched Ben's face playfully.

Ben threw his hands up with his reins still in hand, raising his shoulders quickly with them. "You're the expert." He smiled, and Jenna developed a daring sort of grin.

Pressing her heels into Bentley's flanks, she wheeled the horse into a canter, and she whistled for Fergus and Penny who barked and took off after them.

"Hey! Wait up!" Ben cried, nudging Dani after them down the left path.

****

Bentley and Dani finally slowed gracefully to a halt in a meadow out in the open, the open plain they'd only vaguely seen earlier. The meadow's layout spread wide, giving an airy feel. Eagles and hawks cried and soared over head. Far above, the creek that had followed them seemingly the whole way continued with the forest and the mountains now clearly visible. The sun shone brightly against their bare shoulders, bathing them in the golden bliss of a summer day and a gentle breeze through their hair, giving them a refresh from the constant heat.

"Beautiful!" Ben breathed as they both dismounted, beholding this almost-dreamlike landscape like there was nothing else like it. He continued to marvel as they briefly switched their horses' headgear to halters so they could graze without the bit in their mouths. His complete awe across his face, Jenna found, was quite amusing, and she was internally chuckling at the hilarity of it all.

"Yeah," Jenna agreed, staking the longlines to the ground and bending down to pick something up.

Ben sat down in the tall grass as Jenna flung the stick in her hand as far as she could and yelled, "Fetch" for Fergus and Penny to go rocketing across the open land after it. Bentley and Dani's tail swished at the flies as they continued to graze peacefully, their ears alert and twitching but as calm as could be.

"Ya know," Ben spoke up after a short while, "Texas is great, but it really can't compete with a view like this."

Jenna tossed the stick once more and looked. "Yep, gotta give it to you on that one," she said, smiling into the wide beautiful yonder. Hearing the shifting grasses, she chuckled at the two golden retrievers proudly trotting over to her, carrying the stick in their mouths together, side by side, to bring it back to her.

Ben chuckled with her when he noticed this as well. The simplicity of their amusement felt strangely mutual, but the dogs themselves seemed unaffected by their humorous act.

"So do you ever miss being in Texas?" Ben wondered, rising to take up a stick of his own. "If I may ask." He hurled his away shortly after Jenna, and the two dogs took off once more, splitting off to follow both sticks at once.

"No, it's fine," Jenna replied willingly. "And yeah, sometimes but at the same time, I think it might actually have been good for me."

"Really?" Ben seemed positively impressed by this as his tone lightened when he said this.

"Yeah, it . . . helped me to find my purpose," Jenna confirmed waywardly. "I guess for a long time, I was relying too much on my aunt's guidance that I didn't have the faith in myself to *really* do it." She subtly received the stick from Penny and subconsciously threw it again. "I'd like to think now that the distance helped find the strength I already had."

"Sounds like you've got good self-judgment," Ben observed thoughtfully, fiddling with his for a moment before preparing to throw it again.

"Oh, far from it," Jenna returned certainly. "Though I try to be very diligent about keeping in touch with myself and God." She turned her eyes heavenward in finishing her statement as if something were to suddenly flash across it to confirm the presence that rained down on her along with the sunlight.

"Well, I think you're still on the right track." Ben smiled back at her from where he stood bent over Fergus, running his fingers through the dog's long golden fur. And all Jenna could do was lightly smile back as her thoughts began to wonder of a thought deep inside the back of her mind.

****

"Thanks for asking me to come with you, Jenna," Ben said as they were leading Dani and Bentley toward the stables. "It was fun."

Jenna beamed proudly as the horses hooves clattered against the stone floor, echoing down the long corridor. "No problem. It's the least I could do for my new friend," Jenna answered.

Matt was just coming out of Niki's stall with his pitchfork when he spotted them and came over to follow them to the crossties.

"Have fun?" he asked, casually leaning on the pitchfork. Either for comfort or for show, Jenna couldn't quite decipher which though still figuring it was a mix of both.

"You better believe it!" Ben replied happily as he turned Dani around to face Bentley, positioning her for the second set of crossties. "The countryside here is amazing."

"We took Fergus and Penny with us," Jenna said over her shoulder as she slipped her horse's bridle off his head.

"I thought it was a little quieter around here," Matt realized humorously as Jenna gave Bentley a couple pats and hung Bentley's bridle on her shoulder to loosen the girth and pull his saddle down off his damp body.

****

"Why!" her thoughts screamed. "Why is this happening to me?"

The never ending-pain, the blaring lights, the ear-splitting shrieks, a memory from which she may never wake, a nightmare from which she could not escape. Would there ever be an end? Or will this moment replay itself till it drives her beyond insanity?

"Someone . . . please yank me from this never-ending nightmare! Once and for all!" her throat rumbled in the form of a hoarse cry, which she half-hoped wasn't actually real, but then the pain ensued once more, and she immediately regretted the fleeting thought as the scene became white.

Her neck constricted in an icy breath that she suddenly realized wasn't just in her mind. *What is happening?* her mind wondered a bit distantly.

Gingerly slipping out from under her warm covers, she held her arms tightly against her chest as she shivered, walking across the wood plank floor to retrieve her blue-jean-colored jacket hung on the tall coat rack set to the right of her closet in the opposite corner to her bed. She reached out to take it off the hook, but suddenly, before her eyes, it changed color to her deep navy riding jacket.

"How could this be?" She jerked her hand back as her room faded away and all that remained was the jacket, along with flashes of the accident, which zapped back to her as she numbly stared at it. "How is this possible?" her mind questioned, believing herself to be going mad. But a faint whisper in her ear said, "Come to me!"

And somehow, through the jacket, she caught sight of the smallest light in the distance. She took off, and the jacket burst into a dusty, smoky cloud as she ran right through it to sprint headlong after the approaching light, which grew with every stride till she was blindly consumed by its embrace.

Jenna shot upright once again, but this time she was certain it was over. The slightly chilled warmth creeping in through her window was an indicator. Then she looked down to realize that she'd been pinching herself, subconsciously hoping to find she was indeed awake. The nail mark she left with a slight tenderness confirmed her hopeful desire, and she breathed a sigh of relief in the quietness of the dawn-stricken bedroom.

****

Hope must've heard them before they did because she nickered a greeting with the brightest look in her eyes that Jenna and Matt had never seen before.

"Hey, pretty girl," Jenna whispered to the filly, coming to scratch the horse's cheek lovingly. "Ready to try again?"

Hope just nudged her shoulder, enjoying the attention for seemingly the first time since she'd arrived."

"Let's find out your problem," Matt decided, stroking the filly's neck.

"How's she doing today?" Ryan asked, wandering over to them.

"Better," Jenna replied as she easily slipped the halter over Hope's nose. "She's responded to us a lot better than when she first got here."

"Good." Ryan smiled proudly at his daughter. "I'm glad."

Jenna led the filly out the open door, and they headed for the round pen. Matt opened the fence for her and latched it behind them. She watched Hope's eyes when she picked up the saddle and could instantly see fear and confusion come over them.

"It's like you've never seen a saddle before," she whispered to herself. She dropped the tack and walked over to the gray horse as Matt continued to soothingly stroked her. Feeling down along her left side to her foreleg, she lifted her hoof up.

No shoes.. Jenna thought, recalling their previous discovery, and with those unspoken words, something clicked. *Of course!* she thought.

Setting Hope's hoof down gently, Jenna ran her hand down Hope's back; she put her arms up over her back and put pressure on them. Hope's ear turned back to her, but she remained where she was. Jenna took this as an invitation to push herself up and swung a leg over. Hope stepped about but not at all in a nervous way. Her ears flicked back and forth, but otherwise she calmed once again. *Interesting,* she thought as Matt handed her the lead rope and draped the end of it over Hope's shoulder.

She clicked her tongue and gently squeezed with her legs, and surprisingly Hope began to walk very slowly and smoothly. Matt strode to the fence to climb it so he was right above Ryan, leaning on the fence rung to peer through from the outside in at Jenna and Hope. Jenna worked her up to an incredibly smooth canter before bringing her to a halt and sliding down again.

"Great work, Jenna!" Matt congratulated when he and Ryan crossed the sandy ground to join her in the center once more. "How'd you know that would work?'

"I didn't," Jenna admitted rather confidently. "I think she might've been wild once but then captured and trained bareback," Jenna concluded.

"Must be," Ryan concurred. "Good detective work, slick."

Jenna batted his arm at her father's joke, a humorously amused look unhindered by her desire not to smile.

"Well, girl," Jenna said at last, combing her forelock neatly together on her forehead, "we have work to do."

****

"So let me get this straight," Kate began after Jenna told her the story. "Hope was once a *wild* horse?"

"Yep," Jenna nodded as she continued her long smooth strokes down Hope's beautifully colored body with the body brush.

"But she was eventually caught," Kate continued.

"Uh-huh," Jenna answered.

"But she was only ridden bareback?" Kate finished.

"That's right," Jenna confirmed, turning away from her work at this point. "Well, that's at least what we *think* happened." She shrugged loosely. "Might be why she's never worn a saddle before." Jenna then tossed the brush into the grooming kit on her left next to Kate, finishing her statement.

"And now Jenna knows how we can help her," Matt smiled proudly, putting his hand on her shoulder.

"Girl, you're crazy," Kate said.

"Why?" Jenna asked, smirking humorously as she unclipped the crossties and turned Hope around to lead her into her stall.

"Well, I think it's great news," Ryan remarked.

Jenna let herself out of the stall, walking over to the saddle stand next to the crosstie on the opposite wall and took up the saddle, subsequently setting it up on to the door of Hope's stall.

"Uh . . . what are you doing?" Kate questioned, her tone lost like her thoughts.

"This'll help Hope feel more comfortable around the saddle. Get her used to its strange scent and looks, for when we actually put it *on* her," Jenna replied.

"Oh, gotcha," Kate answered, making the okay sign with her fingers."

"Yeah." Jenna answered, shooting her friend a brief glance as she proceeded to heave the heavy western saddle up onto the open half door of the stall and Hope immediately withdrew in fear with a shrill whinny, backing herself up against the back wall.

****

The blue roan stallion tossed his head and let out a loud happy whinny as a welcome.

"Hello, my handsome guy." She smiled, scratching him behind the ears when he lowered his head into her hands. "How ya doin'?"

The stallion tossed his head happily once more, his long, fuzzy forelock flowed beautifully with every movement. She giggled and ruffled his soft mane. He blew softly into her face then stepped back and pawed the ground, snorting playfully. Jenna laughed and shook her head.

"Okay," she told him, "I'll be right back." She ran to the tack room to get her grooming kit and Bentley's halter and lead. He waited patiently for her to slip the halter over his big head, and she led him out to the post outside the stables.

****

Bentley arched his big neck perfectly and curled his lip up as the cool water hit his bluish-gray coat, intensifying the bluish hue of his fur. He nuzzled Jenna's shoulder thankfully.

Thank you, I needed that, he seemed to say.

"Well, you are very welcome." She told him.

"Who are you talking to?" Matt's voice startled her.

She turned her head to see the younger boy's puzzled face. "Uh, no one," she replied, blushing. "Just Bentley."

"Ah," he said. "I get it, talkin' to the horses again. I should have guessed."

Jenna nodded smiling, a slight warmth increasing at her cheeks, then turned back to her horse.

Matt set a bucket of water down in front of Bentley who bent down to take a drink when suddenly they heard barking. Fergus and Penny took off running across the gravel as that same old maroon truck pulled up followed by a dark blue one, which Jenna was surprised to recognize.

"Hi, Kate!" Jenna greeted as her friend strode up to them. "What's up?"

"Not much," Kate replied with a loose shrug.

"Good morning, everyone!" Ben greeted brightly. "Mind if I join you? I don't really have anything else better to do at the moment. And my part-time job doesn't start for a few hours. How's it going?"

"Of course you can join us, dude!" Matt joked with a chuckle. "And not much, just watching crazy Jenna do her 'horse whispering' thing again."

"Very funny, Matthew," Jenna snickered loosely.

They all stood there for a moment, lost in their own thoughts. Bentley decided to break the silence by shaking his body with a playful whinny, spraying them all with foamy water.

"Hey! Cut that out!" Kate exclaimed, laughing.

"You big clown." Jenna grinned.

"Yeah, no kidding," Matt agreed, wringing out his shirt comedically and shaking the water from his dark brown hair.

"I think it feels good," Jenna commented.

"I don't!" cried Kate, causing Ben to muffle a chuckle into his hand with Matt. "I think it's cold!"

"Okay then, have some more," Jenna called, spraying her friends.

"Hey! No fair! You've got the hose!" Matt cried, shielding his face with the empty bucket in his hand.

Dropping the empty bucket, he took up the full one sitting next to her and threw the water at her, immediately drenching her in suds and bubbles. And so the war began. A bucket here, a spray there, sprinkles and squirts everywhere with echoes and bellows of laughter and joy.

****

Dripping wet and exhausted from running, the four teens gathered on the small patch of grass between the two barns. Matt plopped down and sprawled out between Kate and Jenna while Ben stood over behind him, leaning his right shoulder against the side of barn two, facing the group with their backs to him. Kate sat cross-legged in the thin layer of grass beneath them, and Jenna held an arm over her knee to keep it upright. All were breathing hard as they recovered in silence. Bentley whinnied and snorted throughout their battle as if he'd been laughing too and was now nibbling on what little grass he could reach from where he was tied.

"Wow," Matt gasped.

"That was fun," Ben remarked, turning his back to the barn and using it to slide himself down to the ground to sit up against it.

"Wooph! Yeah," Jenna breathed, Kate nodding her agreement.

Everyone looked up when they heard the sound of another vehicle approaching, but it turned out to be one they didn't want to see.

"Katrina," Kate vocalized bitterly, as they all stood up together.

"What's *she* doing here?" Matt wondered aloud.

"Who's Katrina?" Ben wondered innocently.

"We're about to find out," Jenna said, answering Matt's question as the slim figure of Katrina strode across the gravel toward them.

"Hey, Jenna," Katrina sniffed, the four teens bunching closer together as she strode toward them. "Heard about your new problem horse. Quite a beast if you ask me."

"Well, we didn't," Kate snapped, and Jenna stopped her with the wave of her hand.

"What do you want?" Jenna questioned with some restraint.

"Who said I wanted anything?" Katrina replied slickly. "I just heard about that horse. She came to Prairie Rock too, but Mom couldn't help her. She's just impossible. That horse deserves a bullet in the head or something."

"No, she doesn't!" Kate exclaimed, horrified by Katrina's words.

"She just needs some time and encouragement," Matt protested firmly.

"Ha! I doubt that!" Katrina answered. "Oh, and I heard that, come to find out, you're a Christian."

"My whole family is," Jenna replied dryly. "What's your point?"

"Jenna, isn't it obvious?" Katrina grinned knowingly. "We have both lived here on our family's ranches for *basically* our whole lives, and I didn't know that."

"Only *you* have lived here your whole life," Jenna shot back in a dull tone.

"And why do *you* care anyway?" Kate questioned hotly.

"I don't," Katrina sniffed.

"Then why are you here?" Jenna asked, turning away to run the sweat scraper down Bentley's back.

"No reason." Katrina smiled in her catlike way and turned toward her car. "Oh, and for the record"—she spun around again once more—"if you think that your school bus–sized horse can *really* beat Napoleon, you've got another thing coming."

"Never!" Jenna gritted her teeth, trying desperately to hold back the boiling teapot rising in the pit of her stomach.

"Ha! Dream on!" Katrina scoffed.

"Since when do you know what a good horse is?" Matt demanded.

"Uh, since my mom gave him to me. Napoleon was bred, born, and trained just for me. He and I would crush you in the ring."

"Yeah right!" Kate exclaimed. "Jenna is one of the best riders around."

"Then why don't you enter a show to prove it?" Katrina questioned to Jenna's turned back. "Showcase the talent you *think* that horse has. The Summer Splash Invitational is at least a couple months away. . . if you want."

Before anyone could reply, Katrina slipped into her car and drove off. Jenna heaved a relieved sigh at hearing tires squeal and power away from them.

"Don't listen to her, Jenna," Matt encouraged, coming her side to place a hand on her shoulder reassuringly.

"Yeah," Kate agreed sensitively. "She's just trying to get under your skin."

Jenna turned her head to look Kate in the eyes, almost communicating something through just her eyes.

"You were already thinking about it, weren't you?" Kate said, reading her glance near immediately.

"For a while now, yeah," Jenna replied hesitantly. "But now—"

"You're *sure* you want to do it?" Matt implied to finish her shortened statement.

"Well, no," Jenna replied, dropping the sweat scraper back into the grooming box and loosening the knot on Bentley's lead.

"Well, whatever you decide, I'm behind you 'til the end," Kate agreed.

"So are we," Ben added strongly, placing a firm hand on Matt's shoulder. "Can't believe you have to put up with that *all* the time."

"You have no idea," Jenna assured him as they all walked back toward Bentley's stall.

Chapter Eight

Live and Let Go

"I just can't *stand* her!" Jenna openly complained for only her group of friends to hear. "I know I shouldn't say that about someone, but I don't know how else to describe this feeling I have toward her."

"She bugs you. I understand that." Brian shrugged understandingly. "But part of being in the Lord is knowing when to live and let go."

"Letting go is tough," Matt admitted with a sigh, Jenna's, Kate's, and Matt's gazes dropping toward the floor hidden below the table they all stood around.

"I totally understand that," Brian repeated again. "But just like you, I had to ignore the attacks of the enemy that came to me through the words and actions of my childhood bully."

"I remember how insane Zachery made you at times," Kate recalled. "Guess I should remember that for when *little miss perfect* comes around again."

Brian's brow furrowed slightly at her in a stern glance.

"Sorry," Kate apologized immediately. "But some days, I don't feel like I have the strength to deal with her constant boasting and intentional teasing, especially when it comes to Jenna and her thing."

Jenna's glance dropped away from them at the mention of something she knew immediately.

"She seems to always be throwing punches precisely where it hurts," Matt explained, picking up on Jenna's reluctance to answer up to any of this. "And she doesn't seem to care how it affects her."

"Grace is a gift we *all* are given by God, regardless of whether or not we deserve it," Brian reminded them. "Grace is forgiving the sins committed against us and moving on with humility and patience. Forgiveness isn't easy, but there's no doubt it's worth fighting for. God tells us to fight for those in darkness and to never give up on them. He knows our hearts, for we are his creation. And therefore, he knows what we need even before we ask for it. Trust in him to guide your steps. 'For I know the plans I have for you, says the Lord, plans to prosper you and not harm you, but to give you a future and a hope.'"

"Jeremiah 29:11," Jenna quoted solemnly, regret beginning to pierce her side at this reminder.

"Maybe the Lord is testing you," Brian suggested. "Maybe he's preparing you for something you don't see yet."

At this, the three teens fell silent, all dropping their gaze to ponder this.

"When I go to work every day, doing all the random things I do to make enough money to stay in school, I never forget to enjoy every moment of it, even the parts that I *don't* always enjoy, because I know that God has a *better* plan for my life and that I'm not there yet. He's been teaching me that we all have a role to play and a path to take. Mine has taken me places I never thought I'd ever be. And even while I work to wait, it feels like that path won't change. And that dream seems further and further away. The horizon seems to extend every time I get close enough to reach it before he moves far beyond my grasp once again. Trust me. It's not a great feeling. But that's our nature—to expect things to go one way only for God to surprise us with a change. But what we do with change is the true test of our character. John 16:33 says, 'I have told you these things, so that in me you may have peace. In this world you will have trouble. But take heart! For I have overcome the world.'"

"Well, what about Romans 8:28?" Kate piped up in realization. "It says that 'And we know that God causes everything to work together for good; to those who love God.'"

"Exactly." Brian nodded. "And what *else* does God say about how we should live?"

"Um, how 'bout John 14:16–17: 'And I will ask the Father, and he will give you another advocate; the Spirit of Truth. The world cannot accept him, because it neither sees him nor knows him. But you know him, for he lives with you and will be in you,'" Matt quoted.

"Yes, *that* is a great one." Brian smiled spearing a finger in his direction. "And so you see, guys, grace is a toughy, but in the end, it's a *real* goody."

"You have the worst quotable lines," Kate commented with a humorous smirk. "But we get what you're saying."

"You sure that Bible minister isn't something that should be on your resume?" Matt joked lightly.

"Nah, I'm just a humble advocate for Christ." Brian grinned knowingly with the shrug of one shoulder. "But you guys can be teachers too ya know. Right now even. Maybe Katrina is meant to make an example of you. By advocating to her, you may just find the strength you need to rise above her awful ways. Maybe even help point her to the One that can right her wrongs for the good of her life."

And all that they could do now was think some more on this thought.

****

"Easy, girl," Jenna soothed, rubbing the saddle pad to Hope's shoulder gently. Placing it slowly up onto Hope's back, she weighed a hand on it, and Hope's head eased up at the pressure. Softly repositioning it, Jenna let go of it, and the horse seemed unbothered by it being there.

Matt held the lead rope firmly in his grasp, stroking the filly's soft face with the back of his hand as Jenna then took the saddle off the stand next to her and brought it over for the filly to sniff. Hope touched a nose to it and snuffled at the leather, breathing in the now-familiar scent before turning away. Jenna's eye watched with her peripheral vision as she set the saddle onto Hope's back, her ears merely twitching back toward her in response to this.

"Good girl," Jenna praised.

Weighing down on this brought the same reaction, more defined, yet Hope remained calm all the while. Jenna's heart sang at the progress being shown with this behavior.

****

"There you go."

Matt somehow found the owner of the voice without even trying, stopping at Micah's stall. Jenna stood humming at Micah's head, gently stroking his face with her fingers and holding his head in her right hand.

"How is he?" Matt asked softly.

Jenna just looked with her eyes at him with a haunted look in them.

"Don't worry. We'll figure this out," Matt encouraged having read her mind through her glance.

"He's an old horse, so this should be something to expect." Jenna sighed, continuing to stroke him slowly, the horse's ears and eyes sagging in complete relaxation. "But he's become . . . like a family member, and—"

"It hurts to see him like this," the boy finished for her. "Believe me, I know. I'm worried about him too."

"Hi, guys, what's up?" Ben's voice made Micah jump slightly despite his voice not being very loud. "Oh, sorry. Am I interrupting something?" The young man recoiled sensitively.

"No, not really," Jenna replied lightly, beginning to relax Micah once again as he lowered his head into her hand once again.

"Who's this guy?" Ben asked curiously, leaning against the bottom half of stall door next to Matt.

"Micah," Jenna addressed the horse, looking to him as he gently nudged her shoulder and chest with his head to show his affection toward her. "He's one of our older horses here at Sunshine."

"So where's his owner?" Ben wondered.

"Doesn't have one," Jenna returned matter-of-factly, a hint of sadness ringing along with it. "We rescued him from a harsh owner who worked him too hard. He was at an auction where we bought him for barely nothing at all. He was so old and worn down that no one would really buy him. The auction house was planning to send him to the slaughterhouse, but my dad and I saved him and brought him here. He's been a popular horse for people in my mom's riding academy that she hosts here all year round. But lately he's been struggling a lot with his health, and we've been particularly worried about him."

"What's wrong with him?" Ben asked, developing a haunted look.

"He's got arthritis in all his major joints," Jenna explained.

"Legs, hips, back, all of it," Matt added solemnly.

"*And* he's suffering from an old injury to his tendons."

"Oh." Ben's eyes flashed as he looked to the old horse tenderly. "I take it he's pretty important to you then," he continued, hinting at the way Jenna tended to him even now.

"Very," Jenna confirmed knowingly, glancing to Matt. "Thing is I have a feeling his final day is gonna come soon. And I'm kinda not ready to let him go, but at the same time . . ."

"I know. It's a hard choice," Ben agreed, dropping his gaze to the dusty floor. "I had to make it for my last horse."

"Last horse?" Jenna echoed, looking up to him again.

"Yeah . . . He was my best cross-country horse . . . Rocky." Ben's eyes warmed at the fond memory that panned across his mind. "He was gray, much like Hope but not quite as beautiful. But to me, he was the most priceless thing to me in the world."

"He sounds like a good horse." Jenna lightly chuckled, a certain level of fondness to her tone as well.

"Yeah, I got him when I was ten. My parents hadn't named him, so they let me do it. So I named him after my favorite Rescue Hero, Rocky Canyon."

"Really, you named your horse after a kids' show character?" Matt asked, genuinely surprised and a little bit impressed.

"Well, yeah," Ben validated. "It was my favorite show growing up. And he reminded me of rocks too. It just seemed to fit."

"Works for me." Jenna shrugged. "I've seen weirder names than that even in *my* lifetime."

"Heh, yeah. And he *was* a great horse, the best any boy could've ever wanted." Ben eyes darkened as sadness cast its shadow upon him.

"Bad break?" Jenna implied, leaning her head closer to him.

"Came up lame," Ben returned solemnly. "Then cancer set in, and we made the *toughest* decision in my life to put him down. He was only ten when it happened. I had a special connection with Rocky that I almost feel again with Hope, and the more I get to know her, the more special that bond feels. And the more real it becomes. I've been trying to find a horse as good as Rocky for almost two years now. But just never felt that *spark* until now. I just have this feeling about Hope similar to the one I got when I first met Rocky. Haven't felt it in a while, so it feels great. And I hope that Hope feels the same thing I do."

"I bet she does," Jenna agreed. "Horses can sense things like that, and I believe there's something special about her too. And I know that feeling too." She pulled out the chain concealed beneath her shirt to expose the heart-shaped locket that hung from it.

Stepping back from Micah, who pressed his cheek to her shoulder, she opened the locket and took it off to carefully hand to Ben. The boy studied it carefully to view the image that was inside.

"That was Bentley when we first got him. He was only two years old at the time. He was kind of a gift to me after a rough year. But now I can't imagine my life without him. He taught me some of what I know as well as my aunt. She even showed me some things with him when she'd visited a couple of times."

"Cool. So you *basically* trained Bentley *yourself*?" Ben concluded, putting the pieces together as he handed the locket back to her.

"Pretty much," Jenna confirmed as she slipped the locket back on to her neck and hid it under her shirt again. "My grandma helped me with this locket so I could keep this memory close to my heart. Even though I know that's not exactly how it works in real life, I still like the feeling it gives me."

"I can relate." Ben nodded thoughtfully. "I still have Rocky's old blanket. It's in pretty good shape. I was thinking about using it for Hope. . . if she likes it, that is."

"I'm sure she'll love it," Matt agreed, placing a hand on the other boy's shoulder.

"I hope so." Ben smiled meaningfully. "It's just that it meant so much to be having him here, and then . . . now that he's not . . ."

"We get it. Really we do," Jenna assured him. "Micah's practically become part of the family too. I don't want him to go, but at the same time, I feel like it might be better for him. Then he wouldn't have to hurt anymore."

"Maybe the vet has some ideas?" Matt thought. "Come on, Jenna. We can't give up yet."

"Well, let's at least take him up to the house," Jenna decided slowly. "We could have Mom and Dad come look at him again and see if we should call."

"Sounds like a plan," Matt concurred with a smile growing slightly across his face. "Let's go."

"Come on," Jenna coaxed, gently leading the golden Dutch warmblood forward.

Micah walked willingly with her, but his gait was clearly stiff and painful as he did so.

"So these horses all have problems?" Ben asked curiously as they very slowly walked down the corridor to the exit on the far side of the barn, heading into the gravel drive.

"Most of them," Jenna replied with the shrug of one shoulder. "My mom uses our horses for the academy but will sometimes use our rescue horses if their temperament is good. Bentley's the only one that we don't use for lessons because he's my horse. A lot of times, they let *me* decide unless the situation calls for it, but it doesn't usually happen."

"Selfish with your horse?" Ben wondered, hoping to not offend her in saying this.

"Not really." Jenna shrugged, keeping her eyes forward. "We just have never really needed to use him. Also, he wasn't really trained for that."

"So there are horses here that *don't* belong to anyone yet?" Ben went on curiously.

"Yup," Jenna confirmed matter-of-factly. "Right now we only have five: Kyro who's directly across from Micah, Violet, two stalls down from him, and Melanie and Milo here." Jenna gestured to her left as they passed two stalls containing a paint each, one a palomino the other a blue roan.

"And you find them homes yourselves?" Ben wondered further.

"After we make sure they're ready for a loving home," Jenna answered. "We evaluate them from time to time and work with them often to maintain the continuity of the training we try to instill into our horses. By continuing to solidify the behaviors we want to see in them and discouraging the ones we don't, they'll eventually learn to maintain them on their own. Though it's always good to maintain it anyway."

"Sounds like you've got a good thing for you here," Ben commented thoughtfully. "I'm glad my aunt and I found you guys. Or I'd have had to sell Hope, a perfectly good horse."

"We're glad too." Matt agreed. "Nothing is more special than the bond between a horse and their owner other than family, friends, and of course God, first and foremost."

"You really believe that?" Ben asked, not even a hint of condemnation in his softly questioning tone as they all slowed to a stop in the doorway of the stable.

"Well, yeah," Matt replied with a loose shrug, the sunshine on his complexion seeming to lighten it from the dark shadow of a story that *was* the story of his life from the past. "I mean he's always taken care of me and the Tylers. In fact, I'd like to think that he's the reason I was brought here to Sunshine by my social worker a year ago."

"Social worker? You mean you're not blood related to the Tylers?" Ben echoed, his eyes brightening as he turned to face the other boy squarely.

Matt glanced to Jenna who shrugged innocently. "No. I was orphaned and abandoned before I came here. My dad left when I was young. And my mom passed away from tuberculosis when I was fifteen, a year before I was brought here to live with the Tylers. And I've been here ever since."

"And how long has that been again?" Ben wondered, a haunted look coming over his face.

"Almost a year and a half ago," Matt replied. "My mother has been dead for almost two years now, but somehow from time to time, I *do* still miss her like it happened only yesterday."

"I'm so sorry, man," Ben apologized sorrowfully.

"Thank you." Matt beamed with a gracious nod.

"Sorry I asked," Ben added, scratching the back of his head sheepishly.

"It's okay," Matt replied. "I've gotten better about talking about it. And Jenna was a big help in that." He nudged Jenna's elbow knowingly in saying this. "She's become like the sister I never had."

"And him the brother *I* never had," Jenna added, exchanging a smile with him.

"Heh, I guess you guys don't have to ask for siblings 'cause it looks like you already found it in each other." Ben smiled warmly, a tender endearment reflecting off his hazel eyes at the encouraging thought.

Jenna smirked and punched Matt's left bicep. Matt immediately reacted with a smirk of his own, placing a hand to his arm and rubbing it in slight embarrassment.

"I'm an only child myself," Ben went on, "but my adopted older sister is married with two kids, my niece and nephew. They're just about the cutest two people on the planet. I wouldn't trade that part of my family for anything. It's truly encouraging knowing that you guys have something similar in each other."

"Agreed." Jenna smiled.

Micah nudged her shoulder as if to include himself in the conversation lovingly.

"Aww, Micah, you sweet boy." Jenna sighed, pressing her forehead to his and closing her eyes.

"He really is a sweet horse," Ben concurred, softly touching a hand to his golden neck. "It's a shame he's in so much pain, without a home of his own."

"We know," Matt breathed, heaving a heavy sigh as Jenna stroked his soft face tenderly. "But that's why he's here, to get the love and attention he deserves till either his time comes or he finds a home where he can live out the rest of his life for however long he's got left."

"Right now, I'm just hoping he *has* a life left to live." Jenna sighed, combing his forelock together delicately.

Just then, a cheery tone rang out from her pocket, and she reached down to retrieve her phone from her pocket. Across the screen of her Apple iPhone was a message from Kate saying, *"Hey up for a ride? Brian is off for once and asked to come hang out today. You in?"*

Jenna smiled and replied back, *"You bet! Just gotta finish some things up."*

"So, Ben, up for a ride today?" Jenna offered as they began to lead Micah on toward the house. "Brian and Kate are coming down to hang out if you wanna come."

"Sure, that'd be great," Ben replied brightly, almost taken aback by the offer. "But I'm not sure Hope is quite ready for that yet."

"That's okay," Matt piped up before Jenna could respond in a similar way. "We have plenty of other horses for you to ride. Maybe we can get Dani for you again."

"That would be great! She really was a sweet horse," Ben commented.

"And while you guys talk it out," Jenna cut in politely, "I'll go find Mom and Dad." Jenna then handed Micah's lead rope to Matt and jogged across the lawn for the house.

"So since you're only here for fostering," Ben began as they both stared after her, "does that mean you're indefinitely a foster? Or are they planning to adopt you at some point . . . uh, if I may ask?"

"You're good," Matt answered, shooting him an understanding smile. "And I'm not sure, but it's very possible."

"I noticed that you don't really call Ryan and Ann mom or dad yet either. So it kinda made me wonder," Ben explained simply, shrugging innocently.

"I know what you mean," Matt agreed thoughtfully. "And they've never really confirmed or denied me calling them that, same with Frank. Rose, on the other hand, practically *insists* upon being called grandma."

The two boys shared a humorous chuckle at the thought.

"I don't doubt it?" Ben laughed. "I've met Rose all but once or twice, but she definitely has that carefree and grandmotherly attitude that I kinda miss one of my late grandmothers."

"Sorry for your loss," Matt commented as Micah's head twitched slightly.

"Thanks, and to you for your mother," Ben returned meaningfully.

****

Jenna burst into the mudroom and didn't even stop to take her boots off on the mat. Slowing to a stop in the hallway just outside the mudroom, she glanced about for her parents.

"Mom? Dad?" she called into the silence of the house.

"We're here, Jenna," she heard her mother shout back, and her head whipped to her left toward the sound, and she followed it through the back wall of the living room into the kitchen on the right, just beyond the dining room entrance. She found her mother cleaning the dishes from breakfast on the far side of the room in front of the small sink lit by the daylight flowing in the large window above the sink, granting a decent view of the backyard. And her father was sipping his coffee while leaning back against the counter to her left, the stove to his right side.

"Did you need something?" Ryan asked his daughter, setting his cup down on the counter behind him and picking up the newspaper to fold it more neatly together.

"Yeah . . ." Jenna's voice wondered in a distracted tone. "It's Micah."

At this, both her parents looked her way.

"His arthritis again?" Ryan implied. Jenna nodded sheepishly. They stared at one another for a moment as if communicating through their eyes alone. "All right," Ryan went on, setting the paper down, "let's go take a look." He then strode around the small island at the center of the room toward Jenna, pausing when reaching her to look back at Ann.

"You two go on ahead," his wife answered, glancing back over her shoulder for a moment. "I'm staying here to finish this up."

"All right," Ryan replied compliantly. "You can join us if and when you can. Come on, Jenna."

Their footsteps faded across the wood floor, and Ann soon heard the distinct sound of the front door opening and closing and then silence, indicating their departure.

Chapter Nine

Confessions

Matt and Ben's conversation dropped the moment they heard the door open again. Jenna's gaze caught theirs as Micah stood quietly between the two boys.

"All right, buddy," Ryan said to Micah, coming up to his left shoulder and beginning to feel his hand down his leg, "let's have a look."

Micah's ears twitched back toward him, but he made no other movements. As Ryan reached the horse's knee, the golden Dutch warmblood lifted his foot as if they were going to clean them out. Stepping his hoof forward away from him was the sole indicator that confirmed their suspicion much to Jenna's disappointment. Ryan sighed and shifted back onto his hips, supported by his feet in a composed squat.

"He's definitely inflamed again, mainly on the right side," he confirmed unfortunately. "Probably in a lot of pain too. I'll talk to Ann and see if we can get the vet out here to make a recommendation, but it's not looking good."

Jenna's eyes closed with a heavy sigh, disappointment pouring off her face as she turned to press her forehead against Micah's neck along the hairline of his mane due to her height compared to his.

Micah seemed to recognize her distress because he bent his sturdy neck around to nuzzle her as best as he could reach. Matt's haunted look only slightly brightened at the heartwarming gesture, but even this sweet action couldn't fully lift the heavy weight of sorrow off their shoulders. Jenna bit her lip so no one would see, willing herself not to cry even though she desperately desired to.

"He seems to be in good spirits despite all this," Ryan commented on a lighter note, which still didn't seem to appease their sorrows at all. "He's really trying to live life to his fullest. I'd like to think that we can feel hopeful in that respect."

Yet Jenna's mind could not be put to rest by this, and for a fleeting moment, she could feel herself falling deeper into the darkness of her disappointment.

****

"So what do we do now?" Ben asked as Jenna slowly led Micah back toward his stall.

"We wait," Jenna answered with a half-hearted sigh. "And see what the vet says when he gets the chance to come see him."

"Hey, guys, how's it goin'?" Kate's bubbly tone cut through the thick atmosphere to almost succeed in lifting the mood as she and Brian strode up to them.

"Okay," Jenna answered loosely, guiding Micah's head into the stall and held the door open for him to calmly walk in. "Micah's arthritis is flaring up again. We'll have to get the vet out here to see him again, so we're kind of at a loss here."

"We'll give him some pain meds and treat him with peppermint and lavender to hopefully ease his pain, but all we can do is wait," Matt put in.

"Oh," Kate answered in a flat tone. "Well, shall we tack up for a ride? To . . . distract ourselves in the meantime?"

If that was possible, Jenna thought to herself. "Sure," she spoke aloud. "I didn't ask about Dani, but I think I saw her stuff out, so I think she's doing a lesson today. We can put you on Kinnick today, Ben. He's a really good horse for you too. A great jumper, almost like Hope."

"Great! Thanks!" Ben smiled.

Jenna then turned to Kate thoughtfully. "Prince is *also* doing a lesson today, so he'll have to stay here too," she told her.

"Please let me take Sydney. Please let me take Sydney," Kate pleaded to herself with crossed fingers.

"Ha, okay, you can ride Sydney," Jenna said humorously.

"Yes!" Kate cheered, almost leaping into the air.

"Who's Sydney?" Ben wondered, finding amusement in Kate's reaction.

"She's one of our young horses from our old broodmare," Jenna explained. "She passed away recently, but we've had Sydney since she was born. She's been trained under saddle, but she's still learning how it all works. So we take her out often to continue teaching her."

"And teaching me in the process," Kate joked, giggling.

The friends couldn't stop themselves from laughing too, beginning to head down the corridor together.

"Kinnick's very curious with new people," Jenna explained as they entered the tack room. "But he's very submissive just the same. The only thing with him is he doesn't like a lot of rein in his face. Otherwise, he's okay." Finishing this, she peeled away from the group as they all scattered to head down to the right, reaching the locker on her right, next to the one in the very corner of the room.

"Good to know," Ben replied, watching her from where he stood for a moment.

Everyone began to take out the necessary gear they needed from the lockers in a moment of silence.

"I'll be riding Sky Marshall today if that's all right, Jenna," Brian called over to her from a locker along the line of freestanding lockers nearest to her.

"Fine by me," Jenna replied over her shoulder. "He seems to really trust you when you ride him even though that's not very often And he seems to know that he's your favorite." She smiled back at him humorously to which he gave a light chuckle.

"Yeah well, God didn't create them to be mindless beasts like many'd like to think," he reasoned innocently.

"Very true," Jenna agreed. Her eyes caught sight of Ben scanning the room, still standing where she'd left him. "Oh, sorry. Kinnick's locker is the one against that far wall." She pointed exactly across from her. "The second one from the corner locker."

Ben glanced to his left and found the locker she was referring to, just barely making out the letters on the labeled wooden locker.

"Oh, okay. Great. Thanks." He thanked her with a quick thumbs-up.

"No problem," Jenna shot back as she resumed her rummaging through her cluttered locker. "Micah and the horses in barn two are mostly rescue horses and client horses. All the Tyler horses and a few client horses, like Skipper and Hope, are in barn two on the other side of us. So we'll have to enter from the door opposite the one we came in to get to them."

"Cool, sounds good," Ben replied, distractedly touching a hand to the handle of the locker and looking up at it. He pulled the door open, and the door of the locker next to him fell open due to the corner of a navy-blue material catching the edge of the door he was opening, spilling it out onto the floor as something hard and flat hit the planked ground with it. Everyone stopped to look up. Brian closed his locker to peer around from where he was. Matt appeared far down to Ben's right at the other end of the long wall of lockers with Kate peeking around the corner with him. Ben stared at the item in shock for a moment, but realizing this, he shook himself out of it and stooped down to pick it up.

The wooden frame seemed unharmed, no sign of a chip or scratch. But it was when he turned it over that his eyes brightened at the image he beheld through the crackless glass. In it was a smiling face he knew amongst three others standing next to a solid-white horse wearing a navy-blue blanket to match the color of the girl's riding jacket. The brightness of the girl's smile, frozen in time by this paper reminder, glowed with the pride of joy as she and the other three people in similar attire seemed to be jumping up and down together, singing their happiness for all to hear.

"This is you, isn't it?" Ben asked distantly, staring at the framed image as he felt Jenna's presence join him to look down over his shoulder.

"It is," Jenna replied half-heartedly. "A while back. . . or so it seems." She tenderly took the picture into her own hands and stared at it for a moment herself. A look of longing crossed her face as she touched the fingers of her other hand to the glass knowingly.

Ben's eyes fell beyond it to the floor to find that the navy-blue material had something inscribed upon it, the cursive font, in light blue lettering, reading, *Warrior's Strength SFC 04-15-10.*

"All of this is yours?" Ben implied, squatting down to graze a hand over the words tenderly.

"Sort of," Jenna replied loosely, still staring at the photo. "It was something my dad handed down to me when I first started competing."

"But I thought you didn't compete anymore," Ben recalled, looking back up at her standing amongst the rest of her friends.

"I don't." Jenna shrugged. Then setting the picture down on the shelf inside the locker, she knelt down to pick up the folds of the old blanket and tucked it carefully inside the locker once more.

The two met each other's gaze as they stood up again. "I quit doing it after an accident at a show one summer. I only ride for fun now. . . and for the horses that need it of course."

"Oh," Ben monotoned, eyes lowering.

"Come on," Jenna spoke up after a short moment of silence. "Let's go get the horses ready."

Then with that, Kate, Matt, Brian, and Jenna went back to their lockers, but Ben stared at the locker next to Kinnick's and wondered.

****

Jenna led the way, with the heavy jumble of Bentley's tack in hand, to enter the first barn. Finding a certain skill in struggling to carry everything, she made it to Bentley's stall, somehow finding a way to pull the saddle peg off from the wall so it stuck out for her to put her saddle on and slide her bridle off her shoulder to hang it up next to it. "There's four crossties in here, so I'll tack up Ben in his stall."

"Are you sure?" Ben asked. "I don't mind waiting till you're done to tack up."

"Nah, it's okay." Jenna shrugged, taking the body brush into her hand. "Bentley prefers it this way anyway."

"Oh, okay." Ben shrugged this time, entering Kinnick's stall to let Matt go past with a blue roan paint.

Leading him to the first set of crossties closest the Kinnick's stall, Matt slowly turned his body to the horse's head to line him up with the location of the crossties. Glancing over, Jenna noticed Hope curiously inspecting the saddle still draped over the door, and it brought an encouraging smile to her lips.

"Thought I'd bring him over to join the party," Matt joked with a grin at Jenna who peered over to him from Bentley's stall.

"Yeah, it's a party all right," Jenna answered amusingly, pointing as she continued to brush away the dust on Bentley's blue-jean colored coat. "You can take Kinnick down to the next set of crossties."

"I'm gonna go get Sydney!" Kate called from the other end of the barn as Brian appeared leading Sky Marshall from the other barn to the crossties, about three stalls in from the doors they'd entered from.

"Go get her," Ben echoed as Kinnick gently snuffled at his hand, reminding him to keep working, and he reached up to adjust the straps of Kinnick's halter and clipped on the lead rope. "But isn't she already *in* here?" he finished while peering out of the stall and down the corridor to his left.

"Nope. She's in the temporary shelter stalls outside. We have them for our young horses, and sometimes use them for quarantine and vet calls. We don't usually move them, but they can be rearranged if needed.

"Sydney was born in one of them," Brian added, clipping the crossties on to Marshall's halter. "Marion, her mother, went into labor early one morning while waiting for a checkup one day, and when the vet and I got here, she'd already given birth."

"Jenna and the Tylers didn't even know she'd had her until they brought the vet back there to see her at, like, seven-thirty in the morning." Matt chuckled, embarrassment in his tone. "And they were all amazed that she'd already had Sydney when they didn't realize it." Matt picked up the left crosstie but dropped it when he remembered that Ben needed to get through and nudged Milo over so that the other

boy could lead the colorful paint by them to the crossties across from
Brian and Sky Marshall.

"But you *knew* she was in labor, right?" Ben asked, leading Kinnick
out and down to the crossties. Slowing Kinnick to where he wanted him
to stand, he secured him to the ties.

"We had an inkling," Jenna confirmed, adjusting the saddle, "which
is why we separated her from the rest of the horses to give her some
privacy, but we didn't really know just how close she'd *actually* been."

"Plus, from the sound of it, the labor was quite fast," Brian recalled.
"The vet said she was aged enough and had been bred enough times to
have a quick delivery. And Marion was always in good shape for foaling,
which is why the Tylers kept her around."

"We never anticipated her having Sydney so quickly, but yeah, once
the vet arrived, she'd literally *just* given birth," Jenna finished, beginning
to pull Bentley's bridle on over his draft horse-style head.

"Wow," Ben breathed thoughtfully, pausing before returning to his
task of brushing the dust off Kinnick's multicolored coat. "That's crazy."

"Yeah, wish I would've been there," Matt agreed, beginning to
straighten the saddle pad on Milo's back.

"Yeah, I bet," Ben agreed slowly.

The clopping echo of hooves drew their attention down the wide
hall as they found Kate leading a spritely white horse into the first
crossties they came to.

"Woah, she's beautiful!" Ben breathed even though her features
were a little obscured by the distance between them.

"Yeah, she looks just like her father," Jenna remarked fondly, her
smile fading where no one could see.

"Is he here somewhere too?" Ben asked brightly.

Jenna's eyes lifted then slightly fell again from where she stood at
the door of Bentley's stall. Ben turned her way at her silence. And she
looked up and forced a smile.

"No," she answered finally. "But at least we're glad we have her."
Then Jenna opened the door wide to lead Bentley out into the sunshine.
And Ben's gaze searched the air thoughtfully, his eyebrows furrowed as
he pondered the strange look he'd seen in her eyes.

****

The ground crunched beneath their horses' hooves, the summer breeze beating down heat rays, which warmed their skin in hopes to further pigment their skin to the many hues of a suntan. Sweat at their necks, they found rest in the shade under the line of trees that they strolled through tentatively. But even in the heat of day, their hearts could not be fuller of happiness by the enjoyment of their companions' company and the feeling of height from their calm mounts.

"Hah! Nothing but fresh air and a blue sky." Matt sighed, breathing deeply to show his relaxation.

"So much for silence though," Jenna deadpanned with a smirk.

Matt batted a hand in her direction, and she dodged it instinctively.

"This land is just so peaceful," Ben commented, gazing about in awe. "And you get to see this all the time." He glanced over at Jenna.

"Yup, never get tired of it either." Jenna beamed.

"Ha, if she could, she'd camp out here every night." Matt laughed, Kate and Brian joining in.

"Ha ha," Jenna quoted sarcastically, shaking her head. "But they're not wrong," she had to admit.

"See? Told ya." Matt snickered.

Marshall's head jerked up slightly at the switch of Milo's tail hitting his face.

"It's okay, boy," Brian soothed calmly, giving him a gentle pat.

Ben took a closer look and noted the cloudiness of his glassy dark eyes.

"Is . . . Sky Marshall . . . blind?" he asked in a bit of surprise.

"He is," Brian confirmed. "From a terrible accident. . . Marshall has Equine Recurrent Uveitis, and has gone completely blind because it wasn't caught in time," he explained further, looking at the calm horse tenderly.

"They found this out when his face was severely damaged by a barbed wire fence being accidentally wrapped around his face. The scars have healed, but the damage to his eyes was already done. It's irreversible, so now he must learn how to live with it for the rest of his life. He's in good shape otherwise. And he's a really sweet horse, but he still can be a little spooky."

"His owners rescued him from a shelter, and within a couple weeks, they noticed something wasn't right," Jenna continued his story. "The people that rescued him and brought him to the shelter found him trapped in the barbed wire and had to cut him out of it. And when he was adopted, he'd been recovering from the barbed wire marks since he'd arrived at their farm when they realized his eyes didn't look right and he was acting a bit strangely."

"That's when they found out he had the disease," Matt added. "No one knows what causes it 'cause it's different for every horse."

Sydney pranced about anxiously next to Milo.

"Hey, easy, girl," Kate murmured to her. "I know you're young and eager to run, but some of these guys aren't exactly spring chickens, and one of them is impaired."

"It's okay." Brian smiled optimistically. "Marshall can handle it. I hear Jenna's been working with him at higher paces. And I've been coming by when I can to help since he and I get along so well."

"It's true. Marshall's doing great in adjusting to his new life," Matt affirmed proudly. "He's getting much more comfortable in his 'lack of sight' situation. He might be getting close to going home soon."

"Really? That's great, Marshall," Brian praised, patting the jet-black warmblood's neck again.

Sky Marshall tossed his head in response as if accepting the praise willingly.

"And Skipper's going home today," Jenna added happily.

"Really! That's great!" Kate gushed, looking back at them brightly.

"Yep, we're real proud of him," Matt commented. "He's gotten so much better."

"I bet Mrs. Riley will be very happy to have her boy back," Kate remarked, slowing to be closer to her friends.

"I know," Jenna answered. "She has really missed him."

And after that, silence fell as they rode on.

****

Jenna finished her tight slipknot to the tree branch, securing the lead rope in place so Bentley had enough length to graze while keeping him from wandering off. The other horses grazed around the ground they could reach as well, Sky Marshall and Milo on one tree and Kinnick, Bentley, and Sydney on the other. Ben and Matt lay flat on the ground, shielding their eyes from the harsh attack of the inferno in the sky beating down on them with heat rays smiling down on them. Kate and Brian sat with their shoulders together, using one another for support as Jenna came to sit with them under the tree that hung over the three of them.

"Hah, I could do this all day." Matt sighed loosely, tucking an arm under his head.

"I don't know that your *skin* could," Kate pointed out, exchanging a smirk with Jenna.

Matt sat up suddenly. "Oh, you're right," he quickly realized. "Well, anyway." He shrugged then crawled up under the shadow of the tree, Ben still lying where he was, head supported by his arms in a crisscross fashion.

"So what happened to that white horse in the picture?" Ben asked, craning his neck to look at Jenna directly. "I can't imagine it's Sydney 'cause you looked a lot younger in it. And so happy too."

Jenna's expression fell again, the brightness of her eyes dulling a bit in an emotion of sorrow that Ben caught on to immediately.

"You know how I said Sydney's father is no longer here on the farm?" she asked him rather forwardly.

Ben shifted himself up to face her and nodded.

Scooting closer into the tree's shadow, Jenna began. "Well . . . the horse in the photo was her father," she said. "His name was Samson. His show name was Warrior's Strength."

"Like the words printed on that old blanket," Ben recalled, implying his recollection forwardly.

"Yes," Jenna confirmed simply. "He wore it every time we took him to a show, since we'd won it. You see, Samson was my dad's horse. He rode him for a number of years and took *great* care of him in that time. Then he trained *me* on him. And when I started competing, he was my show horse. We took him everywhere with us. And that photo? It was taken at the Spring Fling Classic seven years ago, where we originally got the blanket. It was my first championship win. Samson and I were the overall champions of that year, and the three people you saw in the picture were some of my show friends. They were there to celebrate my victory that day. We all competed against one another like we always did, but I was the ultimate winner that day. I was celebrating for weeks after it happened." A smile of remembrance came to her lips, but it soon drowned into a look of pain and sorrow.

"Then what happened?" Ben asked curiously, the change in her demeanor disheartening and dreadful for him to feel coming off her.

"Five years ago . . . everything changed," Jenna answered solemnly, a haunted look in her eyes. "I was the last one to compete in the Hemington Way Invitational." And in the moment, the atmosphere darkened. "I was particularly enjoying myself on this day. The jumps were higher than I'd ever jumped before, but I'd been training for months on this particular course. And I felt confident that I could do it." Her smile faded once again. "But something went wrong . . . I don't know if the ground was somehow unlevel . . . or if Sam didn't get a good footing going for the jump. Before I knew it, I was hitting the crest of his neck and lost my left stirrup. Samson took the jump anyway as he always would, and I began to slip. He must have landed wrong on his feet and on the wrong lead 'cause we fell forward over his left shoulder and hit the ground on our side. Samson landed on my leg, breaking it clean in half as he rolled over me quick enough to break my left hip and a few ribs. He probably broke one of my clavicles 'cause I've had it bother me from time to time. His momentum from the roll must have tossed me away from him because all I remember was that I was lying a short distance from him, so he was on my left side. I don't remember much else other than the sound of Samson's painful cries and my own. And Katrina and her friends laughing from where they had been watching my run."

"Oh, Jenna! I can't believe that happened to you!" Ben breathed horribly. "I'm so sorry I asked! I can only imagine how terrible that was!"

"It's okay. It's behind me now." Jenna shrugged, forcing a slight smile. "That was five years ago."

"I remember seeing the news reports about it for weeks afterwards," Brian recalled sadly. "Jenna was in the hospital for weeks, receiving treatment after treatment."

"My nose was broken from falling into Samson's neck, and my elbow was messed up from hitting the ground hard on it. I had scrapes and bruises on my face and arms for weeks. Including this one." She pointed to a subtle blemish on her left cheek that he hadn't seemed to notice until now.

"And Samson?" Ben recalled hauntedly.

Everyone's gaze dropped to the ground.

"Oh." Ben sighed, the realization confirming his dreadful suspicion clearer than words could have.

"The damage was too severe." Jenna sighed, hardly finding the words to say it. "And . . ."

"Sam was twenty-two years old at the time," Brian finished for her. "Many were amazed that a horse of his age could still be jumping at the level that he was at the time. But Ryan took *extremely* good care of him, and he was just an all-around healthy horse for all his life."

"He was one of the greatest horses the Tylers had ever had," Kate chimed in, hollow eyes lifting for only a moment as she shifted her body to sit cross-legged in the grass, hands in her lap. "And he was a *real* crowd favorite in the ring. Everyone loved him. He was practically a legend to the showing jumping community as was Jenna for her amazing skills."

"About a month after I came to Sunshine, Jenna had long since quit competing," Matt put in. "And at the time, she was struggling to work with a horse she met at a horsemanship and riding clinic last year."

"Amir," Jenna recollected, meeting the boy's gaze thoughtfully at which Matt smiled knowingly.

"He's kinda what got *me* my start with working with Jenna and Ryan on the horses," Matt explained. "And what helped me find a passion pertaining to horses."

"Matt's our liaison for equine health and nutrition," Jenna stated in a sort of formal tone.

"I want to go to school someday to become an equine nutritionist to help people who need that level of expertise for their horses and to help the Tylers in their business as well," Matt finished, shaking his head to free the damp strands of his deep brown hair that were plastered to his forehead due to the heat.

"Huh," Ben vocalized intriguingly then turned to his right. "So what about you two?" he asked the Morgan siblings openly. "What's your story?"

The two looked to one another then back at Ben. "Well, he's training to be a vet, and I'm just kinda here to have fun until I decided what to do for a career," Kate answered, pointing a thumb at her brother and then to herself as she spoke. "Also, I'm *her* best friend," she finished, reaching over to wrap an arm tightly around Jenna's neck and pulling her close.

"Got it. So vet, huh?" Ben realized, looking to Brian now. "I'm guessing that's why you were here with the vet when Sydney was born?" His questioning tone suggested his curiosity, which the young man was obliged to answer.

"Yup, and that's also why I'm so busy most of the time," Brian confirmed willingly. "I work a lot of random jobs to keep myself in school for veterinary school, and my parents help me a little bit. But otherwise, I've been essentially paying my way through college as best I can. Hopefully soon, I'll graduate and start an internship with one of the local vets here pretty soon. I think I'll be getting paperwork on who's available to take me on soon, so we'll see what happens with that."

"And you're in school this whole summer too?" Ben wondered.

"No." Brian shook his head. "I was trying to my first year, but I couldn't maintain it. Now ever since then, I've been taking the summer off to work more so I can earn more money to put toward school. I'm trying to graduate without any debt. I've just been blessed by God to be able to stick to that goal so far."

"Just like God has blessed *me* in having little to *no* struggle with my injuries from the accident," Jenna added thankfully.

"Wow, that *is* amazing," Ben remarked, his eyes brightening. "Hey, thanks for sharing this stuff with me." He smiled meaningfully. "I know we've only really known each other for a short time, but I can't help but feel like a part of this group somehow."

"Psh, you kidding." Matt scoffed jokingly. "Of course you're a part of the group."

"I think we've gotten closer to *you* than *anyone* we've ever helped." Jenna commented seriously, fiddling with the blades of grass by her crossed legs.

"Really?" Ben vocalized surprisingly.

"No joke," Matt confirmed. "You're practically a member of the crew."

"Partners in crime," Brian added with a smirk.

"Wow, thanks, guys." Ben grinned, the shimmer of his hazel eyes and the brightness of his freckled face glowing pridefully at this heartwarming statement. "I mean, I know you guys are helping my horse. But I'm glad to know that I've made some new friends too."

"Of course you did!" Kate declared, delivering a friendly punch to the arm, which Ben chuckled at, setting a hand on his arm amusingly.

"Well, we should probably start heading back," Jenna decided, shielding her eyes from the sun above them. "It'll be lunchtime soon, and Skipper's owners are supposed to be coming at one to pick him up."

"Sounds like a plan," Brian agreed, getting to his feet. "Let's go."

"Maybe we can race back," Kate suggested, anticipation and pleasure ringing in her tone as they began loosening halters for their bridles to be put back on and lead ropes untied from the trees.

"Only if you think Marshall can handle it today," Jenna replied, looking to Brian while looping Bentley's lead rope up and tying the end to keep it wrapped up.

"He should be all right," Brian replied, slinging his wrapped lead rope over his broad shoulders like a sash. "I'll feel it out as we go, but he's been quite comfortable today." Then with that, he mounted up, Marshall stepping about as if to steady himself with the added weight.

"So what are we waiting for?" Kate asked, gathering Sydney's reins in a more-organized fashion. "Let's go."

She nudged Sydney forward, and the filly willingly broke into a canter, soon to be followed by the four other horses of the group.

****

"That was a great ride!" Kate remarked as they led the horses into the barn by the order they'd left in.

"Yeah, I think that's the most fun I've had on a ride to date!" Ben concurred.

"We tend to get that a lot," Brian smirked, looking over at the sandy-haired boy as he undid the straps on Marshall's saddle.

"Finally made it back?" Frank implied cheekily as he and the rest of the family entered the stable.

"Grandpa," Jenna dynamically replied, tilting her head back and toward him, an amused grin spreading across her face. "we were only gone for about an hour." She slid Bentley's bridle off his head. "Or two." She followed up slinging it onto her shoulder to retrieve the saddle from his back.

"How was the ride?" Ryan asked, panning his gaze down the long hall at the five of them.

"Pretty good," Jenna replied simply, elbowing the stall door closed and hauling her things by Matt and Milo on the crossties.

"Great!" Ben commented brightly, continuing to untack Kinnick. "We had a race on the way back."

"Really?" Ryan returned impressively, his brows raised.

"Yeah, and Marshall was great!" Jenna reported, coming their way again. "So was Sydney. The dynamic amongst them was very promising today."

"Marshall's been a little eerie of his new situation," Ryan remembered fondly. "It's good to hear he's improving.

"He's got a ways to go in his readjustment, but it's definitely a step in the right direction," Brian confirmed.

"And Sydney's obedience skills were put to the test today, and it looks like she passed." Jenna smiled, glancing far down at the white filly.

"Wonderful!!" Rose beamed. "Now who's hungry?"

"Thanks, Mrs. Tyler, but we wouldn't want to impose," Brian politely declined, Ben and Kate both nodding from where they stood by their horses.

"Oh nonsense!" Rose scoffed. "You're all welcome to join us. I insist."

"It's really no trouble?" Ben wondered, his tone uncertain.

"Of course not." Rose smiled. "You go put your horses out for some grass and sunshine and join us in the house. We have pulled pork and baked beans waiting for us."

"Sweet! I love your pulled pork!" Matt exclaimed, beginning to lead Milo forward toward the other end of the barn.

"Thank you, Mrs. Tyler," Ben agreed gratefully, shooting her a warm grin.

"Oh please call me Rose, son." The older lady chuckled.

"Um, okay." Ben smiled slightly, unclipping the other crosstie to follow the others out to the paddocks behind the two barns.

"All righty then," Ryan said finally. "We'll see you inside."

Jenna shot them a thankful smile as she, too, led Bentley out of his stall and disappeared down the corridor in an echo of clopping hooves and boots.

****

The silver of a big truck shimmered as it drove in slowly. Mrs. Riley with her short snow-white curls slipped carefully from the passenger side, and Mr. Riley appeared out of the driver's seat.

"Hello, Ryan. Ann. Great to see ya," Mr. Riley said, smiling broadly.

"Hello, Mr. and Mrs. Riley," Jenna greeted.

"Oh, hello, dear." Mrs. Riley replied excitedly. "So? Where's my boy?"

"He's in the stables. I'll go get him." Jenna smiled.

"Oh, thank you so much, dear," Mrs. Riley sang, clasping her hands eagerly together. "I can hardly believe that he's finally coming home again."

Jenna beamed and jogged back to the stables to the chestnut gelding's stall at the very back of the first barn. Skipper nickered a welcome, his eyes sparkling in a sort of brightness that seemed to show understanding of what was happening today.

"Hey, boy," she greeted, taking his red halter and snapping his lead rope on. "Time to go home, buddy."

The horse's ears perked forward and searched around as Jenna led him outside.

"Hello, baby!" Mrs. Riley cried when the darkness panned off Jenna leading her horse toward them.

Skipper whinnied a greeting, instantly becoming more alert. Reaching Mrs. Riley, he set his nose in her hand and rubbed his forehead against his owner's chest gently.

"Oh, yes, I missed you too," Mrs. Riley told him, rubbing his neck.

"We both did," Mr. Riley said, aiming this statement toward the Tylers. Skipper nuzzled Mr. Riley's arm playfully.

"I know," he said, ruffling the horse's forelock. "You missed us a lot, didn't ya?"

"Well, buddy," Mrs. Riley began again. "Let's get you home, shall we?" Looking to Jenna, she led her to the little trailer at the back of the truck.

Skipper walked easily up the ramp, and together, Mrs. Riley and Jenna lifted and secured the ramp in place just as Mr. Riley was finishing a conversation with Jenna's family.

"So ready to go, dear?" he asked, turning to his wife with a broad smile.

"Yep," she replied with a huge grin glowing upon her face.

"Well then, I guess we'll be on our way. And thanks again for curing our Skipper," Mr. Riley said, getting back into the truck.

"No problem," Ryan said, putting his arms around his wife and daughter. "It was our pleasure."

The family watched the truck disappear, then Jenna, Ryan, and Matt turned toward the stables.

"I'll go clean up the empty stall now," Matt said, approaching the tool shed just inside the stable entrance on the right-hand side. "Then we can train with Hope and Bentley."

"Okay, I'll help you muck out," Jenna replied, reaching for a pitchfork, which she received from Matt. "Then, I'll work with the other horses, grooming and feeding them when I'm done with each of them."

"Got it." Matt winked coolly.

"We'll *all* help you, Jenna," Ryan offered, her family standing by with him.

"Great, thanks," Jenna replied thankfully, and they set to work together.

Chapter Ten

Finding Courage

Chirping crickets, buzzing cicadas, an otherwise-peaceful night in if not for one little thing. Covers shifted as Jenna positioned herself from her back to her right side. Then suddenly her eyes were awake, and so was she. She silently groaned and rolled onto her back once more, pulling the covers aside. Her door never made a sound as she opened it, much to her relief. Her hands cradled her forearms together by her elbows as her fuzzy-socked feet glided across the wooden floors. Seven or eight paces brought her to another door on the left down the short hall from her own, which she found was cracked with the faintest indicator of light.

"Matt?" she whispered, pushing the door forward a little.

Matt sat on his bed in the left-hand corner on the backside of the room, straight in front of her. The lamp on his stand was lit, and he looked to be holding a shape that resembled an equine science book in his hands.

"Jenna? It's like midnight. What are you doing up?" the boy wondered, immediately closing the book and setting it aside.

"I was gonna ask *you* the same thing," Jenna answered, crossing the floor to the crimson-colored bed and sitting down as Matt shifted himself to sit up and slide back for her to join him.

"You okay?" Matt wondered, his eyes scanning her carefully in the dim light. "You seemed kinda off after seeing that photo of you and Samson."

"I don't know . . . I . . ." Jenna trailed off to slide back against the wall and pull her knees up. "I guess I've just been thinking about what Katrina said."

"About you and Bentley?" Matt interjected smoothly.

"No . . . well, yeah that," Jenna corrected herself with a half-hearted shrug. "But. . . about the upcoming show."

"Thinking about doing it?" Matt wondered, a little more curious this time.

"More like trying to figure out if I should," Jenna corrected. "I mean I haven't competed since the accident. Ever since Samson was put down . . . I couldn't bring myself to compete again even after the doctor cleared me to compete again."

"So what do you *want* to do?" Matt asked her. "If you're considering doing it, there's gotta be a huge reason for it."

"I don't know." Jenna sighed, holding her knees tighter against her chest. "I *feel* like it should be something I should be considering, but at the same time, I'm not sure."

"Sounds like it's a question for our Almighty God," Matt implied heavily, bracing an arm over his right knee, which pointed up for him to steady it on.

"Yeah. . . maybe," Jenna answered, her mind beginning to wander.

"Look, if God's *really* telling you to go for it, we're behind you," Matt told her simply. "And any fear? It's just an attack of the enemy. You were a great jumper at one point. I'm sure that girl is still in there somewhere, and I'd be more than happy to help you find her again. We *all* would."

This statement brought a smile to her lips.

"Hope's greatest challenge has been learning to trust and bond with people," Jenna ventured, gazing out the window along the lengthy wall behind Matt; extending far to his right to bridge the gap between the bed they were sitting on and the closet on the opposite wall from them. "And I think her final test should be something Ben has been meaning to use her for when he and his aunt bought her."

"You want to enter Hope?" Matt asked, his tone brightening slightly.

"With permission from Vanessa and Ben, yeah," Jenna confirmed. "But I've kinda been only contemplating it."

"Probably another thing to take up in prayer?" the boy concluded aloud.

"Yeah," Jenna nodded, leaving a silence amongst the two of them.

"Well, we should probably get to bed," Matt supposed, stretching his arms as far as his arms' length would allow. "*Actually* sleep before the morning comes too soon."

"Yeah, otherwise we'll be nothing but zombies stumbling about the barn." Jenna smirked, reaching the door of the inferno-painted bedroom, and Matt lightly chuckled with her.

"Good night." Matt smiled warmly. "And, Jenna."

She stopped short to look at him once more.

"Don't let fear stop you from doing what you think is right," he finished meaningfully. Her heart warmed with these words, and she could sense a feeling of pride bubble up inside her at hearing it.

"Thanks." She grinned then proceeded to close the door.

****

Staring at the ceiling seemed to calm her spirit 'cause when she closed her eyes, she could hear the squeals of Samson's painful cries.

Her chest felt heavy with the weight of the crush injury, hindering her breathing ability. The scene appeared before her eyes as it had many times before. The same old story, yet it still increased her heart rate just thinking about it. Telling Ben about it, she found, was a whole lot easier than recalling it outright. Suddenly though the tides seemed to change. The winds that blew at her skin during the fall reversed, and suddenly she found herself in the saddle again. But the color that lay below her was . . . blue? Midnight locks flowed like their own kind of banner, and the shimmering bit in his mouth clicked as he gnawed on it calmly.

"Bentley?" she said, finding herself surprisingly able to speak and hear her own voice.

They seemed to be completely devoid of the rest of the world because once Bentley's hooves moved to the beat of a canter, none of it mattered.

****

Sound reached her ears, and her eyes took their time to open. Registering the ceiling above, she wondered for *only* a moment what had happened. *Thank you, Lord, for a different dream,* she prayed thankfully.

Stiffness welcomed her attempt to get up, and she noticed the chaotic state that her ocean-blue covers were now in. Finding little surprise in it due to the busy night in her dreams, she pulled them aside to make way for her feet to touch the floor.

Unintentionally sneaking down the stairs, she was met with the distant chatter of voices in the kitchen, likely her family going about their morning routines and the best place to be for what her mind was needing to speak into words. Softly gliding around the long oak dining table, she strode for the door on the opposite wall leading to the kitchen. The morning sun intensified the light of the wall she was approaching and the dark of the one she was leaving, which concealed the steps behind it. This intense upgrade in lighting launched a new display of the two shades of blue painted in coordination with each other on the walls. Along with the pastel blue of the striped accent wall to her right, leading to the backyard through the simply designed double doors.

"Hey, Dad?"

Everyone looked up finding her standing there.

"I've decided I wanna starting training to compete again."

The look that flashed across their faces was much like that of either surprise or shock or maybe a mix of both. No one spoke for a good long while before a reply finally came back.

"For how long are we talking?" Frank wondered after the forever-long silence.

"Just until the Summer Splash Invitational in August," Jenna answered with a slight shrug.

"And you're sure about this?" Ryan asked, setting his coffee aside. "You haven't competed since the Hemington five years ago." He braced his hands to the counter behind him. "And it was a pretty bad fall."

At this time, Matt had joined them, catching up on the conversation with Ryan's words and his memory of the night before. He placed a hand on her shoulder, and she looked his way to exchange a glance.

"I am. I feel like God *wants* me to," Jenna replied finally.

Ryan looked to his wife thoughtfully.

"Jenna has improved in her riding skills since then," Ann reasoned, shrugging with her fingers out from the mug she was holding on the table. "And her bond with Bentley has become stronger than ever."

"Besides if the good Lord has called this upon her," Rose added forwardly, "then I say we trust what He has in store for our little girl."

Ryan met Frank's glances then Jenna's.

"All right," he gave in finally, coming around the island toward her. "I'll give the board a call and get the registration number and the course-setup specifications."

"Thanks, Dad." Jenna smiled, coming forward to hug him tightly, wrapping her arms around his upper chest.

"You're welcome," her father replied, wrapping her in a hug of his own. "I'll get started on that right away."

They pulled apart, and he set his hands on her shoulders.

"In the meantime, we can start you on low fences to work you back up again. Once you get the chores done, we can get started."

"Okay, come on, Matt," Jenna decided, advancing toward the doorway on a wall to her left from where she was standing, leading to the living room. "Let's go dive in."

"Hey, Jenna, catch!" Frank called, tossing her an apple.

Jenna turned in time to catch it from across the room by the doorway. Matt caught the one tossed his way, taking off after her as Rose snapped at Frank not to throw things in the kitchen as she usually did.

Bursting out the door, they jogged across the dew-frosted lawn, catching the morning sun across their faces as they crunched across the gravel to the stable.

****

The wood of the poles clattered against the brackets setting the height they desired. Matt shielded his eyes to find Jenna in the bright sun. Leading Bentley out of the barn and toward him, he noted a change in wardrobe that her family hadn't seen for years. With cream-colored jodhpurs and a light blue polo, Jenna looked to be in full gear, wearing her old riding gloves and her half chaps over her dusty black riding boots. Her helmet dangled from her elbow, lapping at her side as she slowed Bentley to a stop at the gate entrance. Dressed in complete English-style gear and fitted with leg guards and a breast collar of a deep brown leather, Bentley seemed quite calm despite the change in attire.

"He's like a whole new horse," Matt joked with a smirk.

"Very funny." Jenna chuckled with him. "It's just the gear my folks purchased for me after I'd been training with Bentley for two years. They implied that I was gonna compete again, but . . ." She trailed off to reach over and adjust the breast collar. "At the time I wasn't so sure I'd *ever* get to use it."

"'Cause you *wanted* to? Or 'cause *they* did?" Matt wondered, intentionally hinting at her statement's meaning.

"A little of both, I guess," Jenna admitted with a shrug, still looking at Bentley thoughtfully. She lowered her eyes and met his gaze blankly. "I wanna do this," she reasoned, hoping it would convince more than just herself.

"But you still feel doubtful?" Matt implied, and Jenna's eyes just wandered away from him. "It's okay to feel that way," the boy told her earnestly. "It's only natural given what has happened to you."

"I know." Jenna sighed, combing Bentley's forelock together when he looked her way. "I just wish I didn't have to."

"I bet once you get going, you'll start to feel it less," Matt supposed optimistically.

"I *really* hope you're right," Jenna told him.

"Yeah, me too," Matt replied seriously, "for your sake, if not, mine."

Jenna threw a hand at him, and he dodged it, laughing. Taking a deep breath, she gazed around at the course set before her.

"The fences are set to two feet to start," Matt explained, scanning the course himself then turning to Jenna. "Once we warm you guys up, we'll have you run one jump at a time to get you back into the swing of it and help you feel the jumps as a team. Bentley's done show jumping before, right?"

"He has but not a lot of it," Jenna answered as if coming out of a daze.

"That's what I thought." Matt nodded. "Let's at least get you started. You ready?" He stepped aside to reveal a mounting block that she could've sworn wasn't there before. But still, in the moment, its memories came back to her, and she could recall using it many times in that past chapter of her life. Staring at it a moment longer, she shook herself out of it and straightened up bravely.

"Yeah," she said, then leading Bentley forward, she positioned him next to the mounting block.

Stepping up, it proved to be no issue. But as she placed her foot in the stirrup, a flash of her losing that stirrup moments before her fall zapped across her mind, and her foot jerked against Bentley's side. He jumped slightly while stepping away, nearly dropping her on the ground.

"Hey, hey, easy," Matt soothed, stepping on to Bentley's right side to ease him back over so Jenna could regain her balance.

Adjusting her grip on the reins and Bentley's mane, she placed her other hand back onto the back of the saddle. Jenna smoothly weighed herself on the left foot in the stirrup to swing her leg over and eased herself down into the saddle, picking up the right stirrup easily.

"Okay, go ahead and warm up," Matt instructed.

Jenna just nodded and nudged Bentley forward. Matt strode to the fence and hopped up on to the top rung to watch. As Bentley stepped along the path adjacent to the fence in the counterclockwise direction, Jenna closed her eyes and listened to his hoof beats, timing them rhythmically even at this slow pace. Each beat, each step felt synced to her own heartbeat. Bentley's ears twitched calmly as he strode along. He felt her leg at his side, and he quickened his step to a working walk, his head bobbing a little more noticeably as he went. The metal stirrups and leather contact underneath her brought back every memory of her years as a jumper, the wind at her hair, the sun in her face, but the ones she seemed to recall the most was that of the fall like it was more heavily defined in the back of her mind, engraved there as a remainder of somewhat of a failure that she'd always have to carry with her like a ball and chain to drag her down and hold her back.

Shaking herself out of it, she worked Bentley up to an immediately even trot, posting along his smooth gait in unison with his body. After about two or three laps around the ring, she brought Bentley round in a half circle, changing leads to proceed along the rail in the clockwise direction. After riding this way for a couple more laps, she slowed Bentley to a walk and turned him on a tight, clean circle, reversing to counterclockwise once more. With this act, though, she signaled with her left hand and right leg, asking for a canter. Bentley immediately broke into a calm, clean canter, his hooves beating the ground in a countable rhythm that she wanted to practice counting while she warmed up.

This went on for another few laps before another half circle and a lead change sent them along the same heading, going clockwise once more.

Ryan strode over as Jenna was bringing Bentley down, the horse's nostrils flaring from his heavier breaths.

"Ready to give this a go?" he asked, glancing to the course for a brief moment before turning his gaze on up to his daughter.

"As I'll ever be," Jenna replied simply.

"All right then." Ryan nodded. "Trot along the rail till you get to C, then canter in to the first two jumps after the starting flag."

Jenna nodded and nudged Bentley forward into a working walk, going counterclockwise toward the rail where she began the trot. Reaching the end of the ring, she had Bentley canter halfway around the semicircular bend, turning him about forty-five degrees to reach the green flag where her counting began. Clearing the first jump was a bit bumpy, and she felt herself jostle for position to maintain her balance. But the low oxer that lay before her caught her off guard, and she lowered slightly from her jumping position above the saddle, which bumped her forward into Bentley's neck as he pulled up short in front of the jump. She held tight to his neck to gain the balance to stay in the saddle. Finding the balance she desired, she lowered her legs back to normal position and leaned back into the seat again, a sigh pumping her chest as Matt and Ryan drew near.

"You okay?" Matt asked concernedly though hardly showing how worried he'd *really* been.

"Yeah." Jenna sighed, lowering her hands to put slack on the reins.

Bentley gnawed at the bit in his mouth calmly as if nothing had happened despite his breaths still being slightly more defined from all the exercise.

"We've got a long way to go if I'm gonna be ready in time." Jenna sighed again, her shoulders dropping somewhat in defeat.

"Don't say that," Matt encouraged brightly. "This is just the first practice."

"That's right," Ryan agreed, turning from him to Jenna. "You haven't done this for a few years. It'll take a little time to get used to it again. And Bentley's new to most of this," he went on, placing a hand to the horse's neck. "But he's been in crowds before, so he won't be bothered by that. And he trusts you completely. He knows you'll take care of him, and he'll do the same."

"And just remember who *else* you have on your side." Matt smirked, shielding his mouth with the back of one hand and pointing up with the other, making Jenna smile at the amusing reminder.

"Thanks, Matt," she said with a meaningful tint to her glance.

Matt just chuckled and winked at her to which she responded with the roll of her eyes in a humorous manner.

"Now should we try again?" Ryan began again, gesturing to the oxer once more.

"Yeah." Jenna nodded, turning back his way.

Then turning Bentley on his haunches, she started again. Again, clearing the first fence seemed a little shaky, and she again went for the oxer. Bentley rose up into the air toward her, clipping the rail of the second stand that made the oxer; Jenna tensed at the last second. And as soon as he hit the ground, Bentley abruptly screeched to a halt, sending Jenna flying off over his shoulder to the ground, rolling from her left shoulder onto her back. She immediately got up to dust herself off when Matt and Ryan reached her.

"Are you okay! . . Are you okay?" Matt asked a little more worried this time.

"Uh, this isn't working!" Jenna groaned, the frustration she felt overwhelming her almost to the point of tears. . . though she'd never allow herself to show it.

"Hey, it's okay," Matt soothed gently, trying to sound as convincing as he possibly could. "This is only the first practice. We'll figure this out. Wanna try again?"

"I don't think there's really any point," Jenna replied honestly, taking Bentley's reins to lead him away past Matt who stepped aside to watch her go sadly, trying to think of a way to help as best as his mind could think.

****

"Jenna." It was now Matt's turn to softly knock on the door and peer in.

Finding Jenna sitting on her bed, he could tell she was staring at something. Sliding himself in through the door and sitting down next to her, he found that she held a four-by-four-inch picture of her and Samson wearing a smile and red and green ribbons around their necks.

"He was my best friend," Jenna finally answered in a low voice. "He was my *dad's* horse, but he was *my* best friend, the only one I had until you came along."

"And Kate isn't?" Matt implied, shifting positions with both hands braced to the side of the bed, shaking the whole bed under the both of them.

"Well, yeah." Jenna half chuckled, a smile cracking across half of her face and dropping nearly immediately. "She's another one, I guess."

"Why was he so important to you?" Matt asked almost like he were quizzing her, his brown eyes studying her in the light of the lamps.

"Well, I don't know *exactly*," Jenna admitted with a shrug. "I guess it's just the bond I once *had* with him."

"Exactly," Matt said, earning Jenna's curious glance. "Your connection *alone* is what gave you guys the ability to ride well. God was protecting you, yeah, but your bond always helped too." He paused before continuing, finding very subtly that his statement was helping, "Your connection with Bentley is insanely strong. I *know* it. And that bond is what'll help you find the balance you need to stay grounded."

Jenna's eyes stared at him, inwardly thinking on this, almost leading him to believe that she hadn't heard him.

"I believe God put him in your life for a reason," Matt continued, dropping his gaze for a moment before lifting it to her again. "Just as Hope and Ben were brought here when they were, I think it's meant to be somehow. There's a purpose to all this. We just haven't found out what yet."

Jenna seemed to ponder this further 'cause her eyes searched the air for a few moments more. Then a smile cracked across her face as she leaned over to wrap her arms tightly around him in a hug, catching him a little off guard.

"Thanks, Matt," she told him gratefully, breaking apart so she could hold his arms in her hands. "You really *are* the brother I never had."

"And I'd like to *always* be your brother," Matt responded knowingly. They hugged once more, and Matt finally stood up.

"Don't sweat it about today," the boy began again, placing a hand on her shoulder. "It's probably gonna be rough for the first couple weeks, but we'll get there together. I'm on your side. Always."

"You always were." Jenna smiled knowingly, a reassured look in her eyes, as the boy made his way to the door.

Matt smiled at her one last time, a hand on the door, which he silently shut behind him as he made his way back to his own bedroom, leaving Jenna to think on this some more.

Chapter Eleven

Generating Hope

"Ahn!" Jenna groaned as she was held up again by Bentley stopping short of a jump. A bit of a rage falling over her like a crashing wave swallowing her in the undesired feeling; her acting coaches approaching her.

"You can do this. Don't focus on the jump or what comes after," Ryan reminded her. "The jump is the obstacle, not the landing."

"The smoother you go over, the better you're landing," Matt put in as bubbly as he could manage.

"But I can't seem to *not* think about it." Jenna sighed with a shrug. "Or maybe Ben's heart . . . just . . . isn't in it," she mumbled in defeat.

"You just need to find your middle ground again," Matt answered certainly. "Get back in sync like you always were."

"I don't even know how we ever lost it," Jenna replied flatly.

"Hey, we'll figure it out," Matt told her, reaching his hand up to take hers. "I know you can do it."

"Maybe if we take a break, we can come back to this. We've been at this a while," Ryan suggested. "I need to go to Prairie Rock Stables anyway."

"Prairie Rock? Why?" Jenna echoed, sliding her feet out of the stirrups and sliding her body down off Bentley.

"I need to speak to Verona Dempsey, the show jumping board's sign-up manager. She's currently stationed at Prairie Rock, and she has the paperwork for the sign-up application. I need to head over to get them. Wanna come?"

Jenna hesitated, shifting from one foot to the other.

"Fine," Jenna replied finally, reluctance clearly in her tone. "Then at least we can get those papers signed and return them right away."

"All right, but you know you don't *have* to if you don't *want* to," her father reminded her.

"I know. And I know that Katrina's likely gonna be there, but I gotta learn to deal with her anyway. Part of getting past this issue is to face the source of it, and she's a part of it. If I can't get past her constant ridicule, it won't *matter* how well I ride."

"I'm proud of you for saying that." Ryan smiled, hugging his daughter close. "I know you two have always been rivals and personal enemies. But I'm glad you're trying to get past it all. It's what the Bible commands, to 'love your enemies . . . and forgive those who persecute you.'"

"Well, I don't exactly *love* her," Jenna replied with a shrug as she began leading Bentley out of the ring to the stable, "but I *am* trying to forgive her for all she's done."

"And I'm very glad for that," Ryan repeated. "At least it's a step in the right direction. I'm proud that you're taking it for yourself without being told."

"I've just been blessed to have such great friends that help remind me of what I have," Jenna replied with a smile, "and what I need to work on." She glanced over to Matt in saying this, a touched expression painting itself upon his face. They all looked ahead as they approached the barn.

"You guys go ahead," Matt decided, taking Bentley's reins from Jenna. "I'll clean him up for ya today, then I'll let him out to run with the others horses."

"Oh, okay. Thanks, Matt." Jenna smiled, watching him go as she peeled off her gloves and removed her helmet.

"Then I guess are you ready to go now?" Ryan implied, pointing a thumb over his shoulder.

"Sure." Jenna shrugged. "Just lemme get changed, and I'll be down in a minute."

"Sure thing." Mr. Tyler nodded.

Jenna lowered herself down enough to ruffle Penny's golden fur before jogging off across the gravel, both dogs taking off after her. Then Ryan turned and strode down the corridor himself, thinking all the while.

****

The door closing jerked Jenna out of her thoughts, and she jumped slightly.

"You coming?" her father asked, leaning in on the open window.

"Uh, yeah, coming," Jenna answered, unbuckling her seatbelt and opening her door.

As she stepped out of the car, the wind blew at her hair, somehow stirring up an unwelcoming feeling that radiated off the very building she was about to enter.

Grooms and students bustled about leading horses of all shapes and colors to and fro the corridors that stretched out in front of her and opened up into three more down the short hall to her left.

"Excuse me," Ryan beckoned, grabbing the attention of a young stable boy cleaning a stall near them on the left side of the open corridor. "Can you tell me where, Carlotta Williams is?"

"I believe she's training in the indoor practice ring," the young man answered, pointing down the corridor to his left with the pitchfork's handle.

"Okay, thank you." Ryan nodded, and the boy nodded in response, returning to his work.

Jenna followed her father down about two stalls and turned left where they could hear shouting and the pound of hooves. The room they arrived in stretched out, and Jenna could tell they had reached the right place; the yelling voice clued her in as well.

"Hold him steady!" Carlotta barked, staring pointedly at something moving along the far-right wall.

Jenna could almost follow the laser focus of the Prairie Rock owner and trainer, finding it to be none other than Katrina riding a horse that she guessed was Napoleon. The jet-black horse cantered in a smooth collected gait, stretching himself out easily in every stride. The star on his forehead stuck out like the star from the first Christmas in the Bible, beckoning anyone to notice and revel in its beauty. The only spit of color on this horse's well-built body was nothing more than a half sock on its left hind leg. Cut smoothly on bold edges, it diagonally swooped up from the front of the leg just above the fetlock joint to about a fourth of the way up to the back of his cannon.

"Keep him tight! He can't be loose!" Carlotta bellowed, watching her daughter take the line of jumps along the length of the wall opposite them as Ryan and Jenna made their way toward her at the center of the ring amongst the other trainers barking orders to their students in turn. "And keep your hands up, Katrina. He can't perform with you holding him down all the time!"

"Carol," Ryan addressed her to which the woman's pale blonde curls whipped around in his direction.

She scoffed. "Well, if it isn't Ryan Elliot Tyler." Carlotta beamed offly. "Haven't seen you around here for a while."

"Yeah, I suppose it has." Ryan half chuckled. "I'm looking for Verona Dempsey. Rumor has it she's stationed here for the upcoming show this August."

"Well, you've come to the right place for that—that's for sure," Carlotta replied, almost seeming disappointed. "So tell me," she began, glancing to Jenna briefly, "is your daughter finally coming out of her early retirement to challenge mine again?"

"In a matter of speaking, yes," Ryan replied patiently despite the anger rising up inside of Jenna, which she successfully masked with the curiosity of the action all around her.

Hooves came closer as the black steed slowed to a halt mere feet away from them, turning their attention to the pair. Katrina appeared to be frustrated amongst the proud smirk on her face of showing off her new horse, but Jenna didn't dare say anything. Instead she chose not to meet her gaze and just studied anything but her face, noting the pretty striping on her horse's hooves.

"That last run was atrocious," Carlotta criticized, staring her daughter down coldly. "I want you to do it again. And better. That oxer should not have come down, and your transitions are choppy. You look like a wobbly chicken with no sense of direction."

Jenna could've sworn Katrina's smugness had broken by the look that came to her eyes, the criticism that she'd just received seeming to tear her spirit down a lot lower than Jenna was used to seeing. Katrina pulled Napoleon around, and Jenna caught a brief enraged frown as she nudged him into an immediate canter.

"Push him up! He's lagging!" Carlotta hollered boldly.

Napoleon's gait broadened and smoothed out slightly as she took the jumps from the right side, hitting the line of three from the two on that back wall from where the group of people stood.

"Hands up! And crop . . . through the jump!" Mrs. Williams snapped in time with the horse's hooves.

The snap of the crop to his flank sent the black horse wheeling over the first jump, sending them into a domino effect of failed jumps.

Carlotta groaned, closing her eyes as she turned to Ryan again. "Perhaps the bit of *real* competition will get her in gear to win again this year. We spent far too much on that horse for her not to."

"Well, you know what I always say," Ryan ventured knowingly. "Winning's only half the battle. Showcasing the bond between horse and rider is the other. . . and having fun of course."

"Perhaps, but none of it matters without the pride of victory," Carlotta countered. "The bond isn't worth much if you can't show it by placing high."

Jenna's brow furrowed, which the older lady couldn't see, when she caught motion in the corner of her eye. She found Katrina and Napoleon coming back over to them.

"Well, anyway, about your question," the stable owner began again with a sigh, "I believe Verona is in the office. I'll escort you there." She turned to her daughter pointedly. "We'll continue this later," she finished as she fell in step with Ryan, leaving the two girls behind.

In a bit of subtle rage, Katrina stripped off her gloves and threw down her crop, fingering her helmet strap to unclip it from under her chin.

"You're sitting too far forward," Jenna spoke up, monotoning the whole statement despite her mind screaming in protest for what she was doing.

The clip released, and Katrina leaned forward for the dismount.

"You're just far enough forward that it's compromising your balance and Napoleon's."

Katrina gave her an icy glare as she led her horse right on past her.

"Look, I'm not trying to tell you what to do," Jenna called after her. "I'm just trying to help you improve your form."

Katrina stopped briefly, the girl hiding the brightened expression on her face, but then just kept walking without even turning back. Jenna watched her until she handed the reins to one of the stable hands waiting at the exit, and she walked away to the left, holding her elbows in her hands and her helmet clasped within one of them.

****

"It's so exciting!"

"I know. We couldn't be more proud."

Jenna only caught the last part of the conversation as she entered the Prairie Rock office just a short distance across the hall and a few paces up the corridor from the arena.

"So you'll need to sign here and here." Verona and Ryan looked up from their work when they noticed Jenna's presence in the doorway, Ryan craning around from the chair he was sitting at, elbows braced to the counter in preparation to write.

"Oh, Jenna there you are," Ryan greeted brightly, straightening up. "Ready to sign this thing, honey?"

Jenna stared for a moment at the form on the counter when she reached it, and it brought back silent memories that still seemed to bring back the ones that haunted her. She suddenly blinked, shaking herself out of the daze.

"Uh . . . eh- . . . yeah. I'm ready."

Ryan turned back to the paper, signing his name before passing the pen to her. Taking the small metal writing utensil into her tenuous fingers, she forced them to sign the papers and set the pen down next to it.

"All right," Verona commented, whipping the piece of paper onto the printer below their view from the counter; noises sounded as she then came up again with another piece of paper in hand. "There's a copy for you," she said, sliding it over to Ryan and tucking her deep brunette curls behind her ear for like the third time since she'd arrived. "And you guys have a great day. Can't wait to see your name back on the roster, Jenna." Verona smiled warmly at her, and Jenna forced one back.

"Thanks," she answered quietly.

"Yes, thank you so much. You have a great day too," Ryan added. "I guess we'll be seeing you soon."

"In less than two months," Verona confirmed, her green eyes sparkling. "Good luck out there, girl. Happy for ya." The middle-aged woman's hand touched Jenna's arm almost at the shoulder, her thumb softly caressing her skin.

This action only seemed to provide a small amount more of reassurance as she forced a slightly wider smile.

"Yeah, thanks," she answered softly.

"Bye, guys," Verona beckoned one last time as they headed for the door.

Jenna glanced back briefly then closed the door behind her.

****

"Wait, so you actually tried to *help* Katrina?!" Kate gasped, rubbing down Prince's silky coat from the dust still on it.

"Well, yeah," Jenna admitted, gesturing her hands out while still holding Bentley's body brush and curry comb, standing where she could see her. "And from the sound of it, I *had* to do it. She was having a rough practice. 'Course her mother wasn't being all that helpful."

"Carlotta Williams is a trainer through and through," Matt spoke up from Kinnick's stall. "And I heard she's *totally* hard core. And you gotta be pretty tough to withstand her coaching."

"Which is why I'd never train with her," Jenna decided. "She's too focused on looking good and winning shows to teach good horsemanship to her students. She's just like Katrina."

"You mean, *Katrina's* just like her *mother*," Kate corrected.

"Okay, yeah, that," Jenna complied with a shrug, stroking the brush down Bentley's hindquarters. "Still, I feel like I *needed* to do it even though my heart still despises her."

"Brian would be proud though," Kate remarked, tossing the brush into the grooming kit and taking out the hoof pick. "He'd be glad that you're trying to 'get along' with your enemy versus reacting to her insults in anger."

"Yeah, he would," Jenna agreed lightly.

"You okay?" Matt wondered, stopping his work with Kinnick on the crossties to step a few paces toward her in Bentley's stall.

"Yeah, fine," Jenna replied, blinking out of a daze.

"You sure?" Kate wondered, wandering over to peer inside the stall door. "You've been on a space roll for weeks now. Where's your focus been lately, girl?"

"Everywhere and back, I guess," Jenna replied.

"Apparently, Space Cadet," Matt joked then proceed to dance in slow motion, singing "Space Cadet" all the while.

Jenna just shook her head at him in humorous amusement.

"Still, seriously, what is your deal?" Kate wondered, turning her serious glance on Jenna. "Is there really *nothing* that's been bugging you?"

"I guess since Hope's been here, it's just got me thinking about stuff," Jenna admitted, letting herself out of the stall with the grooming kit. "And since talking with Ben about Sam, I'm kinda starting to miss him all over again."

"Oh well, I guess I can give you that one," Kate surrendered tenderly with a shrug.

"We get that you're missing him," Matt spoke up, his eyes soft and meaningful. "But let's stay open about this stuff, okay? What happened with you and him all those years ago is behind you even though it was painful."

"I know. You're right." Jenna nodded at the ground. "But I just need to figure out how to shake it off again."

"Don't worry, Jenna. We got you," Kate answered, nudging her friend's shoulder with her own brand of swagger. "We're in this together, homie."

"As long as you never call me that again." Jenna smirked.

"Okay, you got it," Kate responded, holding her hands up in a gesture of surrender.

"All right well, let's get these guys out to the pasture to graze, and then we can sweep the halls and clean the stalls."

"Yes, captain!" Kate announced as she and Matt saluted to Jenna like military officers.

Jenna rolled her eyes knowingly, finding some humor in the gesture.

"Come on, guys," she said, strolling down between them to grab Prince's and Bentley's halters.

****

Jenna's laughter echoed through the air, the pure bliss of joy ringing in the atmosphere, Samson's smooth angelic gait giving the illusion that they were flying versus cantering. A jump over an oxer seemed to launch her into another reality as she watched Samson's white coat shift to grey as if the jump itself was creating the change. Bentley's hooves were what hit the ground next, and suddenly she felt taller, a more real feeling coming to her as they moved toward the next jump. The water on the other side of the fence shimmered, and she knew what was coming. One stride, two strides, three strides, and they were there. Bentley's hooves left the ground, and they flew higher than she'd ever thought, and for a moment, her heart sang the praises of the feeling it gave her.

A jerk brought them down again, and suddenly a squeal rang out as they hit the ground, and she then realized she was back the way she'd fallen when Samson crashed. But instead Bentley lay in his place, squealing and thrashing to get up again. Tears blurred her vision as she could just barely lift her head to see such a horrifying sight.

"NOOOOO!" Her lungs sustained her cry better than she'd realized, and she couldn't stop herself from screaming the word at the top of what her lungs could handle.

"No!" she cried, shooting upright.

Jenna almost choked on her own breath as she came out of it, realizing now what had just been. Her body relaxed a little then tensed back up when she threw her head up to the right, tossing the covers aside.

****

The gravel crunched under her feet. The lights above the stable doors led her to her destination as the horizon was slowly reaching out to her in a brow of pinkish red, signifying the coming dawn. Pushing the doors aside, she stood there a moment with her hands to both doors, her breaths abrupt and slightly gasping. Bentley looked up from his hay, calmly nibbling the wisps in his mouth as he nickered a greeting. Jenna's guard dropped as she closed her eyes, lowering her head in relieved sigh.

****

Jenna braced hard as Bentley refused the jump for the third time. Jenna groaned as she recovered her posture.

"This isn't working. He's not in it," Jenna complained, about to dismount.

"Just run it one last time," her father suggested. "See if we can get something going."

Jenna reluctantly complied by turning Bentley on his haunches and walking him to the rail on the far left end of the ring.

"Hey, guys, how's it going?" Ben greeted, strolling up to Matt and Kate.

Another ruckus rang out as Bentley refused once again, bringing the boy to attention.

"They're trying to get Bentley to jump so they can get him ready for the upcoming invitational in August," Matt told him, his chin resting on his arms crossed over each other and anchored to the fence rung so he could peer through at them.

"She *actually* entered?" Ben said, eyebrows raising to know this.

"Yeah, but unfortunately, Big Ben's not having it." Kate put in from where she sat on the top rung of the fence, both teens staring out at the rocky practice session.

But the lens with which Ben saw things caught his attention nearly immediately, and he strode over to the gate.

"Hey, Jenna!" he called after Bentley refused once more. He raised a hand to her and waved for her to come over.

Bentley turned and strode calmly over to him, Jenna's face telling all her thoughts at once.

"You seem a little tense," he told her gently. "Are you all right?"

"Wish I was better." Jenna sighed, stroking a gloved hand down Bentley's crest once.

"Hmm," the boy thought, placing his thumb and forefinger to his chin, eyes settled on the ground. "Maybe you need a change of pace," he thought for a moment. "Do you guys have another jumper I could borrow?" Ben asked brightly a moment later, looking to Ryan.

"Kinnick, he's one of our best." Mr. Tyler nodded.

"Great! Thanks!" Ben smiled.

"I'll come help you," Matt offered, falling in step with him as they trudged through the sandy ground to the gate.

Jenna stared after them, her brow furrowed.

"I don't think it'll help all that much." Jenna sighed finally, lowering her gaze. "Bentley doesn't really seem into it."

"Just wait and see," Ryan told her knowingly, holding his hand on her knee. "You might find it more helpful than you think."

And Jenna's gaze lifted to watch them some more.

"Well, while they do *that*, I'm gonna run into the house real quick.." Kate decided, hopping down off the fence on the opposite side of them. "Stock up on the latest *Rose Original* and family gossip while I'm at it."

"Haha, okay." Jenna chuckled lightly, watching her stroll away, her smile fading to a blank thoughtful one as to what her other friends were up to.

****

It was no surprise to see Ben reemerge with Kinnick, the paint's many colors brightly shining in the glow of the afternoon sun. But the snowy sapphire companion that came from the shadow of the calico-colored gelding caught Jenna's attention. Matt and Ben led the two horses out and through the gate, Matt handing the reins to Ben to go close the gate behind them.

"Sydney?" Jenna gasped, surprise bursting on to her face like a party favor. "Guys, what is this?"

"We think it's time to bring out the big guns," Matt replied as they led the horses closer. "In this case, us."

"But how is *this* gonna help me?"

"I was gonna surprise you later," Matt began. "But I think now is more important."

Jenna gave him a strange look, and he continued, "We've always been saying that we should get Sydney into the show jumping world to do well by her father, so I thought it was time."

Jenna's head cocked.

"Matt has decided to enter the competition with Sydney."

"I figure that if you're gonna face your fear of competing again, might as well not let you do it alone." Matt's brown eyes met Jenna's green ones, a smile cracking across her face.

"And I'm just here for moral support," Ben added, "so to speak."

"For what?" Jenna wondered, arching an eyebrow for him to see.

"I think the reason Bentley won't jump is 'cause he's feeding off your current anxiety from your previous accident," Ben explained. "I think he senses that you're worried about something and, thus, is afraid of it in turn."

"But I've been with him since forever," Jenna countered stiffly. "He should trust me enough to just do it, shouldn't he?"

"Horses still feed of human emotions, Jenna," Ben reminded her, "which means you could have the strongest bond, but a lot of times, they may *still* play off your emotions for that reason alone."

"Hmm, I guess you're right," Jenna admitted after a moment's thought. "I, of all people, should know this—I deal with horses all the time."

"I think this instance is a little more personal," Ben supposed, "which is why it was an oversight. Happens to the best of us."

"All right." Jenna shrugged loosely. "So what's the plan?"

"We turn it into a game." Ben smiled in a bout of pleasure. "Well, so to speak."

****

Kinnick's nostrils flared, his eyes bright as he sailed over the next jump, hitting the oxer at the opposite length of fence, clearing it perfectly. Ben craned his neck to the right around to spot the next jump, lining the horse up for the three-jump combination. Kinnick's body rose up to meet with Ben's body on each jump, flowing over it to make a unified display of the performance leading into the wall obstacle three or so lengths away. A wide semicircular turn brought them to another oxer, setting up a clean approach to a vertical fence. The glassy surface of the water sparkled with the dancing reflection of the horse and rider as they cleared the full extent of the jump that followed the vertical. Then came another clean turn and the final two vertical fences, ending the round with the thud of hooves.

Ben smiled as he brought Kinnick down to a halt, applause ringing out to add to the boy's pride.

"Ohhhh! That was amazing, man!" Matt praised, throwing his hands in the air excitedly, having to then settle again to calm Sydney's nervous pacing from foot to foot. "Oh, easy, girl. You're okay," he soothed, stroking her soft neck.

Jenna concealed a smirk into her hand, away from Matt so he wouldn't see.

"Anyway, great job, Ben," Matt commented once again.

"Thanks. Would you believe this isn't even my passion sport?" Ben replied, beaming humorously.

"What!" Matt breathed, his jaw dropping at this thought.

"Could've fooled me." Jenna shrugged in amused agreement.

"Yeah, you should put me on a cross-country course and see where my *real* strong suit is." Ben cracked a smile wider than before, his eyes showing the enjoyment he'd taken with Matt's reaction.

"I might've known," Jenna replied. "I mean you *did* say your last horse was a cross-country racer."

"Oh well, when you put it that way," Matt joked, shrugging as though he'd known all along simply making Ben and Jenna laugh.

"What?" the boy wondered, seemingly unaware of their reason for laughter.

"Okay, now it's your turn, Matt," Ben said finally.

"Ben's time was 13.2," Ryan spoke up, holding the timer up. "And the higher the jumps are, the longer the time will be. But for now, we'll just practice at two feet."

Matt shot a grin at Jenna before nudging Sydney forward into a working walk. Starting her at an even trot, he smoothly transitioned her into a trot, which he then turned into a slow canter at the far-right end of the ring.

"Get her going a little faster there, Matt," Ryan advised, holding the timer up in preparation to start it. "Give her some leg."

Jenna could see success when Sydney's gait quickened. Matt peeled her away from the rail, and Ryan started the timer as soon as he passed the starting flag, clearing the first vertical jump. Seven strides later, he was soaring over an oxer made up of two verticals like all the rest. Rounding the two verticals on his right, they met another oxer that he wasn't prepared for, hence the clatter of the pole behind them. The vertical/oxer line along the rail came as no surprise though, and he cleared them with little issues though coming off the oxer, Sydney threw her head up and whinnied, her excitement bubbling over, and Matt had to lift the reins to calmly guide her head down again. The line of three flopped as they knocked down a pole from both oxers but cleared the vertical in the middle, proceeding to clear the wall about five strides later. They made the circle around to the last oxer, which would then lead to the vertical into the water jump, into the last two verticals, only knocking down the last one.

Sydney shook her head, her silvery mane flopping against her damp neck as she slowed to a stop in front of the group. Matt craned himself back to look at all the poles he'd knocked down, having lost count in the moment.

"Swift work, Matt," Jenna teased, lightly chuckling.

"Okay, well, not my best run." Matt shrugged, his honesty a little comedic. "But we'll get it next time."

"You better if you expect to beat us." Jenna smirked, allowing Bentley to stroll forward with a little pressure from her leg.

"Matt got a 14.4, but because he knocked down four obstacles, he's got sixteen faults."

Ben and Jenna snickered while Matt groaned.

"Looks like *I'm* gonna need to work my tail off if I'm gonna have Sydney ready in time," Matt figured, scratching the back of his head.

"You mean so *you'll* be ready in time." Jenna smirked, glancing back behind herself at him.

"Didn't I say that?" Matt wondered sarcastically though looking to be serious.

Jenna just turned front and nudged Bentley into an immediate trot. Bentley's canter started comfortably at her command, and the internal click, like a metronome, began. *Please, Lord,* she prayed deeply, *please go over.*

The counting in her head started as she turned Bentley toward the first fence, and she lifted herself out of the saddle for the initial jumping action to occur. She opened her eyes to realize that she'd cleared the fence, and Bentley's ears flicked back toward her gently as they made an approach to the incoming oxer. Feeling the inaccuracy of Bentley's stride, she pressed her leg into his side to lengthen his stride; they fell in line with the oxer to land precisely on the other side. Jenna's tense grip released slightly, her breath having seemingly found her again.

Bentley must've felt this change because making the smooth circle around to the next oxer, they cleared it with no trouble, Jenna finding it almost exhilarating. As they reached the vertical oxer line, Bentley's forepaw came in too low and knocked the top rail off the vertical, and Bentley stumbled a bit, Jenna's heart catching in her throat, but she felt his stride smooth out to find his footing again, and he flew over the oxer to finish the line. As he wobbled a bit, with a quick sigh, Jenna gave him more pressure that set them up for the set of three. Almost like a seesaw, Bentley easily hopped over the three jumps, only knocking a rung off the vertical in the middle. Bentley's hooves found the ground and carried them all the way to the wall of fake bricks in three long strides.

The final oxer came as no surprise and didn't slow them in the least, but after approaching the vertical, they cleared it. Then the forward momentum stopped below her, and suddenly air brought her down in a splash of clear blue.

"Jenna!" Matt cried, he and Ben jumping off their horses to race across the sand with Ryan.

Chapter Twelve

Breakthrough

Jenna's breath flowed back into her with a loud gasp as she came up from the surface of the water jump, a shocked daze across her face as she sat up again. Bentley made a low squeal and stepped anxiously back from the fence he'd stopped himself from jumping. He twitched his ears back in fright as Ryan came to take his reins and calm him down again.

"Jenna, are you okay?" Matt asked, both he and Ben peering over the low vertical at her as she began to strip herself from the shallow rectangular pool.

Jenna shivered from the initial chill of the cool water, taking the end of her ponytail and wringing it out to keep the water in the pool.

"At least I don't feel hot anymore," she answered finally, her tone surprisingly bright.

"Phew!" Matt sighed, lowering his head thankfully. "Thank goodness," he finished while extending a hand to her.

Taking it, she pulled herself up out of the water and carefully stepped over the rungs of the two-foot jump. Then in a bit of humor, she shook herself so that she could spray Matt and Ben with the remaining water dripping off her clothes.

"Hey, quit it!" Matt shouted, chuckling while shielding his face with his hands. "Heh, now we know where Bentley gets it."

"That would be a disqualifying round, ya know," Ben remarked, cocking a smirk, "taking a dive for the water jump."

"Ha ha," Jenna mocked with a smirk of her own. "Still I feel like that's the *most* progress I've had for weeks." Her eyes thoughtfully searched the ground in saying this. "And that's because of *you*, guys." Her gaze found theirs, and the two boys looked to one another, adopting a collective grin.

"It worked!" Matt beamed, he and Ben draping arms over one another's shoulders, Ben ruffling Matt's hair in victory.

"Should've known you too would gang up on me." Jenna laughed, shaking her shirt out as best she could while wearing it.

"Hey, at least it was for a good cause," Matt returned with a shrug involving his hands as well.

"I had no idea Matt was going to compete in the show too," Ben informed her. "But when he came to help me get Kinnick, he told me his surprise, and we decided it was the perfect time to roll it out on you."

"Well, congratulations," Jenna snickered in a formal tone "'cause it worked."

"We know. Isn't it great?" Matt beamed, leaning an arm on Ben's shoulder casually, his leg crossing over the other to proudly demonstrate the pride of their hearts.

"You know," Ryan spoke up dynamically, "I'm starting to wonder who this girl is and what she did with my daughter, Jenna Tyler."

A suggestive grin shone down on her, and she couldn't help but laugh. "Dad." She sighed humorously, coming in to hug him tightly.

"I'm really glad to see you're improving, sweetheart," Ryan told her earnestly, releasing his grip to set his hands on her shoulders. "And for you to finally feel good about yourself again. The pressure has been on lately, and I know you've felt stressed by it all, but I praise God to see it finally starting to come to an end."

"Yeah, me too." Jenna smiled.

Bentley strode forward toward her as if to apologize by nuzzling her cheek gently to which she touched a hand to his face as he did so. "Yeah, I forgive you, boy." She grinned, scratching behind his ears.

"Jenna Tyler, what happened to you!" Kate demanded, marching over to them and looking Jenna up and down disgustedly. "You're soaked! Did you hit the deck again!"

"Yeah, I did, but I'm all right," Jenna said, still wearing her smile from before.

"Positivity? After a fall? Okay, who are you and what did you do with my best friend?" Kate stalked up, their noses almost touching as she spoke, Jenna leaning back from her a little.

"I guess I just found something I hadn't felt for a while," Jenna admitted calmly, her eyes soft.

"The thrill of competition?" Matt implied, sharing a confident fist bump with Ben.

"No, the thrill of the moment," Jenna corrected as though it was just now that she realized it. "The rush of adrenaline, that feeling like you're flying, that passion for what you're doing. It's something I haven't felt for a while. . . ever since Sam." Her eyes wandered down then back up at them. "It's a feeling I'd almost forgotten."

Matt, Ben, and Kate stood back thoughtfully.

"There she is," Matt said.

"What?" Jenna asked in a half-chuckle.

"The Jenna we all know and love," Kate replied, meeting Matt's glance knowingly.

"The version of you we were looking for," Ben finished proudly.

Jenna's chest fluttered with a warmth that brought the realization to light. She placed her hands to her face as her eyes glistened. "Oh, guys," she managed to say, coming forward for a group hug with her three friends.

"So why *did* Bentley stop?" Matt wondered, after they'd broken apart again. "If you'd have made that jump with the last two verticals, you'd have had a good run with only eight faults."

"But more than what you'd done, but I think it's 'cause he's never seen a jump like this before," Jenna guessed. "Sure, we've jumped streams and creeks before, but this is something new to him."

"Well, we'll just have to work on him with that too then," Ryan remarked, coming alongside his daughter.

"Ryan! Time for you and the kids to come in for lunch!" Ann called from the house.

"Oh guess she's right," Mr. Tyler concurred and shielded his vision from the sun above. "Looks like it's time to call it. We'll be sure to try this again later if we have time."

"Okay. We'll untack these guys and be in in a sec," Jenna replied.

Ryan nodded and began to head toward the gate to cross the gravel to the house.

****

"So what would you like to do for your birthday, kiddo?" Ryan asked from the kitchen, opening the fridge to retrieve a few bottles of Gatorade and returning to the dining room. "I know we've been kinda busy lately, but it *is* coming up soon, just another week or two." He handed a bottle to Jenna and tossed another one at Matt like a football across the table who dramatically obliged in catching it.

"It's three weeks from now," Jenna corrected. "And I'm not a kiddo anymore. I'm gonna be eighteen."

"I know," Ryan replied anxiously. "Yeesh! You kids grow up so fast! I don't think I can handle it!"

"Oh, you'll handle it just fine," Ann countered easily, brushing off his statement. "We're just so proud of what wonderful godly people you've become."

"Even though we haven't really been acting like it lately," Matt specified as the three friends' eyes lowered.

"Don't feel bad, you guys. I'm sure we all fall from whatever grace we believe in," Ben spoke up. "I'm not really anyone to talk, but I'm starting to understand your God more and more by just listening to you and your family. I've heard that song that says God knows us by name and that being famous doesn't matter because we already *are* famous *because* he made us and loves us."

"'He Knows My Name'?" Jenna wondered, her thoughtful eyes settling on him.

"Um, yeah, I think that's the one," Ben recalled. "Sung by some Francisco Beeta—"

"Francesca Battistelli," Jenna corrected, smiling at the boy's amusing attempt at pronunciation. "She's a Christian artist we listen to a lot."

"Yeah, that's it." Ben smiled, pointing to her happily. "Good music. Gotta say."

"Heh heh. Yeah, Bentley thinks so too." Jenna chuckled, recalling her horse's response to hearing them.

"We know. You sing them to him all the time," Matt remarked with a smirk.

"And to answer your question, Dad," Jenna retracted as they all began to sit at the table, "I have no idea. I've been so busy lately that I really haven't had time to really think about it. There's still a lot that needs to happen with Hope for her to be ready to go home. And training needs to remain a priority if I'm gonna do well at the show next month."

"Oh, I hear ya," Frank spoke up fondly. "Ya know your father was once like that. When he'd be competing all the time and doing whatever young boys do at your ages, he would be managing so many important things that a lot of times, he'd forget all about things like that. We'd find ourselves *asking* if he wanted to do something for his birthday. And one year, all we did was take him on a ride down the mountain trails that you kids take all the time for fun."

"It's true." Ryan chuckled, seeing the memories return to him in his mind's eye. "I hardly had any time to think on it too much before I was off doing something else. One of those years, I was proposing to your mom, believe it or not." He looked to his wife, pulling her close at the hip in finishing this, a knowing grin between the two.

"Yup. Ain't no one immune to the busy nature that God no doubt puts in our lives," Frank stated with a sense of ease, relaxing back into his chair. "But yet we still find time to honor God and bless others."

"I guess mainly what I want is to spend it with my closest friends and family," Jenna decided thoughtfully. "Maybe have an all-nighter in our upstairs family room?" The girl's eyes suggestively sought out her three friends in saying this.

"Absolutely!" Matt exclaimed.

"You know it, girl," Kate smiled, shooting a finger gun at her with a wink.

Then Jenna turned to Ben.

"Me?" the boy vocalized, placing a hand to his chest. "Well, yeah! I'll check my schedule, and let me know the date, I'll see if I can make it."

"Great! I'll text it to ya as soon as I can," Jenna replied brightly, the spirit of the room lifting.

"Sounds good." Ben grinned, passing the carrots to Ann, and Jenna's smile could subtly indicate her satisfaction of this response.

****

Stillness . . . peace . . . Jenna shot upright in a flash. If she'd made a sound, she wouldn't have known. Silence continued, so clearly no one had been disturbed by it if it'd happened. Sliding out of bed, she paced forward then back, hands shaking, eyes blinking, thoughts racing.

No! The breakthrough has already come! her mind assured her. *Hadn't it?* She paced a second time. *Was it all just a dream?* Her fingers fiddled with themselves, slightly twiddling the tips of the stray blonde hairs that snuck over her shoulders, bringing little comfort.

Finding herself at the window, she pinched the thin drapes in the thumb and forefinger of her right hand, peering through at the dew-frosted lawn, the twin barns connected by the tack room to the right of the rounded gravel drive and then the jumping course just beyond the gravel, meeting up with the corner of the first barn. Jenna's green eyes stung with the light's harsh attack, but could it also be the tears that foreshadowed the coming emotion building up within her? *It must be.*

She turned with her head bowed and strode in the darkness back to her bed, a sinking feeling in her chest as she lay down again.

****

"So I think Hope's ready for the next step," Jenna was saying, leading Hunter's Chase down the corridor to his stall.

"Really? You think so?" Ben vocalized, his tone brightening.

"Yeah, I think she is," Jenna answered.

Chase suddenly stopped, stamping his forefeet out in a wide stance, his head frozen up.

"Keep going," Jenna told Ben easily who'd jumped slightly at the horse's abrupt action, reaching a hand up to softly rub the palomino's pink nose. "Chase's a little spooky, but he's getting there. We're trying to teach him to stay calm when new or unknown things scare him."

"Oh." Ben blinked, gathering his thoughts. "Well, anyway, does that mean we can try Hope out undersaddle?"

"Probably," Jenna answered, continuing to rub the horse's nose behind her field of vision who by now had calmed him to the point of lipping at the air below her fingers. "She's beginning to get used to the saddle, and we've managed to get her used to the girth around her body," Jenna continued as she eased Chase to walk forward once again. "Lately we've been using feed bags to give her the feeling of a rider's weight on her back. If we take her out to the arena real quick, we can see if she'll let us ride her."

"Sounds good." Ben smiled. "I'll go grab her gear and meet you at her stall."

"Okay," Jenna replied, reaching Chase's stall as Ben peeled away in two backward steps to head back down the corridor.

****

Hope's mouth eased open for Jenna to place the bit easily in its proper place to secure the straps around her well-shaped head, the filly's chewing motions giving them the indication of ease.

"Good girl, Hope." Jenna beamed, rubbing her hand over the horse's nose from where her head was draped over the girl's shoulder. "That's probably the fastest she's ever taken the bit before." Her gaze met Ben's, and his hazel eyes lit up.

"Really!" He gasped. "That's awesome!"

Hope shook her head in a way to shrug off his comment, which only made the two laugh at the hilarity of it.

"Would *you* like to do the honors?" Jenna asked, stepping so her back was to Hope's shoulder and gesturing to Hope's bare back while still holding the reins in her grasp.

"You bet!" Ben replied eagerly, coming forward calmly. Easing the saddle pad out from under the saddle, he turned back to catch Jenna's glance.

"Just set it up onto her back and put a little weight on it," Jenna instructed, answering his unasked question.

Ben positioned the pad to where the withers sloped down to her back and pressed both hands down on it. Hope's head rose, and her ears twitched back toward him.

"Good, now go for the saddle, and do the same thing," Jenna continued.

Repeating the process brought the same result, and Hope *still* did not react beyond her head raise and ear twitch.

"Good. Now just slowly tighten the girth from one side to the other until it's tight enough. The pause in between allows her to settle in to the tension of the girth before tightening it once again."

"Makes sense to me." Ben shrugged, tightening the girth up one hole from the left side. Making his way around, he tightened the girth another hole from the right; Hope's head lifted more abruptly, and she stepped away from the pressure.

"Easy, girl," Ben began softly.

"Good, that's good. That's the reaction we wanna see," Jenna said. "She's responding to the pressure correctly, and as she gets used to it, reward her for standing still."

"I can do that." Ben grinned brightly, giving her a thumbs-up. He then turned back to Hope and eased his fingers under the girth. "Okay, I think it's tight enough."

"Good, and she doesn't seem to have developed the habit of faking us out when tightening it, so let's continue to keep it that way. You hold on to her, and I'll bring the mounting block over."

"Has she been trained on it yet?" the boy asked, his sandy hair and hazel eyes glowing in the sunlight.

"Yeah, we've been trying to get her used to it for when you go to ride her," Jenna answered, beginning to drag the black three-stepped block over to Hope's left side. "Have a go."

Ben hesitated. Handing her the reins, he placed his helmet on. Looking at the crop in his hand, he hesitated a moment longer while staring at it.

"You know what?" He dropped it to the sand and looked at Jenna. "I don't need it. Hope needs to trust *me*, not my will."

This only broadened Jenna's beaming grin and Ben's as a result. Stepping up onto the mounting block, Jenna pulled Hope's reins over her head so Ben could reach them. Grabbing a hold of the filly's mane and placing his left foot into the stirrup, the boy eased his weight down on it and watched Hope's ears as he stretched his leg over and lowered himself into the saddle. Feeling the sensation of his leg at her sides, Hope stepped about nervously.

"Keep your hands quiet and your seat deep," Jenna advised calmly.

Adjusting his grip on the reins, he held them still and relaxed into the seat of the saddle, Hope's nervousness fading away once more.

"She hasn't fully got the concept yet. But at least, she understands that she's not in any danger," Jenna stated, adjusting the position of the stirrup iron.

"I honestly can't believe she's made it this far," Ben admitted in a mount of awe. "I had all but given up on the fact that she'd *ever* be rideable. But somehow *you* found a way. I guess I owe you a lot *more* than just a thank you."

"*You* don't owe *me* anything," Jenna countered meaningfully. "I merely just found the oversight that everyone else couldn't seem to find."

"Yeah, but if you hadn't, I'd have had to say goodbye to her, maybe forever." Ben's gaze lowered. "I'd have given up on her when I didn't *need* to."

"We *all* are a little rough around the edges," Jenna replied. "But only God can only see the diamonds in us."

"Because He made us," Ben said, almost suggestive of something.

"You're learning," Jenna smirked.

"Might have gotten a little curious," Ben joked, touching a hand to his face modestly. "Guess you guys are starting to rub off on me."

"Hey, at least it's not a bad thing, right?" Jenna shrugged.

"Nah, not really." Ben shrugged as Jenna adjusted the slack of the reins in Ben's left hand. "It's actually become kinda good for me, ya know?"

"Glad to hear it." Jenna beamed. "Now take her around in a circle on that end of the arena, around the three-jump combination."

"You got it." Ben pointed Hope straight over to the right side of the arena and nudged her forward gently, allowing her to walk at her own pace. After a few slow laps, Hope's gait quickened, her ears tracking everything around her as she upgraded to a trot.

Jenna caught movement in the corner of her eye, which she definitely confirmed as Matt and Kate. Hope's head jerked about as she broke into a choppy canter, which eventually smoothed out as she calmed down again.

"She looks great," Matt commented, suddenly appearing next to Jenna, pulling her from her thoughts.

Turning her gaze from the gray horse, she met his gaze with a smile. "Yeah, she's really improved from when we first got her back in May," Jenna agreed, her eyes finding the filly once more. "It's already July, and we're finally preparing her for her final stage of her training, and then she'll be ready to go home again. Feels like things have gone by so fast. Before we know it, we'll be back in school, and I'll be a senior this year, which means I'll be able to work with the horses full-time."

"Uh, yeah, and then I won't have any company against you know who," Kate complained in her usual sassy manner.

"Yeah, well, things are changing," Jenna replied. "And this time, I think it's for the better."

"And you won't be alone," Matt said. "I'm graduating late because I *started* school a year late, so you'll still see *me* in the halls of Riverton High School."

"Great, I feel *so* much better," Kate deadpanned, waving jazz hands in the air.

"Hey, I said it." Matt shrugged with an amused smirk.

"Anyway, we're glad Hope's doing better," Kate said, turning to Jenna. "A real breakthrough has happened. . . with her *and* you."

"Why me?" Jenna questioned lightly.

"Well, lately you've been kinda struggling, what with all this reminder of Sam and what happened to you back then. It's good to see you getting past it again."

Ben by now had switched directions and worked Hope up to another steady canter, which the teens could see looked much more relaxed and free-flowing than before.

"Hey, Jenna!" Ben called, cantering to the edge of rail and pointing to the first jump of the course.

"The fences are low enough," the girl thought aloud. "Go for it," she called to him.

Making one last round, he turned Hope toward the first fence, the filly's ears perking forward at it. Jenna and her friends slid over to be next to the water jump as Hope sailed over it perfectly. Ben pulled her up and to the right, just before hitting the oxer along that same line and walked her back around to the where the others were standing.

"That was incredible!" Ben breathed, his amazement beyond awe at this moment.

"She looks very sound on her feet," Matt commented.

"And smooth in her gait," Jenna added.

"Not to mention you both look wonderful together," Kate agreed dreamily.

"Thanks, guys," Ben replied, chuckling a little at Kate's response. "She seems to *really* trust me now."

"And that's a great thing to see," said Jenna proudly. "I think it's time we got her out of the farm and into the elements."

"Really?" Ben asked, leaning forward slightly. "Like going *out.*" Jenna nodded.

"Woah, cool," the boy breathed.

"Wait here, and we'll get our horse's ready," Jenna replied as she, Matt, and Kate began the trek back toward the barn out of the arena.

"Okay, we'll be here," Ben replied, giving her a thumbs-up.

Chapter Thirteen

The Other Side

"Hope's like a totally different horse from the one I met back at the shelter where we found her," Ben remarked, looking to the filly as she stepped carefully down the small incline of the path with the other horses. "She's become the horse I'd always hoped she'd be."

"I bet," Jenna figured, letting Vinny, the Tylers' black paint, lazily tromp along next to Hope. "And she seems very well acclimated with the other horses here at Sunshine. She's truly become a great horse because we all saw the beauty in her. We saw through her rough exterior to find the potential that she no doubt has."

"Yup, she's a keeper." Matt sighed deeply. "Savor that, and always treasure the bond you share with her. That's where your strength will come from. . . other than God of course."

"Yeah, you know what? I will." Ben smiled, lifting his gaze to them.

"So what do you plan to do when Hope is finally ready to come home?" Kate asked, craning her head back as Prince held his forward heading.

"Well, like I've told Jenna, I want to look at training for the next cross-country meet, but if I've learned anything from this process," Ben ventured thoughtfully, "it's that I'll wait till *she's* ready before we *actually* start competing. Listening to Hope and meeting her necessary needs are my top priority until I'm confident she can fully handle it all. We'll work toward competition until it feels right, and then we'll slowly start trying it out just to get her used to the atmosphere. I want her to one day be my go-to cross-country horse so I can make it all the way to the top, maybe even get to the Olympic levels someday."

"Very ambitious," Jenna commented, grinning at him from the corner of her eye.

"I try." Ben smirked, shrugging one shoulder. "But I know Hope's confidence comes first. I know she needs to feel safe in order to perform well. So for the next few months, my focus is gonna be on *her* and our bond. I wanna have as strong connection as we possibly can in practice before we try out the real thing. And I think going to church and meeting people. . . good people will help with that."

"Totally!" Jenna confirmed. "Getting in touch with the Father through strong Christian people is a *great* way to start. They'll definitely give you guidance into connecting with God's heart. After all David in the Bible was a 'man after God's own heart,' and that's still true for us today."

"I'm glad to serve a God who's like that," Matt remarked, the sunlight sneaking through the trees dancing across their skin as they went.

"Me too," Kate agreed. "He's the one person I can count on even if others fail."

"Yeah, I think I might be able to grab a hold of that." Ben smiled, the tint of his hazel eyes bringing forth an unsettled feeling to Jenna that got her attention.

"Rough home life?" she implied thoughtfully, feeling in his insecurity.

"You could say that." Ben sighed, his eyes hitting the ground. "My mom and dad are working through a divorce. I don't want them to do it because it feels wrong, but . . ."

"You have no control," Jenna finished for him.

"Yeah," the boy replied, meeting her gaze with solemn eyes. "My sister, Jessie, and I have been trying to get them to work it out, but we've had little success, and I'm afraid it might be over soon."

"I'm sorry you're walking through a dark time, Ben," Jenna told him softly. "I pray that God will heal your broken family. I may not know the situation, and that's okay, but I do know that the Lord has you in the palm of his hand, and he knows the desires of your heart if you're willing to ask him for them."

"Thank you." Ben smiled, a sense of reassurance returning to his face. "I hope I can ask him in time."

"It's *never* too late with God," Jenna emphasized, reaching a hand over to his. "He'll work it out. I promise."

"'And we know that God causes *all* things to work together for good,'" Kate quoted, now on the far side of the group as they walked in line with one another.

"'To those who love God,'" Matt finished meaningfully, both looking over at Ben to their left on the other side of Jenna.

"It's Romans 8:28, a verse in the Bible," Jenna explained, turning from her friends to Ben. "It's a good verse to memorize, just one of many promises God has made to us as his children."

"I got looking at a Bible once," Ben mentioned, his eyes dropping into his lap. "But then I realized I didn't even know where to *start* looking for answers."

"You can come around here *any* time," Jenna offered forwardly. "My family is the most scripture-savvy bunch I've ever met. We'd be *more* than happy to help you navigate the vast reaches of God's Word. And help you find the peace of mind you need to work through this."

"Thank you," Ben answered. "I might just take you up on that one of these days."

"I'm glad you're willing to give this a try." Jenna smiled earnestly. "Not many have the faith for that."

"At this point, I'm about ready to try anything," Ben replied, an openness to his tone as they rode on.

****

"Training's been going great with Bentley," Jenna commented, her brow shimmering with sweat as she pulled a dining room chair out to drink some water from the bottle Ryan had handed her. "We just made it to three and a half feet today."

"I know," Ryan answered proudly. "Can't wait, you'll do great at the show."

"I'm still knocking fences down though. I feel like even though we're doing better, we're still struggling in a way, but we'll get there."

Everyone looked toward the kitchen when the phone rang.

"I've got it," Ann said quickly, sliding her chair back and hurrying off to retrieve it.

"I wonder who could that be?" Frank remarked openly.

"Probably another client," Jenna supposed, wiping her forehead with her athletic towel.

****

"They've been talking for a while now," Matt stated, listening to Ann's voice from where he lay slouched upright on the couch against the wall.

"It may well be an academy matter," Frank guessed, laying back against the other couch set perpendicular to the one Matt was sitting on, positioned nearest to the door leading to the kitchen so that their backs were to it.

Ann finally returned, and her gaze immediately fell upon Jenna.

"Jenna, it's Vanessa. She wants to ask you a favor," her mother said.

Jenna stared at her for a moment before getting up out of the old rocking chair in the corner of the living room and walked by her mother to the kitchen.

"Hello, Vanessa," she said, picking up the phone.

"Hi, Jenna," Vanessa's voice sounded cheerful and excited. "I have a favor to ask."

"So I hear," Jenna replied humorously.

"I wanted to know if you could enter Hope in the Summer Splash Invitational."

"Um, sure, but I'd have to ask my folks about it. They might not want to pay the fee to enter."

"Oh, don't worry about that. I'll pay for it, Hope *is* my nephew's horse, but I'm as responsible for her as. . well. . . he is."

"Does Ben know about this?" Jenna sounded worried for a moment.

"Oh, sure," Vanessa replied easily. "In fact, he suggested it. I talked to your mom about it earlier. And she said it would be fine as long as you agree. But I was just wasn't sure if Hope was ready for that and if you would be willing to ride *two* horses in the show."

"Oh, okay. Um . . . well . . . I think Hope can handle it," Jenna thought. "She's been doing really well lately. Ben and I have *really* been working on her in the ring since we can *finally* saddle and ride her. I think she'll be ready for her final test soon, and I guess a show is about as good a test as any."

"Then would you be willing to ride?" Vanessa wondered hopefully. "But of course, I wouldn't want to pile on to your busy schedule."

"Well, sure. I'd love to." Jenna shrugged despite knowing that Vanessa wouldn't be able to see.

"Oh, that's great to hear. Thank you so much!" Vanessa sighed, sounding quite relieved. "And good luck. Sorry I asked you on such short notice."

"Oh no, that's okay," Jenna assured her. "I know how busy our lives are, but it's okay. Besides, Hope and I work well together, so I don't think we'll have too many problems."

"Oh, that's good. I'm glad you understand," Vanessa's tone lightened. "Not many do these days."

"No problem." Jenna beamed, a warmth rising in her chest. "And ya know, at the end of the show, if all goes well, Hope *might actually* be able to go home with you if you want."

"Sounds good to me," Vanessa answered brightly. "I'll have my trailer with me in case that happens."

"Okay, and I'll be sure to bring all her things with us so we can just hand it all off to you versus having you come all the way *here* to get them."

"Thank you. That would be nice," Vanessa replied. "Have a great rest of your day. Goodbye."

"Buh-bye." Jenna put the phone down and thought for a moment, a small smile bending her lips up as she returned to the living room.

****

"She really said that?" Kate asked, impressed by the story that Jenna and Matt had just told her.

"Yeah," Jenna replied thoughtfully, her focus on Chase.

"But it's great news, right?" Matt asked, studying her to read her expression.

"Actually yeah, it is," Jenna answered, her small smile returning.

"But I didn't know a rider could *have* two horses in the invitational," Kate remarked thoughtfully.

"Well, believe it or not, it's legal," Jenna replied.

"Seriously?" Kate said in disbelief.

"Yep." Matt nodded. "It doesn't matter who's *riding* the horses as much as it matters who's sponsoring them."

"Hope's name will be registered under Vanessa's stable name," Jenna explained simply. "And Bentley's will be under Sunshine's. I'll just be the rider for both."

"Huh," Kate replied thoughtfully. "Well, good luck then. I'm cheerin' you on." She shrugged.

"Thanks." Jenna smiled. "But we won't need it. We've got something better than luck." She smiled, and her two friends developed ones of their own. The group then fell into silence as Jenna continued to rub Chase's face in tight circles.

****

"Jenna!" Ben's voice called in echoes toward the tack room door.

"I'm here!" Jenna's voice called back.

Following it with incredible accuracy, he turned the corner into the open tack room door. The young man's gaze panned around from left to right until it found that familiar blue polo and slim figure that he'd gotten used to, and he then began an approach to peer into the locker she was rummaging through.

"What'cha doin'?" he asked, craning his chin up to view what she was focused on.

"I'm working on clearing out Hope's locker," Jenna replied, standing up with a bit in one hand and a lead rope chain in the other, raising each to look at before setting them into the cardboard box at her feet. "Just so I can have it organized and ready for transport."

"Transport?" Ben echoed lowly.

"Didn't you hear? After the show, Hope *might* be able to go home with you guys," Jenna replied, turning his way after sticking Hope's saddlebag on the peg inside the locker.

"Really!" Ben gasped. "You mean she's almost done with her training?"

"If all goes well at the show. . . maybe," Jenna responded, her eyes lowering thoughtfully for a brief moment.

"Wow! I mean . . . this is . . . Wow!" Ben's stammering brought a hand to the boy's head and a wider smiled to Jenna's face, painting it with a form of joy that brought more meaning to her victory with the beautiful filly and adding an extra sense of pride she hadn't felt before till now.

"This great news!" Ben breathed. "Thank you. Thank you so much!"

"Don't thank me yet," Jenna advised, still humorously smiling at him. "We still need to see how well she responds to the activity of the showgrounds."

"Right, better keep working on her to try and prepare her for the busy sights and sounds of the show ring," Ben recovered quickly, resuming his calm modest demeanor.

"She'll need it if she's gonna do well out there." Jenna chuckled and finished putting things away by setting Hope's neatly folded stable blanket into the box and pushing it into the locker with the toe of her boot.

Closing the door, she proceeded to walk down the line of lockers to where Samson and Kinnick's were then over to Bentley's locker on the opposite side of the room. She opened the first locker on her right from the corner one, and the dim light from the rafters above lit up an image of Jenna standing with Bentley. Green grass, blue sky, a smile on her face as she held Bentley's lead rope up from where he was grazing on halter and lead.

"When was *that* taken?" Ben wondered, leaning in for a closer look.

"Last year," Jenna answered fondly, kneeling down again.

Ben now realized the scribble of writing on the bottom right corner of the image, the frame only covering the faulty edges of the handwritten script, leaving it exposed enough to read.

"Janice Devino. Sunshine, 2016," he read, squinting to make out the intricate ink text. "Friend of yours?" he implied, glancing down on her.

"Just a photographer," Jenna replied loosely, standing up with a blanket draped over her arm. "It was one of the best days ever."

Taking the photo down off the shelf, she turned it over on to her arm, holding it steady with that hand as she opened the back of the framed photo. She lifted up the frame's back, and there was another photo of Jenna depicting her smiling at the face of a bright copper chestnut, which appeared to be quite expensive even from the crude quality of the picture itself. Jenna willingly let Ben take the photo into his hand to look at it a little closer. He noticed a man looking to be of Argentine descent, beaming a glowing smile at Jenna and the horse from the background on the far-right side.

"The horse's name is Ameridian Prince," Jenna explained, gesturing her chin to the photo. "He was a horse I saved from going to the slaughterhouse last spring."

"Wow! He's beautiful." Ben breathed. "Wait. Was he the one they mention in the article about you? The one my aunt found that led us to here?"

"Probably." Jenna shrugged one shoulder. "It was a big deal for a while." She bent down to sift through the box once again. Setting the blanket aside, she pulled something else out of the box and handed it to Ben. The thickness of it and the notable text told him that he was holding a newspaper and stamped across the front page in big bold letters was the headline: LOST HORSE IS *LOST* NO MORE! The image of Jenna and Bentley was slapped across the page under it with the other image of her and Amir under it on the right side of the article itself.

"The article was written the day Amir won his first big show jumping comp in over a year," Jenna went on. "Amir was a high-end show jumper that wasn't performing like he used to. He was traumatized by an electrical failure during one of his runs in the summer of 2015. His Argentinian owner, Constantine Martinez, was originally bringing him to Prairie Rock for discipline reinforcement in January 2016, but his trailer accidentally rear-ended a minivan on their way there. No one was hurt or killed, but everyone was a little shook up, including Amir. My dad, Matt, and I were heading into town when we were stopped by the police to wait for them to clear the area. We were there when they got Amir out of the trailer. Once they got him out of that trailer, there was no *way* they were getting him back into it."

"So what happened?" Ben asked, his eyes searching her carefully.

"Well, eventually, I got tired of watching them fight with him." The girl shrugged. "I was slowly able to calm him down enough to wrap my jacket from the car over his eyes and lead him back into the trailer again. To this day, I have no idea why they took him out of it to begin with. There would've been a lot less fuss if they hadn't."

"Maybe it was to show off your mad skills," Matt's voice startled the two of them, and they looked up to find the boy standing in a confident wide stance with his arms crossed proudly, Kate at his left shoulder.

"Only *you* say that." Jenna smirked.

"Only because it's true," Matt shot back then began an approach. "So whatcha doin anyway? Besides reminiscing?"

"Well, I was cleaning up Hope's locker so it's ready for transport for when we go to the show," Jenna explained. "And now I was gonna get Bentley's stuff out to clean before we practice again today."

"Sounds fun! Count me in." Matt smiled, heading down the line of lockers and stepping over the long bench to access the fourth locker on the freestanding lockers just beyond them.

"What are *you* doing?" Ben asked, arching a brow at him.

"Getting Pinto Beanz's stuff out," Matt replied, pulling a saddle and bridle out of the locker as he turned back to the other boy. "Looks like it's a cleaning party before practice."

"I'll do Sydney's!" Kate called, racing over to the filly's locker excitedly.

"All right." Ben shrugged as his friends kept going. "Guess I'm in too." He finished making his way over to Hope's locker once again.

Chapter Fourteen

Past and Present

"Janice Devino was the photographer on the story at the time." Jenna went on as they scrubbed at the leather straps with the saddle soap and sponges in their hands. "Apparently people that saw me handling Amir got talking about it, and eventually the media got involved. After I calmed him down, Constantine decided to bring Amir to *me* at Sunshine and asked that *I* work with him instead."

"That's amazing!" Ben remarked, his eyes glowing.

"Oh, it was," Matt confirmed. "It was like the closest thing to dealing with royalty!"

Jenna just smiled knowingly at him.

"All I *really* wanted was for Amir to get the best shot he possibly had," she said, turning her gaze to Ben. "I wasn't really expecting him to put that shot on me."

"Well, it must've paid off," Ben said, his eyes thoughtful.

"Mm, maybe." Jenna shrugged.

"I'm just glad I was there to see it!" Matt spoke up again. "So cool!"

"I bet." Ben beamed understandingly.

****

One, two, three, and jump! Jenna's mind counted, following the strides of the white filly gracefully weaving round the series of jumps that would be the course with which she herself and Matt would run on in the coming month swiftly approaching their midst.

"Awohh!" Matt groaned as Sydney knocked over the last rail of the final vertical fence.

"Haha! That's only eight faults this time." Jenna chuckled. "You're getting there, Matt."

"I'd like to get one with *no* faults." Matt sighed, walking Sydney past them to then line her up amongst Hope and Bentley.

"Ben's been riding Hope for some of our practices, but I'll need to start riding her more to practice if we're gonna ride well together at the show," Jenna said, adjusting her grip on Bentley's reins and swinging her leg back over his back, her feet hit the dust enough to raise a cloud, which scattered the sand under them.

"Can't wait to see this," Ben commented, holding Hope's head as Jenna made her way around them to the filly's left side.

"I've ridden her in front of you before," Jenna replied, slowly pulling herself onto the horse's back from the mounting block and settling herself into the saddle.

"I know, but I mean at the show," Ben corrected himself. "You guys look so good here. And I know Hope is *my* horse, but I'd like to think that she'll do better with you out there."

"What are you talking about?" Jenna asked, staring at him rather boldly. "You're a *great* jumper and an awesome rider. She'd do just as good with *you* as she would with me. Maybe even *better* with the strong connection that you two have."

"Yeah, but show jumping's not really my thing." Ben shrugged loosely. "With cross-country, you get a change of scenery all the time. The courses are *always* changing. They're different every year too. It's so much more exciting that way. Show jumping, to me, just feels confining."

"It's okay if it's not your *favorite* event," Jenna replied. "But you're skilled enough that you could do it easily."

"Glad *you* think so." Ben smiled up at her, his reassured expression pure and genuine.

"So, Jenna," Matt's voice spoke up, earning their glance. "Bet you can't beat that," the boy finished, leaning his head back against hands crossed back to cushion them in a sort of cocky demeanor.

"I guess we'll just have to find out." Jenna smirked back.

Ben's hand slid off of Hope's rump as she walked away, proudly watching his horse's every response thoughtfully.

"Okay, Jenna, we're up to four feet, three inches," Ryan reported, raising the last jump a couple pegs. "If you can make this, we'll be ready to go to five feet for next time."

"That's the height they're running at the level we're in," Matt added.

"Which is the level I used to jump at," Jenna confirmed, Hope standing calmly facing the group and gnawing on her own bit.

"All right, let's see what ya got," Ryan announced, gesturing to her.

Jenna tightened her calves into the filly's sides, and she responded appropriately by walking forward. Matt and Ben swiveled around to watch as Jenna brought her around behind them on the rail, working her up to a trot. On the far corner approaching the starting flag, Jenna asked for the canter, which Hope willingly gave, much to the girl's surprise and relief. Jenna's two-point position over Hope's saddle granted the filly space to move under her. She landed the jump and, four strides later, cleared the oxer.

We're gonna make it! she thought. Samson's squeals rang out in the back of her mind, and she tensed up, Hope's ear's twitching nervously. *No! That's not today!* she demanded of herself.

Hope stumbled after the second oxer, and Jenna tried to keep her head up so she could successfully regain her balance. Turning into the vertical/oxer line, Hope's balance improved, and they cleared them, no problem. Landing out of the oxer, she glanced over briefly to find the three-jump combination, mentally charting out her course for which Hope's approach would need to follow. *One, two, three, four. One, two, three, four,* her internal timer ticked.

They jumped one, two, and three, and yet no poles hit the ground. Matt and Ben found it growing increasingly difficult to remain calm, the boys each fidgeting with the anticipation pounding through them as an adrenaline rush. Over the wall and around, the oxer nearest to them remained standing.

Jenna reached the next vertical jump where they could get a good side view, and Matt could've sworn he'd seen a flash of Jenna jumping Amir in just a similar way over a jump much like the one in use right now.

Lengthening her stride, Hope reached the water jump in one long stride, sending her over it and on through the final two jumps. A hoof clipped the final jump, but to their amazement, it never fell.

Jenna then realized that she'd been holding her breath and released it in the relief of finishing the course.

"What!" Matt cried, astoundment stamped across his face, eyes wide and jaw hanging open.

"That was incredible!" Ben breathed in agreement.

"I'll say," Ryan concurred, pride glowing across his slightly aged face. "I'd say our girl is finally back on her game."

"Um." Jenna looked back over her shoulder to discover that all the jumps were still standing. "Well, I guess so." She shrugged, finally lifting her gaze up to them again.

"Dang, watch out, Katrina, 'cause here she comes!" Matt marveled.

"Okay, well." Jenna chuckled quickly. "I wouldn't go *that* far just yet."

"Why not? Looked pretty good to me. Right, Ben?" Matt asked, glancing to the older boy expectantly.

"Agreed, you looked amazing!" Ben replied, his gaze on Jenna. "Couldn't have done it better myself."

"Yeah well, I think you could've." Jenna snickered modestly.

"Only heaven knows." Ben shrugged, his ease a welcome surprise.

****

"Hey, girl!" Kate greeted brightly, waving when Jenna opened the door. "Look who I found on the way in." She pointed back behind her in subtle form as she turned back to where another figure stood.

"Ben!" Jenna breathed, her eyes flashing. "You came."

"'Course I did," the slightly older boy replied earnestly, holding a box in his hand. "Wouldn't miss it for the world."

Kate shot her a smile as she slipped by her into the house. Shaking herself out of a dazed stare, she pulled herself back into focus. "Uh, anyway, thanks for coming. Come in."

Ben smiled and climbed the stairs to enter the house, and Jenna shot a glance out across the yard before reentering the house once again.

****

"Okay, do mine next," Kate decided, handing her a small present wrapped in a red-and-blue-striped paper. The three teens slid closer to her as she began to fiddle with the edges, the flatness of it thick enough to measure about a half an inch or more, the size being no more than four and five inches on all four sides.

"I bet it's a tiny handbook," Matt joked, leaning in closer over her left shoulder.

Jenna just elbowed him playfully at the suggestion. Finally peeling away the paper, she saw the image of a red chestnut horse frozen mid-jump with a rider dressed in red, filling the small sturdy page.

"They're trading cards for the U.S. Olympic show jumping team throughout the years," Kate explained, her excitement growing as she spoke. "My dad helped me track down a bunch of them from years past for ya. There *might* even be some limited edition ones in there somewhere."

"Wow! Thanks, Kate!" Jenna breathed honestly. "This is great! Thank you." Jenna wrapped her right arm around her friend as best she could while still holding some of the cards in her grasp. The girls pressed a cheek to one another's in an awkward hug that seemed to work only for them.

"You might already be able to guess mine." Matt scoffed, handing her a brown bag with white handles and a decoration of blue crimped ribbons.

Taking out the tissue paper with a quick glance at him, Jenna carefully peeled away the layers to only find a tiny box in the bottom of the small bag, which seemed almost too big for such a small container. Setting the bag on the floor, she took the lid with one hand and held the bottom in the other, stealing another glance at Matt before the lid released and she could peer into the small box. The soft fuzzy bed of fluff held in its cottony embrace the faces of two familiar shapes that she found to be herself and Bentley."

"It's to update your locket space," Matt stated openly. "I know you've always been wanting to add a more current photo to it since it has another slot to put one in to make it double-sided."

Jenna's gaze softened. Pulling the locket out from under her shirt, she balanced the box on her knees as she reached back to unclip the locket from her neck. Matt took the box into his own hand, and taking the photo out, Jenna fingered the locket open and stuck the photo within the slot on the free-moving side of the locket's heart-shaped divide. Now the photo of two-year-old Bentley accompanied itself with the current-day Bentley with Jenna smiling at the current version of her beloved horse in the frozen memory.

"It's perfect." Jenna sighed. "Thank you, Matt." Hugging him almost brought more meaning to it even just in Matt's mind.

"I hope you like mine. I kinda got it a little late, so it might not be all that good," Ben admitted, passing her the large flat package.

"It's mainly the thought that counts," Jenna replied, tearing away the blue and green paper, the green side of it glaring against a glass surface, which didn't really grab her attention until it was laid away from the glare's view to reveal what lay beneath it.

Hope's posture was frozen over her in a vertical jump with none other than Jenna in her saddle, her determination forever captured in this snapshot of her victorious run just a few days earlier.

"I had it made yesterday," Ben said, his arm rested on his knee from where he sat on the edge of the coffee table, which he'd been amazed that the Tylers had permitted. "I managed to get this shot when we were training the other day. The photo's not that good, and the frame feels off, but I still thought you'd like to have it as a reminder of what you did for me."

Jenna feared she'd cry, given how her eyes stung. Or maybe it was just the glare of the glass messing with her eyes, but either way, her heart melted into her chest.

"It's . . . beautiful." Jenna wished to sound less shocked than she was but simply couldn't deter herself from this feeling that came upon her. "I . . . sometimes the imperfection of it is what makes it even *more* perfect." She looked up to meet his gaze with big green eyes. "Thank you." Jenna wrapped an arm up over his shoulder with the picture still in hand, so that their shoulders were the only thing to touch, giving more of a neck hug than anything.

Releasing him once again, she held the picture in both hands to look at it once again. "It looks amazing," she said, observing the variant grains of the wooden frame's detailing, caressing her fingers down the right side of it. "It'll go great with the image of Amir and me," she finished, looking up to him again.

"Eh, I hoped so." Ben shrugged earnestly.

Ann leaned in to her husband's head, keeping her hand up on Ryan's draped over her shoulders like a shawl from where they sat together on the couch closer to the wall to the left of the one the teens were sitting on, facing the TV on the opposite wall.

"This stuff is amazing!" Jenna commented, glancing round at all she had received around her. "Thanks for it all!" Her glance panned around the room at her friends and family, thankfulness and joy upon her face with their endearing expressions of her company thanking her back.

"Okay, so who's up for a game of charades?" Matt suggested in pleasure.

"I'm not really all that good at charades," Ben admitted, scratching the back of his head sheepishly. "But I'll give it a try."

"Yeah, you will!" Kate agreed confidently. Then shielding her mouth from the rest of the group, she added, "You'll be fine. We're not the best at this game either."

Ben chuckled, his gaze hitting the floor with the blinking of his eyes.

****

"Uh . . . uh . . . eh . . . a bird!" Matt blurted out, watching Jenna flail her arms about in an up-and-down motion.

But then Jenna lowered her hands as if she were holding something and dragging the tips of her fingers across it in a graceful manner.

"Harp, harp player . . . Oh! An angel!" Matt shouted.

"There you go." Jenna giggled, dropping her act immediately.

"You call *that* an angel?" Kate remarked, mimicking her friend's movements.

"Made sense to me." Jenna shrugged, coming to sit back down between Matt and Kate on the couch once more.

"At least it was better than Matt's interpretation of a chimpanzee." Ben smirked.

"Hey? What can I say? I go bananas for bananas," Matt joked, starting another round of laughter, then Jenna turned Ben's way.

"Okay, Ben. Your turn," she addressed him.

The boy's gaze lit up at the mention of his name, but he got up off the floor between the TV stand and the couch they were sitting on to grab a folded piece of paper from the cluster sitting in the middle of the coffee table in front of him. Standing up to read it, he tossed the paper aside onto the coffee table so no one would see what it read. Then taking on a heroic pose with his fists to his hips, he mouthed a bunch of words with the point of a finger to the air. Finishing this, he dropped down a little, holding his arm out as if his forearm was a gun, a steady hand hovering over it as if searching for something.

"Buzz Lightyear?" Jenna answered, more surprised that the character was even in the list of words. "Who came up with that?"

"What? At least it was a fun one to act out." Frank shrugged.

"Grandpa!" Jenna beamed, holding back another chuckle.

"Hey, you said there's no rules on what we choose as long as it's fun." Frank shrugged again.

"Gotta give him that," Matt remarked with a shrug of his own.

"Well, it's getting late," Ryan said finally, stretching. "We should all probably call it a night." He rose from his seat and stepped around his family to head back beyond the open living space to the first door of the hallway stretching down to the rest of the bedrooms and the bathroom on the far end of it.

Frank rose shortly after him and headed downstairs, the two women of the house rising shortly after him.

"We'll help you kids get settled," Ann told them.

"I'll go get the sleeping bags in my closet," Jenna decided, heading off to the second door down from the one Ryan had left from.

Entering her own bedroom, she crossed the floor to the closet in the back-right corner of the room. Sliding the door aside, she rummaged amongst the few crates lined against the back of the shallow closet. Looking up for only a moment, she caught something hanging on the very far left end of the long rod, which she soon recognized held an expensive white and navy-blue attire she hadn't seen nor worn in seemingly forever. Shaking off this thought though, she grabbed the straps of the rolled-up sleeping bags and returned to her friends. When she arrived back, her friends were clearing space for them to set them out.

"I got the sleeping bags," Jenna announced, tossing a purple one at Kate.

"Nice!" the dark-skinned girl cheered in, catching it. "I love this one!"

"And Ben's gonna use one of mine," Matt told Jenna, rolling his red one out between the TV stand and the coffee table.

"Good thing 'cause I only have two." Jenna smirked. "Ben would've had to sleep all alone in the guest room."

"Oooh, the *guest room*," Matt mocked spookily. "You say that like its haunted or something."

"It could be," Jenna joked humorously.

"Ha! Whatever, girlfriend!" Kate scoffed.

"Okay, okay, shh." Jenna snickered. "Let's not disturb anyone while we're at it."

"Right, don't wanna scare the ghosts away," Kate emphasized with a smirk of her own. "Then we won't have anyone to come and get us while we're sleeping."

And Jenna just had to roll her eyes at her friend's amusing statement.

****

Silence surrounded them, the rumble and crash of the storm outside pounding at the walls and roof, which protected them from its wrath. Yet a distinct atmosphere hung overhead, but only one seemed to feel it's beckoning.

The white and gray horses, joined by Hope, danced round her head, their neighs and squeals all ringing at the same time. Jumps and cracks shattered the empty air, her mind's self demanded her physical self to cover her ears to block out the sound, yet it still sounded as clear as ever.

"I'm done with this!" she cried, her tone trying and failing to scare away the darkness that reached its shadowy fingers for her very soul. "You can't control me!" she screamed into the darkness, almost trying to convince even herself. The noise grew louder and louder, like a train rattling down the tracks toward her, showing no signs of stopping. Her body was aching as a spotlight of blue and red charged in her direction.

"No!" Jenna found herself upright.

"Huh! What? What is it?!" Matt wondered groggily, thrusting himself up at the sudden noise. "Jenna? What's wrong? Why are you awake?" the boy asked, more awake now at seeing her as Kate sat up from across the room from Jenna. And Ben was pushing himself up off his stomach to his knees inside the large sleeping bag.

"Sorry," Jenna apologized quickly, hugging her knees to her chest. "It's nothing. Let's just go back to sleep."

"I'm not so sure it *is*," Matt countered, sitting up more and sliding forward, stopping her from her attempt to lie down again. "What's going on?"

Jenna's gaze fell away from them. Her jaw tightened, and her forehead sank onto her knees.

"Come on, Jenna," Matt coaxed, almost begging now. "We wanna help you."

Ben and Kate shot a glance at one another, turning them back to their friend.

"Whatever it is, we can handle it," Matt continued, sliding over to her all the way to sit beside her and place a hand on her shoulder.

She finally looked up at him with haunted eyes that surprised him, a lightning flash defining the characteristic glisten of them in the barely visible darkness.

****

"How long as this been going on!" Matt gasped, the light of the lamp illuminating his shocked look.

The distant growl of the fleeing storm filled the silent gap for the lack of a response. Jenna sat sheepishly across from him in the corner of the same couch he was sitting on closest to the wall behind it.

"Seriously how long?" Matt repeated.

"Ever since that day," Jenna quietly admitted, her gaze remaining unbroken from the floor.

"Why haven't you said anything?" the boy gasped. "We could've helped you a long time ago!"

"I don't know. I guess I've just been trying to convince myself that I'm fine when really, I'm not in the slightest." Her gaze lifted but fell just as quickly.

"Well, you must be more *fine* than you think," Ben spoke up softly, earning Jenna's tearful glance. "It's no secret that there was something off about you throughout this whole process," he said. "But now that we know why, we can understand more how strong you *really* are."

"How am I strong if I can't admit that I have a problem?" Jenna questioned, her defeat unmistakably plastered to her face.

"Because you've overcome challenges despite it," Ben told her. "You've been facing your fear of what happened to Sam by pushing through and doing it anyway. You've chosen to pluck up the courage to jump again. And not just with *my* horse but yours too. You've taken on anything that has come your way despite the struggles you face at night. And if you can do all of that, there's no reason you can't completely overcome this."

"He's right Jenna," Kate agreed in a soft meaningful tone. "God wouldn't have brought you this far only to let you fall."

"And if *you* can power through what scares you *and* inspire others to do the same, I'd like to think you can do anything," Ben finished.

"Philippians 4:13," Jenna recalled thoughtfully, her eyes softening.

"Uh, what?" Ben asked, puzzled.

"It's a verse from the Bible," Jenna explained, her demeanor shifting. "It says, 'I can do all things through Christ who strengthens me.'"

"That's right," Matt concurred. "And that's why we *know* you can get past this." His hand adjusted its grip on her shoulder. "Let hope guide you." He paused, thinking on this statement carefully. "Okay, not the horse, but I guess that could work too while on the jumping course."

Jenna shared a light chuckle with her friends, this fact lightening the mood in an instant.

"Well, now that we know the problem," Kate spoke up, "we can start to help it get better, starting with you telling your folks all about it."

"I know, and I'll try to tomorrow," Jenna replied honestly. "But the sun'll be up soon. Let's try to get some more sleep before then."

The friends shared a collective nod and laid down, their thoughts fading as their dreams resumed.

Chapter Fifteen

Lost!

Silence ensued upon the tribunal of adults. Jenna's sheepish gaze turned away from them in a shame. Kate, Matt, and Ben snuck glances to one another from where they sat in a line down the long dining room table as if feeling guilty of something. But after a forever silence, Ryan silently rose from his chair at the end of the table. Walking around to the other end, he took Jenna's hand and pulled her up from the chair, pushing it back away from her, and wrapped her in an embrace, his arms stretched all around her as he held her close, tears glistening in his own eyes.

"I'm so sorry we missed it," he said, a shakiness to his tone. "We should've been paying more attention . . . I . . ."

"It's okay." Jenna sighed, filling in where her father trailed off. Releasing each other, their glassy eyes met. "I had been *choosing* not to show it. I know now that I should've said something. I guess I was afraid that I was a lost cause."

"Jenna," her father answered lightly, tucking her hair behind her ear with his right hand, "you are *never* a lost cause to our Father or us."

They hugged once more, a flurry of emotion sparking something over everyone that they rose to join the father and daughter in an embrace that was shared by all of them. Not one eye was dry in the moment, and as they all parted, tissues were distributed to bring the moment to a close.

****

Stepping out onto the porch granted them the fresh air to clear away their sorrows. Sipping on the hot coffee and cider that Rose had prepared, they watched the morning sun's infiltration continue, starting the day that lay ahead of them.

"Eighteen years starts today," Frank stated, turning his head in Jenna's direction. "You ready?"

"Yeah, I . . ." Jenna's response trailed when her eye caught something in the distance. "Is Dani on the *other* side of the fence?"

The family looked up quickly, staring out past the right side of the barn to find the black mare standing amongst something jumbled up at her feet. Standing quickly amongst them, Jenna left her position, strolling forward into a run down the steps. Matt leapt over the top of the porch's wooden railing as the rest of the group rushed after Jenna to cross the gravel to the pastures behind the stables. Matt stumbled forward out of the first barn after Jenna, holding a lead rope in his grasp. Looking up at his friend, he realized she'd stopped, then looking beyond her gave him the answer.

Dani nibbled on the long wisps of grass just outside of where the fence stood, dividing the space between the pasture and the ditch beyond it adjacent to the gravel road that ran beside it. Brambled branches and splintered wood lay among the remains of the wooden fence, metal wiring twisted in with it.

"A tree's down," Matt stated as they made a slow approach to the black mare.

"And the electric fence is down," Jenna realized, observing how a section of the twisted wire had wrapped itself around the horse's front legs at the fetlock and halfway up the length of her cannons.

"I'll go shut off the fence," Frank offered, turning to leave.

"Wait!" Jenna's voice brought everyone to her attention as she counted the herd. "Some of the horses are missing!"

"Okay, uh, I see Cota, both Cairos, Violet, Prince." Kate pointed out each one as she listed them off by name.

"Major, Pinto, Sandy," Matt continued.

"Melanie's over there," Rose called, pointing to the palomino paint over amongst the others.

"The fence is broken right where the pastures meet," Ryan observed, looking at the broken fence more closely. "That's why Mel is in with the others."

"Chase is here. So is Niki," Ann reported, shielding her eyes then looking to her husband.

"I saw Hiccup behind Kyro," Frank called, making his way back over to them.

"And we know Dani's still here because she's tangled up in the electric fence wire," Jenna finished.

"Who does that leave us with?" Matt wondered, trying to recall.

"Well, um, let's see," Jenna thought. "We have Checkers, Milo, Zelda."

"Lead Zeplin's gone too," Kate interjected quickly.

"Kinnick, Vinny, and—" Jenna's body stiffened, her eyes widening.

"What? What is it?" Matt asked quickly.

"Did anyone see Micah?" Jenna asked icily, terror gripping a hold of her at the thought.

Matt looked up, shielding his eyes. "I . . . I don't see him," he stammered, squinting to see.

"Marshall's gonna too!" Kate gasped. "That's not good."

"Wait. Anyone see Hope?" Ben asked, peering out himself.

"And where's Bentley!" Jenna cried, desperately searching for her horse's distinct color and shape.

"They must've all gotten out," Frank supposed, "from the broken fence. Look!" He pointed down, and they all came to find where his finger indicated.

"Hoofprints," Ryan interpreted by the distinct shape. "It must've happened late last night when the storm hit. It must've knocked the tree down, and the horses escaped."

Matt searched up and around, his eyes panning around the open land to notice only one thing.

"Jenna?"

Looking around, they soon found her grabbing horses and leading them to the gate.

"Right, let's go, guys," Matt decided, beckoning to his friends. "We'll get the horses inside and get them all fed and watered. The adults deal with Dani and the broken fence."

"Frank, Ryan, do what you can here," Ann said. "We'll help the kids bring in the horses." Then the two older ladies took off after the teens.

Jenna had just gotten Chase's halter on when footsteps pounded up behind her, earning her gaze.

"Jenna, let's just run them in. Don't bother with the halters. Just open up all their stalls and close the front stable doors.

"Oh, right," Jenna realized. "Come on, Matt!" Leading Chase through to his stall, she quickly ran him inside and latched it closed. "I'll handle barn two," she told Matt. "You take barn one. We'll close them in as soon as we open the gate to let them in."

"Got it," Matt replied, dashing out and around to the other door.

Fumbling with each latch, Jenna threw open each stall door, only opening the ones they needed. Reaching the far end of the stable, she pulled the heavy doors together and looped the lead rope around it in a slip knot to keep it in place since the latch was on the other side. Then working her way down the longer end of the stable, she came out the side she'd started from just as Matt reemerged.

"Mom, now!" Jenna called.

And Kate and Ben opened the gate to let the horses come charging in. Rose and Ann waved with arms up to shoo them out of the pasture and into the gated enclosure that corralled them by the barns. And together, Matt and Jenna sorted them into the right barns, slowing them to the point that they could walk them down the corridor and into their corresponding stalls, which the horses knew all on their own.

"Phew, glad that's over," Matt breathed, wiping his brow with the back of his wrist.

The group turned at the sound of hoofbeats, finding Ryan and Frank leading Dani down the corridor toward them.

"The fence is badly damaged," Frank reported. "But it should be nothing we can't fix."

"We have to saddle up immediately and go find Hope and the others," Matt stated.

"Yes, but we don't even have a clue which way they went," Ryan reasoned.

"Well, there were hoofprints outside the fence. Is that clue enough?" Ben wondered.

"We don't know how far away those hoofprints go, or if they can be tracked," Ryan replied. "Fergus and Penny aren't exactly hunting dogs."

"But there's got to be *some* way to know where to look for them," Kate protested.

Matt's glance wandered once again.

"I'm sure there is," Ryan continued. "But until we track them from the road, we can't just go out willy-nilly to try and find them."

"Hey, guys," Matt spoke up. "Where's Chase?"

And everyone looked up at him in confusion.

****

Matt's fingers touched the open stall door, a purple lead rope still tied to the vertical rungs that made up half the wall.

"I'm telling you he was here," Matt insisted, studying the surface he was touching carefully.

"And wasn't his tack sitting here before?" Ben recalled.

"I thought I heard something about Jenna wanting to do some more work with him today," Kate remembered. "But why now?"

"Uh, guys," Ben addressed them from the other side of the barn. "Jenna's not out here."

"Then where could she have gone in such a short amount of time?" Frank wondered openly, then Matt's thoughts hit a brick wall.

"She's gone to find Ben," the boy realized aloud.

"And she decided to take *Chase* of all things!" Kate cried. "She knows that horse is afraid of his own shadow. What is that girl thinking?"

"It doesn't matter now. We've gotta go find her," Matt decided.

"Agreed. That means we *all* need to saddle up," Ryan declared, "and fan out across the area where they *might* have gone in."

"Right. Let's go," Matt called.

"I'll take Dani," Ben offered. "I've ridden her before."

"Go for it," Frank grinned, handing him the horse's lead.

"Wait," the boy vocalized in realization a moment later, stopping everyone in their tracks as they all turned to face each other again. "I don't know this area very well. How can *I* be helpful here?"

"You can ride with me," Matt said. "I'll saddle up Pinto, and we can go look for Jenna together."

"Okay, sounds good." Ben nodded, taking Dani back out and around to the set of crossties nearest her stall.

****

"Ben! Hope!" Jenna sighed, listening to the lonely crunching of Chase's tromping hooves. *The hoofprints led me into the forest,* she thought. *But where did they go from there?*

The marshy ground showed more markings, but many of the patterns resembled nothing other than the specific details of the ones she searched for.

"Kinni! Marshall!" Her shrill whistle merely echoed in the silence, not even returning its own voice. *What was that? A twig?* Her head whipped over to her right. Chase stopped, his breath silent yet audible and his ears twitching about to find any more noise.

"It's okay, boy. We're okay," Jenna soothed, squeezing her leg on him to go forward.

The palomino advanced with a lowered head, his steps slow and almost stalking. Ears twitching, his head bobbed slightly and panned from one side to the other. *They've got to be here somewhere,* she assured herself. *We've been trekking for like ever. We have to be getting close to finding at least one of them.*

The darkened shadows of dusk lowered over them like a coming fog, adding a murky haze to their field of vision. The sun's rays retreated from the darkness, coming to quench the light of day until the fiery celestial body were to return the following morn. *Maybe this is the time to head back to search again tomorrow.*

Pulling Chase up seemed to be a huge mistake because at the moment, the world seemed to laugh at her attempt to return home. Fluttering shadows screeched over Chase's head, and he reared violently, his own squeal ringing out as she tore forward through the woods. Appearing to have gained the ability to see in the dark, the horse galloped through the brush and woods, weaving through in a mad sprint.

Jenna ducked what few branches she could see, the sting of the invisible ones attacking her skin with the whipping wind with which their speed was achieving adding to the adrenaline that gripped her through her pounding chest. Suddenly the sting bombardment ended, and instead, a bash to her shoulder derailed her attempt to pull up, and her chest lost its breath upon impact with a hard surface. The light divide between her body and head lasted for a short time to her relief, but pushing herself up to all fours proved difficult for only a second. Seething, she maneuvered her body around to sit on the muddled forest floor to inspect the radiating pain on her upper shin.

Pulling her phone from her back pocket, she turned the screen light up to the top and turned upon herself. Noting the circular shape of the mark on her pants, she reckoned a surefire explanation was plain to see.

"Of course I take the spooky horse," she cursed to herself. Finally gaining the courage to stand, she found that her sore knee didn't seem to deter her all that much or impede her movement quite as much as she'd originally thought. *Okay, now what?* she thought, looking around again.

****

"Okay, we found Marshall and Kinnick," Matt reported, leading Pinto Beanz back out of the stable with Ben and Dani at his side. "And Frank and Ann found Checkers, Vinny, and Milo."

"I found Zelda," Kate announced, leading the copper chestnut Appaloosa by them, the mare calmly walking alongside Prince.

"That just leaves Micah, Zeplin, Hope, and Bentley," Matt noted.

"And apparently now Chase," Kate added bluntly.

"Uh, I think you need to try again, son," Frank countered, pointing subtly over across his body to his right with his left finger as Rose and Ryan arrived, each leading a horse at their sides.

"Zeplin and Micah, thank goodness!" Matt sighed.

"We still can't seem to find any sign of Hope or Bentley," Ryan reported. "And since apparently Chase is *still* missing, that means Jenna must still be out there. We'll need to call in the authorities if she doesn't return soon."

Attention was brought to alert in seconds; a golden shape charging down the lane rang alarm bells in the very back of their minds.

"Chase!" Matt screeched.

The palomino abruptly staggered to a stop, his panic sending him up in a full rear for them to discover that his saddle was empty.

"Woah, woah, woah, easy," Matt soothed, eventually talking the horse down enough to take his reins and calmly stroke his face. "But if Chase is here . . ." he trailed, looking up at the group hauntedly, "where's Jenna?"

"Forget waiting," Rose spoke up determinedly. "Contact them now! Get a chopper in the air and find her!"

Ryan's eyes closed painfully, his brow's intensity furrowed. "Then it's settled," he said, opening them again grimly.

****

"Hah!"

Another scratch and rustle shot her glance to her left while her body creeped away to her right. The sound drew in her breath to avoid revealing herself, but seeing no form of motion coming her way, she slowly backed away from it until her sight diminished. Tearing away from the small clearing that Chase had left her in, she sprinted for an unknown and unseen destination, which she yearned to be anywhere but here. As she dared herself not to scream, her booted feet leapt her across a ravine that she almost didn't see coming. Hitting the side of it, she lost her momentum, and the lack of footholds gave her an uphill battle of failure as she only slid down into the muddy stream that flowed barely visible in a dark night. Squelching underneath her seemed to give her a chill, the pointed nip of the cool night starting to get to her with no sun to bring the thaw. Trying to view a route up the slope, her eyes having become accustomed to the darkness by now, she found her search to be in vain.

"Now what?" She sighed abruptly to herself.

Vaguely feeling the water's current, she discovered the level was just high enough to flow over the top of her boots, allowing her to feel the direction from which it came. She glanced up to her right, and she saw the ridge sloped up to a rock ledge, which she was amazed to see in the complete darkness that surrounded her. *There! That's my way out!*

She climbed the staggering slope, nearly hitting the ground many times as she trudged toward its source about a half a mile up the rocky incline.

"Ahn!" Her knee struck the rocks, and the cool of the water splashed at her forearms. *The rocks are so slippery, gotta play this smart if I'm gonna get out of here without breaking my neck in the process.*

Stone-cold hands touched the surface of the rocky face. The ground around it she found easier to grip. With hands spread apart, they weighted her body against it. Earth crunched, muscles tensed, pull by pull, the end was near.

Jenna caught herself from falling as her hand slipped backward toward where she'd been. A small sigh and on she continued, pulling her upper self forward to balance on solid ground.

At least now I can try to figure out where home is, her mind reasoned, glancing back down to where the ravine dropped out of the overall layout of the land. Alertness was demanded with the sound of rustling returning. Creeping around the other side of the rock wall, she turned quickly to scramble up the side of it, fumbling at the top and looking down again. *Something's coming, but what?*

The rustling ended with the emerging of a long stealthy body, the fur of its hide a distinct color that, even in the midnight darkness, could be defined as a rocky tan. Paws were spread to the forest floor to bring balance to its four-legged base of support. Shimmering eyes were mustached by whiskers, and peeking white shiners revealed themselves with the creature's quiet pant. Jenna's blood ran cold where she lay against the top of the rocks to avoid detection.

Mountain lion, her mind breathed icily. A twitching action occurred at the big cat's behind, his eyes lifting as it sniffed the air. Jenna felt her eyes pop wide with the panic setting into her heart, quickening its pace in the process. Quietly crawling back away from the edge, she stood and reached the edge of the structure, looking down into the darkness of the barely defined stretch of land below. Looking back as she heard the animal's low growl, she found she had only one way to go.

Taking a seat, she slid down the side of the rock. Hitting the ground on her feet, she ran forward to wherever she could to escape the pounding paws tearing after her from far behind. The land seemed to run in slow motion as she seemed to be going at hyper speed, her legs carrying her across the uneven ground, yet she cared not about the possibility of falling and twisting her ankle. The terror of escaping created that "flight or fight" instinct that she'd always said pertained to the horses.

Guess it's not just for horses, she vaguely remembered herself thinking. A hard structure seemed to reach up to catch her foot because she found her face meeting the ground once more. She could've sworn to have heard stomping around her head, but was it just the pounding dizziness of her fall? Or had the creature finally caught up to her? A screeching cry rang out, and a growl responded, stomping continuing, resembling somewhat of a fight.

Heavily turning herself onto her back, she saw the darkness shake violently with blizzard shapes that hazed about wildly. Midnight black thrashed about at the lighter-colored shape just beyond it. A violent twinkle shot the creature's way with another shrill cry.

"Bentley?" Jenna vocalized hopefully. The thrashing lurched forward toward the creature, the distinct hiss returning with the pearly white teeth that uttered it. The smaller animal backed itself against a wall behind it, the thrashing figure edged closer. Anger and rage seemed to attack the big cat with a fiery vengeance, which seemed to finally pay off as the more-defined shape stepped on its front paws in a wayward manner and took off. Hooves hit the ground, and silence fell with it.

Jenna cautiously stood, her gaze locked on the darkened shape cut out of the forest scenery. "Thank you."

Shimmering eyes turned her way. Curious and brave, they came closer to nuzzle her fingers.

"Wait a second. Hope?"

The filly blew in her hair, nibbling the leaves and twigs from her loose hair as if to clean her off from the harsh conditions she'd found herself in.

"*You* saved me," Jenna realized aloud, a smile immediately breaking upon her lips. "Thank you!" She couldn't resist a hug around the horse's neck, which she seemed to return by tightening her head around and down the girl's back.

"But if you're here, you must be trying to find the way back home?" Jenna realized, breaking the embrace to look at Hope.

Flowing locks of midnight tossed in a form of nod as a howl soon rang out.

"Oh, great, wolves," Jenna cursed. "Don't want one of *those* to find us. That cougar was enough for one night."

Hope's hoof stomped with an added bit of a snort, which then reminded her of a voice of wisdom she'd heard all too recently.

"Let hope guide me," she quoted, searching the air thoughtfully.

Hope stamped once more, her foot beating the ground in a more-anxious manner.

"All right, let's go find home together," she said, hopping herself up onto the horse's back.

Hope stepped into a walk, through a path only *she* seemed to know.

****

Heaviness attacked her eyes with a passion, the sole intent being to pull her into the comfort of sleep, which she knew she could not have until they were safe. She reached a hand up to rub away the tiredness; a yawn sucked in more air than she was prepared for, and her cough soon followed.

Hope trod on nonetheless, finding her way around things that might trip her up otherwise. Jenna peered into the night. No trees or shaded structures rang true in any form of recognition.

"I . . . I don't know any of this place . . . or . . . where these paths lead," her voice shook with the night's chill against her skin. "I don't know what to do. Hope, what should I do?" Laying down against the horse's crest with this statement, a tear escaped her, soaking into the gray filly's already sweat-soaked coat. But with her silence, the horse kept moving on, finding no reason to stop as the night still burned on.

****

Matt stared out the end of the barn, his eyes glazed with worry as he turned back into the stable laid behind him. Chase nibbled on the wisps he'd plucked from the hay net, his demeanor long since calmed with the feeling of home.

"Where could they be?" Matt whispered almost to himself. "They've been gone all night. Who knows what could happen out there?"

"If Ben and Hope are still out there, they're *bound* to find her themselves," Kate assured him, successfully hiding the doubt she still felt deep inside.

"I'm more worried about what might find Jenna before *they* do," Matt corrected hopelessly.

"Or if they'll make it back in one piece," Ben added.

Lights shone across the far end of the stable, and they all looked to follow them out. The three teens shielded their faces as a breeze was kicked up by a spotlight hanging over head. They powered their way over to the Tylers who stood to meet the officer stepping out of the patrol car that had just pulled in with its red and blue lights.

"We've just received word," the officer began, approaching the family. "No sign of the girl or either of your horses. The forest is too thick to see them from overhead. We may have to wait until the morning to send a ground team in."

"Morning? We can't wait till the morning! It might be too late by then," Matt protested.

"Wait. Look there!" Ben pointed, shielding his eyes from the powerful spotlight. An odd slow-moving shape, lit up by the subtle glow of the moon, heavily strolled down the lane, a lump laying on top of it.

"Jenna!" Ann gasped, taking off in a run toward the odd figure.

Jenna felt a warmth that defined the ground as bright as day, and she looked up to be blinded by a giant star, which she found wasn't a star at all. Figures racing toward her ignited a feeling within her chest, which brought a sudden burst of energy to sit up again. Anticipation overcame her, and she slid down off of Hope just as her family reached her.

"Jenna!" her mother cried, immediately wrapping her in a tight embrace, her hand wrapped up around her daughter's head as she buried her face into her child's neck.

Ryan surrounded his wife and daughter in a hug that held them both, his face pressing to his daughter's head in a tender kiss as he laid his cheek across it. The rest of the family gathered round, and as Jenna came out of her parents' embrace, the others lined up for a group hug of their own, first her friends and then her grandparents.

"But the horses are still out there," Jenna realized, coming out of her last hug.

"They're not," Ryan assured them. "They're fine. The only ones we were still looking for were Bentley and Hope, but it appears you found Hope."

"Well, actually, *she* found *me*," Jenna corrected with a light chuckle. "Good thing too. She saved me from a mountain lion attack. . . And. . ."

"Mountain lions!" Ann gasped.

"It's okay. I'm okay," Jenna spoke up quickly. "Just a bruised knee is all. I'll be fine."

"Well, either way, it's good to have you home again," Matt commented with a shrug.

"But what about Bentley?" Jenna began again.

And the answer came in the form of a distant whinny. A charging blue beast cantered down the length of lane toward them, a white ghost of a shadow at his side.

"Ben!" Jenna screamed, racing to him.

The stallion slowed at seeing her approaching meeting in the middle as the girl threw her arms around his neck in the tightest hug that almost suffocated herself. A glistening crystal trail down her face soaked into his bluish-gray coat matted with dust, dirt, and mud shaded in sweat. Crimson stripes at his feet turned his bluish fur as a form of dried purple or oozing red, painting the ground with it in each step.

"Oh, Bentley, you're hurt." Jenna slid down to inspect them, but the horse just blew a snort and tossed his head in response. "Well, at least you don't seem bothered by it." Jenna smirked, standing once more.

Bentley's big head rested on her hands with a gentle sigh, his forehead pressed to her chest lightly as though trying not to compromise his owner's balance. Another breath blew at her hair, and she looked that way.

"Syd!" She gasped, then looking into Ben's soft blinking eyes, she could almost read them as a mental response. "You brought her back with you." Tears welled up, and she hugged his head once more. "Thank you!" she breathed.

"Didn't even realize she was gone in all the excitement." Matt vocalized, suddenly appearing at her side. Then the two friends looked to the two horses standing safely with them on their home land.

Chapter Sixteen

The Final Test

Opening the closet gave off a more surreal feeling than it had before. Her thoughts wandered, falling back to that astronomical day not long ago.

****

"Everything looks great here, Mr. Tyler," Dr. Vanderbeak announced, strolling out of the stable with Ryan, Matt, and Jenna.

"Really?" Jenna responded. "Even Micah? But what about his joints?"

"I'm not sure what you mean," the vet replied, turning to her. "Old Micah's bones are as strong as ever!. Whatever happened to him out there last night, something must have really *been working in his favor."*

Unbeknownst to the vet when he turned away, Matt and Jenna's glance met, a knowing grin fell upon their collective response.

"I'll let you guys know if anything happens to come up on my tests from the samples I took," Dr. Vanderbeak informed them while climbing into his vehicle to leave. "But it looks like everyone's doing just fine. Ben's scratches are very *superficial and'll clear up in plenty of time for the show."*

"So we can still train?" Jenna wondered.

"Oh, absolutely," the vet replied, draping his arm over the side of the vehicle's open window. "Call me if something doesn't look right, but from what I can see, everything looks good here."

"All righty, thanks so much, Ed." Ryan beamed, shaking hands with the middle-aged man.

"My pleasure," Dr. Vanderbeak replied. *"Anything for my best patients and friends. You take care now,"* they bid him farewell with a clean bill of health, and it proudly glowed across Jenna's face. recalling how relieving the news had been.

****

The thought came back to her with a certain joy that curved her lips up at the mere thought. She reached for the back of the closet for the protective clothing bag, and it crinkled as she brought it out from where it had been stashed.

"I don't need my name in lights," the song on her phone sang. *"I'm famous in my Father's eyes / Make no mistake / He knows my name."* She pulled the zipper down and exposed the fancy well-made materials.

"I'm not living for applause / I'm already so adored / It's all His stage / He knows my name." Stripping off her clothes and putting these on reminded her of the many times she'd done it before.

"He calls me chosen, free forgiven, wanted, child of the King / His forever, held in treasure / I am loved." The powerful voice gave her a new strength somehow, raising it that much higher when she looked into the mirror.

****

The grip of her hand on the banister, the delicate sweep of her feet down the steps . . .

Everyone looked up when they heard her footsteps come down. Hair pulled back into a tight bun, fancy navy-blue riding jacket and white jodhpurs worn with tall black boots,. . . a look long since returned.

"Jenna, you look wonderful," Rose swooned at her granddaughter's beauty.

"Completely stunning," Frank added.

"Thank you. . . both of you." Jenna smiled, hugging both of them.

Matt stepped up to her, wearing his riding attire in a red jacket and cream jodhpurs.

"You look great, Jenna," he said, beaming.

"So do you," Jenna replied. "Looking spiffy in your new gear. It's a good look for you."

"Yeah well, highly doubt it'll ever happen again." Matt chuckled. "Don't know how you pull it off so easily."

Laughter was shared between the two, and the family collectively enjoyed the quiet moment together.

****

"Today's the day," Jenna whispered to the horse, "the day we get to show everyone how hard we've worked."

Bentley blew in her hair, the horse's mane done up into stiff fancy braids and his saddle and saddle pad gleaming clean in the morning sunlight. Matt strode by, leading Sydney out to the waiting trailer fashioned for the coming occasion as Bentley was.

"I'll come back for Hope," Matt called over his shoulder.

"Okay," Jenna walked Bentley out after him to be loaded into the trailer while Ryan and Frank loaded the last of their things.

"Are we ready?" Ryan asked.

"Nearly," Jenna answered, smiling at her father. "As soon as Matt comes back with Hope."

"Good." Ryan beamed, wrapping his arm around her shoulders.

****

"Welcome, everyone, to Riverton's Summer Splash Invitational."

Crimson-red and navy-blue banners decorated the fences and around the outdoor arena. A big white banner on the judges' booth read, "SUMMER SPLASH INVITATIONAL" in bold blue lettering. The sun shone brightly over the showgrounds, and the people gathered in the stands to watch.

Jenna's green eyes scanned the crowd carefully, finally spotting Kate, Brian, and their parents sitting in the front row and saving some extra seats. When she turned toward them, Kate waved her arm up excitedly. Jenna waved back grinning wide.

"Okay," her mother sighed. "This is it. Good luck."

"Thanks, Mom," Jenna replied.

"Good luck is right," Rose agreed.

"We're gonna go and sit with Kate and her family, okay?" Frank said.

"Okay," Jenna smiled as Rose, Ann, and Frank strode toward the stands.

"Why don't you get Bentley warmed up. I'll go check you guys in. And they'll be starting in about an hour," Ryan said, handing her Bentley's reins. "Be careful."

"I will." Jenna nodded as she took them and swung them over her horse's head.

"I'll say."

Jenna turned around, and suddenly Kate was standing right behind her, the girl's normally proud smirk upon her face.

"Glad you could make it," Jenna replied, hugging her friend.

"Girl, you seriously didn't think I was gonna miss this?" Kate replied, her personal swagger returning. "You're sadly mistaken. Or I guess you could say delightfully mistaken.

"Hey! Tyler!" a male voice called, two girls amongst him when they looked toward the sound of the voice.

"Hey, Bennett!" Jenna replied casually as they met the young man.

"Aw, come on, you were supposed to say, 'Hey, Tyler!'" the boy complained humorously, leaning back on his heels in disappointment.

"Well, well if it isn't Tyler Bennett. Fancy meeting you here," Kate joked, comedically taking on a prim and proper persona.

"Yeah, yeah, ruin the moment, why don't ya?" Tyler scoffed in sarcastic annoyance.

"Been a long time, Jenna," Dylan Summers spoke up. "What changed?"

"I see you still kept your black locks, looks like things haven't changed a bit," Jenna commented.

"Nah, it's just been boring without you," Tyler replied. "Things haven't been the same since you 'retired' five years ago. Has it *really* been that long?"

"Believe it or not," the other Hispanic-looking girl answered.

"Denali Jay Pierce, you're back on the circuit," Jenna noted. "Decided not to quit after all?"

"Yeah, we found a better instructor, and now my skills have *mucho* improved," Denali replied brightly. "But I am surprised to see that you're back. When you left after your accident with Sam, I was almost certain it was for good."

"Well, a lot has changed lately." Jenna shrugged, a hand resting on Bentley's shoulder.

"Like what sort of things?" Tyler piped up expectantly. "Hmm?"

"It's a long story," Jenna admitted, meeting Matt's brief glance.

"Long story, huh?" Tyler mused, looking to be unconvinced.

"Seriously, you have *no* idea," Matt agreed.

"Wait. Who are you?" Tyler wondered, pointing to the other boy.

"I'm Matt, Matthew Bartlett," Matt introduced himself, shaking hands with Tyler. "Pleased to meet you."

"My family has been fostering him for about a year and a half now," Jenna explained, gesturing to Matt as their hands dropped.

"Wow, things really *have* changed," Dylan noted; hinting at the shadow over Jenna's shoulder, which turned out to be Bentley.

"Oh, right, guys. This is Big Bentley," Jenna announced, setting her hand back onto the blue roan's shoulder. "But the name he's regularly known by is Bentley."

"Big Bentley, huh?" Tyler thought, looking Bentley over thoughtfully. "Cool name. Oh! Have you met *my* new jumper? He's amazing! You'll see."

"Yes, see you level out your jumping accuracy." Dylan smirked, arms crossed playfully as she glanced at Denali who just muffled a giggle into her hand.

"Right, ha ha, very funny!" Tyler sighed, shrugging his hands up with his eyes.

"Anyway, it's great to meet you, Matthew." Dylan chuckled once more, turning the boy in question. "The Horse Girl really *has* gotten an upgrade."

"Sure has," Matt agreed. "And wait'll you see the roster for today."

"Something tells me that it's gonna be a surprise we won't forget," Denali smiled.

"Probably." Matt shrugged.

"Well, we should probably go warm up," Jenna decided, preparing to mount.

"I got you!" Matt offered coming to her side. "Ready?" he asked, bracing her leg.

"Yep."

"One, two, three!" the two counted and acted together, successfully reaching Jenna to her desired position astride her beloved steed.

"So now what're *you* gonna do, Matt?" Jenna wondered, staring down on him.

"Well, first, we're gonna get Syd and Hope out," the boy replied. "Then *I'll* use the mounting block in the training ring."

"And *I'll* bring Hope in with us so we can warm her up too," Kate added, swinging a small end of the lead rope in her hand coolly.

"Wait. You have *two* horses?" Dylan questioned, looking to Jenna.

"Well, she's not really *mine*," Jenna began. "She's a client horse that will *essentially* be taking her final test today. If she does well here today, she'll finally be ready to go home with her owners."

"Cool!" Tyler gushed.

"So this *Hope*, is she beautiful?" Denali wondered.

"You be the judge," Jenna answered, gesturing her hand up. The gray flurry of a horse stepped down the ramp gracefully, ears twitching about and eyes bright with all the activity commencing around her.

"Woah," the three teens breathed together.

"I know, right?" Kate added, amused by their response as she brought Hope to a halt before them.

"Lucky duck to be dealing with *that*," Tyler commented, pointing to Hope. "How long has she been at Sunshine for?"

"Um, the whole summer I guess?" Jenna recalled. "We got her back in May."

"Dude!" Tyler breathed, his hand finding his head in the surprise of this. "We need to stay more in touch 'cause wow, that's incredible."

"I'd tell you the story," Jenna returned, "but we better go. We've lost enough time gabbing as it is."

"Right, good point. See you in there!" Dylan called as the three kids turned to leave.

****

"Ms. Tyler, Matt, meet Gunthar's Garland," Tyler declared, sitting atop the dappled buckskin proudly.

"Pretty colors," Jenna remarked. The dappling of brown and black coupled with the characteristic tan hue and black points that the nature of a buckskin would have made up the appearance of this horse that Tyler so proudly praised about.

"Gotta say," Matt smiled from Sydney's back, "he's definitely handsome."

"I'll say," Kate agreed, leaning against the fence to peer through at them, still holding Hope's reins easily in her grasp. "Tyler Bennett, you've got a pretty handsome guy right there."

"Thanks." Tyler beamed, his eyes closing with his proud grin.

"And I see you're still going with good old Danish Midnight," Jenna observed as Dylen walked the black and white mare over to them.

"Well, she may be up to ten now. But she's still got a lot of years still in her. Right, baby?" She rubbed the horse's neck she shook it in a way to look like either a nod or a shake of her head.

"Is that a yes or a no?" Kate smirked cheekily, the mare just repeating this action.

"I guess we'll never know." Dylan chuckled, scratching her horse's neck.

Hearing an approaching snort, Kate turned around, and the others looked up. Sandy-umberish in tone with hints of reddish pink or rose gold, the flowing white or cream of the animal's mane and tail waterfalled over its shoulders and behind, beauty symbolized by the delicate detail of her soft face and gently eyes and a sturdy body structure that screamed its own form of perfection.

"Woah!" Matt breathed.

"She was an import from my country," Denali explained, rubbing the horse's nose.

"Rusty Savannah hasn't changed at all." Jenna smiled. "Except for maybe just gotten more beautiful."

"You *know* this horse?" Matt asked, looking to her with wide eyes.

"Of course I do," Jenna replied, leading the way on the rail to warm up. "Rusty was brought to Sunshine to be retrained as an advanced jumper for Denali's family. They got her when she was two, but whoever had her before was trying to make her into a Western riding horse, and she really wasn't built for it. Plus, her heart seemed to be for jumping 'cause she'd always jump our fences and run away to jump more. So we had to work with her on some things to really get her ready. That was a year or two before you came along."

"So you trained her horse, and then a year or two later you had the accident with Sam?" Matt reiterated.

"One year exactly," Dylan corrected, following just behind Matt and Sydney.

****

"Jenna helped us all at one point," Dylan went on, her breath in tune to her posting on Daina's steady trot.

"She helped each of *us* improve when she used to compete all the time," Denali added.

"'Course we would've figured it out anyway," Tyler put in, bouncing a little more than he should before readjusting his seat.

"So when she left due to the accident, we kinda had to forge on without her, improving on our own skills in other ways," Dylan went on.

Jenna started the half circle to change directions, which then changed for all the rest. Laughter caught Jenna's ears, and she noted the familiarity of it.

"Ugh, not *them* again," Dylan groaned, holding their gait.

"Who is it?" Matt wondered, turning toward the sound.

"It's Katrina Williams and her best friend, Cheryl Conway. They're practically the showground divas around here," Dylan explained, her midnight brows furrowed.

"Well, I know who Katrina is," Matt replied. "But I'm not sure I know who Cheryl Conway is."

"Lucky you," Tyler grumbled.

"Playtime's over, kiddies," Cheryl announced smugly, leading her chocolate-colored stallion in with Katrina and Napoleon.

"You can't just kick us out." Dylan protested, pulling her horse up.

"We can if it's our turn," Cheryl shot back immediately, her eyes challenging the other girl's.

Dylan sneered and gripped her reins tighter. "You don't own the place!" She snapped.

"Oh, right, 'cause you *do*?" Cheryl snickered and cracked a grin to Katrina, who wore an almost stoic one.

"We're not going anywhere, Cheryl, so you'll just have to share the ring like everybody else," Jenna told her, bringing Bentley to a halt.

"Ugh, you were right, Katrina." Cheryl sniffed in clear disgust. "Retiree girl really *has* returned with a gargantuan runt of a horse."

A boiling teapot began to scream at the back of Jenna's mind, but her face remained calm.

"You don't know whatch'er talking about!" Matt exclaimed, his anger left unrestrained.

"No, Matt." Jenna stopped him with the wave of her hand. "She can say what she wants. Doesn't make it true. Let's keep warming up. They know they can't win as long as we don't let them."

And with that, the group returned to the rail at a canter with Katrina staring after them unbeknownst to their knowledge.

****

"Up next is Number 210, Matthew Bartlett, on Hail Sydney!" the male announcer declared over the microphone.

Matt guided Sydney into the open ring, Jenna's breath sighing out of her in the wait to watch this moment play out. Matt approached the first jump, and Sydney anxiously stumbled into it. Her head held up, she took the jump and knocked down the first pole, and regaining a footing, they worked their way over the next jump and the next and the next. Knocking the first oxer jump seemed to give them time to adjust in order to clear the rest of the course with ease.

"That was Number 210, Matthew Bartlett riding Hail Sydney! with a time of 18.6 with, it looks like, eight faults," the announcer called.

"Well, not my best, but we made it." Matt shrugged, coming out by Jenna with an off grin. "We survived!" the boy announced, throwing a hand in the air as he rode away past her and Hope, insisting that Jenna laugh at his amusing statement.

Hope jumped and stepped about anxiously, her ears and head searching the area with the swell of the crowd above them.

"Easy, girl, we're okay," Jenna soothed, relaxing in her saddle.

"You're up soon, riff-raff," Cheryl commented, leaning over to her. "Hope you get luckier than your *last* time on the course."

Jenna blocked out the sound of her cackling tease to listen to the inner song that played in her head. *"I am a child of the King,"* her thoughts proclaimed.

"Maybe it's time to lay off for a while," Katrina suggested when Cheryl recovered. "Your teasing's clearly not working."

"Oh, what, are going soft now too?" her friend mocked. "You realize she's the only one here who *used* to be a challenge for us. And *now* suddenly she decides to just show up and take over? She needs to be reminded of her place. She gave up her place in this world the moment she ran away scared after one little fall. And so she can't just waltz in here out of the blue and take over what she left behind all those years ago like some kind of goody-two-shoes jockey."

"But if your teasing's not having any effect, why bother?" Katrina shot back pointedly.

"Time conquers all, Katrina," Cheryl returned bluntly, "as long as you have the sharpest points."

Katrina's brow furrowed and, her gaze wandered out to the open arena.

"Famous in my father's eyes," Jenna thought, eyes closed to make her completely devoid of the world around her. *"Just you and me and Him."*

"Now, next up, we have Cheryl Conway, Number 203, riding Hershey."

Jenna's eyes popped open at first hearing the announcer's voice crack over the mic, bringing her to attention.

"Watch and learn." Cheryl smirked, kicking her horse into a forward walk, sneaking glances at both Jenna and Katrina on either side of her.

Reaching the open gate, she rode on through, the sun gleaming upon her proud smile as she looked to the judges' booth. The head judge gave her a nod, and Cheryl faced forward and forced a canter. Hershey's head bobbed heavily as he was pushed forward, his ears lying back for a moment and his head lowering a bit. Cheryl snapped the crop to his side, and he picked up his pace. Snapping it again just before the first jump granted her the opposite result of what she wanted; she fell forward and hit the horse's crest full on, gripping his neck to stay on.

"Ugh, come on! Get moving. Let's try that again!" Cheryl demanded, kicking Hershey's sides repeatedly.

Yet the horse stood still in front of the jump, looking around like nothing was happening. "Ugh, you."

The snap of the crop just earned her a half-buck, nearly unseating her again as people in the crowd began to laugh at the girl desperately trying to stay on. Finally, the head judge rose and waved a hand to dismiss her.

Sneering, she allowed Hershey to stroll down out of the ring. Walking by Jenna and Katrina, she wouldn't even meet their glance.

"I could've told her that her approach was the wrong call," Jenna spoke aloud to no one in particular, Katrina's brow tightening. Jenna craned her neck to search the crowd as best she could, hoping to spot Ben or Vanessa, but her vision could not seem to find them.

Did they decide not to come and didn't tell us? she thought, scanning the stands again. But when she approached the gate with Hope, she saw them both slip in to sit down next to her parents; she heaved a sigh to show her relief.

Hope suddenly jittered her feet under her, stepping about anxiously with her uneasy demeanor and twitchy ears, which Jenna had to relax into until the filly calmed again.

"All right, girl," she whispered to the filly, "this is our time to shine. Let's make Vanessa and Ben proud."

Hope perked her ears forward and snorted nervously. *Okay, let's do this then*, seemed to be her answer.

Jenna smiled and patted her neck gently.

"Now, folks, it looks like we are in for a little treat. Jenna Tyler, one of our past champions and most talented jumpers, returns to us, riding a horse famous for being *'a lost cause'*, Hope Shines, horse number 212," the announcer called.

Jenna pressed her leg into Hope's side, asking for her to walk forward into the ring. Hope's body tensed, but Jenna gripped the reins and whispered soothingly to her.

"It's okay," she murmured softly, her eyes front.

The head judge beamed, rising to give her the signal to begin.

"Okay, let's go!" she whispered, asking for the canter.

Hope smoothly transitioned into her long flowing canter, the pace quickening with the excitement of the crowd. Jenna sat deeper into the saddle until she started her approach to the first jump. Air tugged at loose hairs as their flight began, hitting the ground to stride three more times for the next.

"Good girl," she breathed. "Keep going."

Making their way around, Hope lunged forward and clipped the top of the second oxer, bringing down a pole. But Jenna's mind barely heard it hit the ground as she guided Hope around to the vertical/oxer line along the rail opposite the stands closest to where she'd started. Coming off the oxer, she led her to finding the focal point of the triple-jump combination, which came one after the other in clear, clean leaps.

Bounds later, the wall showed before them and was gone once again. Hope's head went up off of it, and Jenna lost her line. The filly's head aimed away from the jump, and Jenna feared she couldn't correct it in time. Assuming her two-point position and pulling her head in toward her left hand, she clenched her eyes closed and prayed, *Lord, get us through.*

Hope's warm body and saddle leather raised up her legs, and Jenna peeked an eye open. There was an almost slow-mo feel as they sailed through the air to the rapid flash of cameras capturing the perfect shot. Hope's hooves hit the dust and turned sharply into the vertical water jump shimmering through. Laughter rang out in the back of her mind as she rounded the last invisible curve to the final two verticals, crossing the finish with a swell of applause.

"That was Jenna Tyler on Hope Shines, with a time of 15.3 seconds and four faults," the announcer said in a surprised tone. "And what a run! On our roster next is returning champion, Number 205, Katrina Williams riding her new horse, Napoleon Bonahoof."

Katrina glowed with an off-tone but proud smile when she rode into the ring on Napoleon. The young steel-black colt with a star and bright eyes pranced into the center of attention with a brand of confidence that didn't seem to mirror that of his rider. Jenna had guessed he was a Dutch warmblood, but the shape of his face and the build of his limbs and the handsome stature just begged another look.

Katrina nudged him into a canter at the head judge's command and turned into the first fence. Napoleon seemed to float smoothly over it and kept that elegant form, maintaining it with such ease that almost made Jenna graciously jealous. Jenna noticed how much difficulty the approach was for the second oxer jump and that she caught Napoleon on the wrong lead. *That almost* never *happens!*

Napoleon stumbled, coming off the vertical in the vertical/oxer line and knocked over the oxer and nearly unseated herself from it. The triple-jump combo wobbled with the colt's head shaking in the air, and out of that came a launch of a leap over the wall. *She's so out of control! What's going on out there?*

The pole seemed to fall right out from under Napoleon when he jumped the vertical, and two strides later, he stopped as the pole rolled to a stop about a yard from where he stood. Katrina no longer sat on his saddle as a result. The sole indicator of her fall being her boots flying over Napoleon's shoulder and neck, poles clattering to proceed the crash to the inevitable splash.

Not even wasting a second, Jenna leapt down off of Hope and ran out across the sand, the fleeting thought in her mind of what she was doing becoming clear for only a moment.

Katrina's surprised gasps almost sounded like sobs as she came up from the surface of the water jump's pool soaking wet and probably embarrassed. The collective gasp rippled through the crowd with only a few echoes of laughter ringing out.

Dylan and her friends collectively groaned in pure disgust at the dying laughter of the one standing at their left, drying a tear.

"You'd think she'd have even just a *little* sympathy," Matt commented to the others dryly at Cheryl's infuriating response.

"There's no soft spot in her heart," Dylan sighed, groaning once more. "Not that we've seen anyway. But to be fair, Katrina isn't exactly the nicest person either."

Katrina spit out some water that'd been in her mouth for this short time when a figure appeared above her, and she found an outstretched hand extended to her. Genuinely sympathetic eyes met hers, and soft ones at that, as Jenna stood there over her, waiting for her acceptance to come.

"Why do care enough to help *me*?" Katrina snapped coldly but took Jenna's hands regretfully.

Jenna pulled her up out of the water and on to dry, sandy land. "Because it's the right thing to do," she replied, pressing Napoleon's reins into the palm of her hand and leaving her to the officials that now surrounded her and Napoleon.

"Why did you do that?" Dylan asked her when Jenna strode up to them.

"Because no amount of awful behavior will change another person's heart," Jenna replied simply.

"You can't *possibly* think that girl can change," the black-haired girl questioned.

"Nothing is beyond the Lord's reach," Jenna answered in an innocent way. "Besides, I've been where she's at." With this statement, she strode over to her father to accept Bentley's reins and a kiss on the forehead.

"Well, folks, it looks like Prairie Rock is dropping out of this one," the announcer narrated. "Up next, Jenna Tyler returns riding *her* horse, Big Bentley."

As Jenna eased herself up into the saddle, Bentley tensed, but Jenna softly murmured their favorite song soothingly, and he relaxed. Walking him to the open gate was no trouble, and he stood there staring into it with twitching ears and laser focus.

"We're in this together, okay?" Jenna whispered to Bentley tenderly.

And the stallion just shook his head to agree. Walking forward, Jenna exchanged nods with the head judge.

And taking off, Bentley's stride lengthened to the broad gait, which was his canter. He sailed easily over the fence, then the second, and the third; the speed of light could not have described it. The next jump, a big oxer, loomed ahead, but neither of them minded. Bentley stumbled and almost lost his footing. But Jenna remained there, shifting her weight to keep his head up and falling in sync with his gait once again.

Bentley regained his balance to clear the next jump with at least a foot to spare, Jenna's world turning to one that only seemed to encompass herself and Bentley's heavenly smooth gait. Counting his strides became a fleeting thought, the timing of the jumps just falling into place. The stallion's hooves beat the ground, but to Jenna, they were floating on air, hardly even *touching* the ground if that was possible. Slow motion seemed to occur once more as she heard the echoes of her own laughter.

Could it have been a mere dream? Or a recollection of what had already been? Or was she, in fact, hearing her own voice in the current day? The dreamscape of a land, seemingly all their own, faded into screams and cries of joy and triumph, the flags of the finish point flapping by them in crossing it.

"That was Jenna Tyler on Big Bentley with a time of 15.3 seconds, and *no* faults!" the announcer said. "Unbelievable! Talk about a comeback!"

Jenna glanced back to find that the truth was real. No poles had hit the ground.

"Now, we would like all the participants and their horses to come line up in front of the judges' booth for awards," a female announcer requested over the mic.

Ryan and Matt escorted Sydney and Hope over to Jenna at the designated area, just in front of the finishing flags. A female judge came forward to meet them, glancing over to the remaining judges and nodding.

"All righty then," the announcer began, taking up his notes. "Due to the disqualifications, two of our eight riders will not be placing today."

Matt and Jenna exchanged glances, and the announcing continued. "But without further ado, in sixth place, we have Number 385, Tyler Bennett on Gunther's Garland!"

Applause rippled through as Tyler waved to the crowd and accepted his pink ribbon.

"In fifth place, we have Number 301, Denali Jay Pierce on Rusty Savannah," a female announcer declared as more applause sounded, the volume increasing.

"Fourth place," the male announcer continued, "is Number 225, Dylan Summers on Danish Midnight."

"Third place goes to Matthew Bartlett on Hail Sydney!" the female announcer added.

"For first and second place," the male announcer began, "Jenna Tyler on Hope Shines and Big Bentley!"

They finished together, creating an uproar of triumphant praise. Jenna's face lit up when she heard her name. Her gaze caught Matt's, equally ecstatic and completely dumbfounded by the hype. Hugging Matt tightly, she turned and threw her arms around Bentley's neck.

"We did it!" she gasped, almost in shock. "We really did it!"

Bentley tossed his head and whinnied, the judge coming over her with ribbons and the trophy.

"Congratulations!" the lady judge said, beaming as she handed Jenna the ribbons.

Jenna pinned the red and blue ribbons on the horses' bridles, then another judge gave her the trophy. Jenna's family and friends flooded from the stands to join them, and some photographers arrived not long after, taking pictures. Jenna and her family gathered around the horses to have a couple pictures taken.

Chapter Seventeen

Overcomer!

"You did it! You did it!" Kate cried, wrapping her friend in a hug and shaking her at the shoulders.

"I know! I know!" Jenna replied happily, releasing her to hold both her friend's hands.

"Man, what an upset," Kate gushed. "Cheryl and Katrina *both* getting knocked out of the competition within *minutes* of each other. Can't imagine what that feels like!"

"Well, they can't win *all* the time," Jenna replied with a shrug.

"Yeah, no kidding." Matt grinned. "But not bad for third place," the boy added, admiring the white ribbon on Sydney's deep umber bridle.

"Congrats, Jenna," Frank said, grinning proudly.

"You looked great out there, dear, on *both* horses," Rose added.

"You were amazing, honey," Ann remarked, hugging her daughter.

"Thanks, everyone," Jenna answered. "But I couldn't have done it without Dad and Matt's help and Ben's."

"But even though Syd's heart's not really in it," Matt spoke up, "I think I kinda wanna try her at cross-country like Ben. Show jumping's a little too *showy* for me."

The friends all shared a round of laughter

"And Bentley and Hope were great too," Jenna went on. "They're *both* incredible horses."

"That's good to hear," Vanessa commented in a relieved tone, earning their attention. "So she'll be okay in the ring, then?"

"She was great!" Jenna confirmed, rubbing the gray horse's neck proudly. "She just needs a little encouragement—that's all. But otherwise, I'm confident that she'll be a *great* horse for competition."

"That's great!" Ben nodded thankfully. "And I think I can give her that. You looked great out there on both of them by the way."

"Yeah, you did."

Jenna swung around in surprise as the tall, slim figure of Katrina Williams stood before her. Jenna stared in disbelief, but the look in the other girl's eyes showed a genuine seriousness.

"I was watching you closely out there on both Bentley and Hope," she said in a low voice. "And I could see that they both wanted to jump. I could also see a little fear in Hope's eyes. But then again, I also still saw the willing trust too."

"Thank you," Jenna replied softly, finding genuine truthfulness in her words.

"And I . . . I want to apologize and . . . ask your forgiveness. For all the things I've said about you . . . your home . . . and Bentley. He's a magnificent horse. Better than I expected," Katrina remarked, looking up at him.

"Okay, apology accepted," Jenna replied mindlessly, still shocked by what was happening.

"And . . . I would like to know," Katrina paused a moment before continuing. "How do *I* become a Christian?"

Jenna was so shocked to hear Katrina, of all people, say this; words failed her.

"And I would like us to start over . . . as friends."

"I . . . I . . ."

"Please, Jenna." Katrina's blue eyes searched Jenna's green ones.

"I . . ." Jenna sighed. "I guess I could . . . try."

Katrina sighed with relief. "Oh, thank you, Jenna!" She cried, hugging Jenna tightly as tears began to stream down her cheeks.

Jenna hugged her back, still shocked from hearing and seeing all of this. *Am I in a dream?* she asked herself, but she had to admit it felt good. This moment was one she found she'd been hoping for one day, and it seemed to go on forever. And she even discovered herself to be hugging Katrina tightly back, tears soaking her cheeks. But they weren't tears of fear or sadness, but of joy. She had never felt so peaceful in her life. It was as if a weight had been lifted off her shoulders.

At last they broke their embrace and smiled at each other for the first time. Somehow they found themselves laughing together, and everyone around them began to laugh with them.

"Thank you for giving me another chance," Katrina said at last as they broke apart. "One of our horses is having a foal soon. My parents are giving it to me when it's born. And I think I'm going to call it Second Chances."

"Ms. Williams, I think that's a wonderful name for a foal," Frank smiled.

"And the Bible says, 'Trust in the Lord and do good; dwell in the land and enjoy safe pasture. Delight yourself in the Lord and he will give the desires of your heart,' Psalm 37:3—4," Ryan quoted.

"What does that mean?" Katrina asked.

"It means that you should try to be really good at something but also do it for the glory of the Lord," Jenna replied. "He loves you, Katrina. He knows you by name because he made you. You don't have to be famous in the world because you are already famous in God's eyes."

"How do you know?" Katrina asked, slightly dubious.

Jenna reached into her bag and pulled out her iPhone and played "He Knows My Name" for everyone to hear.

"This is how I know," she said simply. Jenna began to sing along as the chorus played and watched Katrina's face listening thoughtfully.

"Can we get together more so I can hear more of this song again?" Katrina asked at last.

"You can buy it in the iTunes Store on your phone," Jenna replied.

"Can you show me?"

"Sure."

Katrina smiled and took out her phone and, handing it to Jenna, stood at her shoulder to watch. Jenna pushed the button to wake it up.

"What's your code?" Jenna asked, handing the phone back to her.

"Oh, here." Katrina typed the code and opened the iTunes Store.

Jenna took it from Katrina and typed in "Francesca Battistelli."

"Is that the artist's name?" Katrina asked, reading it over her shoulder.

"Yep," Jenna confirmed.

"What is the song called?"

"'He Knows My Name.'" Jenna selected it from the list. "There you go." Jenna said, putting the phone into Katrina's hand. Giving it back to Katrina, she pressed the *buy* button then the word *play* showed in its place. She then exited out of the iTunes Store and opened the music app to play the song.

"Thanks."

"You're welcome."

There was a silence among them.

"Oh, and, Matt, there's something we wanna show you," Ryan spoke up and glanced around at his wife and parents.

"Um, okay?" the boy replied, stepping toward them.

Shooting another grin at Ann, Ryan retrieved the long white envelope that poked out of his shirt pocket and handed it to Matt. The young man stared at it for a moment before hesitantly looking up at Ryan.

"Go on. Open it," Mr. Tyler coaxed, waving at hand at him.

Matt looked down at the envelope in his hand and slowly began to peel it open. Lifting the flap and sliding its contents out, he unfolded the trifold of paper and studied the text printed across the page. Matt's brow furrowed as he looked closer and flipped through the short thickness of the papers in his grasp before his eyes lit up and lifted to the Tylers.

"These are adoption papers," he breathed.

"We figured what better time than the present." Ryan grinned.

"We always knew it was in our future to adopt you, Matt," Ann added, leaning in to her husband. "And the Lord's perfect timing has brought it to this day."

"All that's left to do is to sign them with your social worker and return them to the court," Ryan finished. "Then you'll be *officially* family.

"Not that you weren't before of course," Frank deadpanned, earning him a hearty chuckle.

"No way!" Matt cried, looking from the papers to the Tylers then back again. "Thank you. Thank you so much." The boy's shoulders dropped as he broke down in tears to come hug Ryan and Ann, his words almost trailing off into sobs as they held him close.

"Well, I should probably go take care of Napoleon now. Mom's *not* gonna be happy that I lost today. And Napoleon's probably gonna be a little antsy if I don't give him his carrots," Katrina said.

The girl turned to go but stopped and turned back around. "Would you maybe wanna teach me how to use your training methods and stuff on Napoleon? He kinda gets a little jumpy before competitions, and it kinda makes me a little nervous."

"Um, sure. When would you like to start?" Jenna answered.

"As soon as possible." Katrina beamed. "Matt can come too. Maybe he can teach me something about the essential oils and herbs you use and how to use them."

"Sounds great." Matt grinned happily.

"Can I come too?" asked Kate hopefully.

"Sure, Kate," Katrina replied, shrugging. "*Everyone* is welcome." She glanced past the group to seek out Ben who lit up at her genuine smile in his direction.

"Well, I guess we can start today if you want," Jenna said. "We could try something with him right after we get Hope ready to go home with her owners."

"Really? You would really do that?" Katrina asked excitedly.

"Why not?" Jenna shrugged. "I don't have anything better to do."

"Jenna, you totally rocked it today!" Dylan praised, her three friends racing up to her. "And . . . what's *she* doing here?" Dylan's eyes stared pointedly through to Katrina's soul, and she held back the desire to respond.

"She's . . . on our side now. It may take time for you to trust her, but *I* believe she's ready to start changing," Jenna spoke up.

The three other teens stared for a moment, Dylan especially remaining hardened to the idea, but searching around Jenna's face, she finally softened and gave in with a sigh. "All right, I'll play along." The girl shrugged.

"Hey, wait," Ben realized now. "You guys were the ones from that photo with Jenna and Samson, aren't you?" he asked, pointing to the three of them.

"Yup, that's us." Tyler smirked, draping both arms up over the two girls' shoulders to assume the same poses from the photograph.

"So ready to get started?" Jenna asked, turning back to Katrina after an amused chuckle.

"Oh, Jenna, I think that's a great idea!" Katrina took her hand gratefully.

"We can go down to see Napoleon right now if you want," Matt suggested. "And Jenna can join us when she's finished here. Right?"

"Sounds good to me. It shouldn't take too long," Jenna answered.

"We'll see you there," Kate said, and she and the group of teens headed off toward the barn.

****

Jenna walked up into their trailer, the gray filly in her new travel blanket and boots preparing her for the journey ahead. She secured them in place and went up to the horse's head. Grasping her halter, she began the T-touch on her cheek.

"Well, girl," Jenna said finally to the filly, "time to go home." Jenna untied the lead and led her back down the ramp as Ben wandered over to them.

"Hey, pretty girl," he greeted, smiling broadly.

The filly perked her ears forward and stepped toward Ben as if understanding Jenna's words. Ben smiled and scratched her under the chin.

"Yeah, you know who your owner is," he told her.

Jenna handed him the lead.

"Come on. Let's get her things ready to go," Jenna said.

****

They had just unloaded the last box, when Vanessa drove her SUV up with her trailer behind it.

"Ready to go, Ben?" she asked when she rolled her window down.

Ben scratched Hope's forehead. "Yeah," he replied.

****

Hope walked confidently up the ramp with Ben. The filly whinnied loudly to Jenna. *Goodbye, Jenna, and thank you!* she seemed to say.

Jenna smiled then helped Ben put the ramp up.

"Goodbye, Jenna," Ben said. "And thanks for everything."

"No problem." Jenna smiled. "It's what I do."

"Maybe I'll see you again some time?" Ben implied hopefully.

"You know where to find me." Jenna grinned. "And, again, you're welcome anytime." She watched happily as Ben hopped in and Vanessa's vehicle disappeared over the distant hill, and prayed a prayer only her heart and Bentley, in his champion attire, could hear.

"Thank you, God, for giving me the best horse in the world," she whispered. "And thank you for a nice *new* friend." Then she walked off toward the stables to join her friends.

****

"Hey, Jenna, come look at this!" her father called.

Matt and Jenna Tyler thundered down the stairs to weave around the dining room table to the kitchen. Ryan stood on the opposite side of the room, looking down at something in his hand and looking up with the motion and sound of their presence.

"This came for you from an old friend," he finished, holding up a newspaper.

Jenna stepped forward, and Ryan handed it to her; reading the headline made her heart skip a beat.

LOST CAUSE NOT SO LOST!

"Ben won his first championship with Hope," Jenna breathed, "last month." Her eyes lifted toward him.

"A year from the Day," Ryan nodded.

"Hey, Horse Girl."

Jenna's glance whipped to her left. Sandy brown hair and hazel eyes met her, tenderly embracing her green ones with pride she'd seen so recently yet seemed like so long ago.

"Ben," Jenna gasped, tears welling up as she strode forward to hug him. "You were here the whole time!" She sniffed, playfully punching his arm. "Why didn't you just tell me yourself?"

"Where's the fun in that?" Ben smirked cheekily.

"You've been hanging around Matt *way* too much." Jenna grinned, shaking her head.

"Eh, what can I say? He's grown on me." The boy shrugged.

"Ah yes, the thrill of friendship." Matt sighed humorously, resting his chin resting in his hand, his elbow on the kitchen island.

"At least you're family life is back in order." Jenna recalled happily, causing Ben to chuckle blinking his gaze at the ground bashfully.

"Yeah... well anyway I stopped by to give you this to add you your success story hall of fame."

"You *know* that's not a thing, right?" Jenna hinted, folding the paper up again.

"Not yet it isn't," Ben replied. "But I'm telling you, it could happen. Amir, Hope, and now Marshall? You're on a roll, and it shows. God has blessed you beyond measure. I say we make it more official."

"By creating a horse hall of fame?" Jenna implied sarcastically, her smile more like that of a smirk.

"Sure, why not! I mean you're practically famous. Why not take it to the next level?" Ben reasoned.

"Well, we'll see," Jenna replied, finally turning his way. "I just hope you can stay around more often. The cross-country circuit is crazy, and even though Matt's not in the big leagues like you, I still miss both of you when you're off at competitions without me."

"Don't worry—you're not missing much." Matt chuckled. "Just some one-on-one guy time."

"That's what I'm afraid of," Jenna countered, rolling her eyes.

"Hey, I never said it was a *bad* thing." Matt shrugged innocently.

A knock at the door halted their conversation.

"I got it," Jenna said, sliding by Ben to leave the kitchen.

Opening the door, she was met by . . .

"Hey, girl, hey! What's up!" Kate and all their friends, past and present, stood on the porch with smiles of pride and anticipation in them telling her all she needed to know.

"Here to go for a ride?" Jenna implied easily.

"Aw now, how'd you guess?" Kate gasped, faking her surprise.

"Hey, Matt, Ben, who's ready for a ride?" Jenna called back into the house.

"I'm in!" Matt's voice called back.

"Me too!" Ben agreed. "Right after we grab one of these amazing blueberry scones!"

Appearing in the doorway with faces painted blue, they both licked their fingers and froze with everyone staring at them.

"What?" the two teenage boys asked blankly.

"Better watch out, or Bentley will eat you up," Kate joked.

"He's gotta catch us first!" Matt called, pushing past the dozen or more group of their friends to leap over the banister and leading the charge across the yard to the stable, laughter and joy filling the air with the sound of horses serenading this heartfelt emotion, proving once again the fondness that is no lost cause.

~A Lost Cause~

CPSIA information can be obtained
at www.ICGtesting.com
Printed in the USA
BVHW030010250220
573206BV00001B/39